THE HONOR OF AN HEIR

LINDARAE SANDE

Twisted Teacup
PUBLISHING

The Honor of an Heir

V1

Cover photograph © Period Images.com

Cover art by Twisted Teacup Publishing

Edited by Katrina Teele-Fair

http://www.lindaraesande.com

ISBN: 978-1-946271-49-5

Twisted Teacup Publishing, Cody, Wyoming

ALSO BY LINDARAE SANDE

The Daughters of the Aristocracy
The Kiss of a Viscount
The Grace of a Duke
The Seduction of an Earl
The Sons of the Aristocracy
Tuesday Nights
The Widowed Countess
My Fair Groom
The Sisters of the Aristocracy
The Story of a Baron
The Passion of a Marquess
The Desire of a Lady
The Brothers of the Aristocracy
The Love of a Rake
The Caress of a Commander
The Epiphany of an Explorer
The Widows of the Aristocracy
The Gossip of an Earl
The Enigma of a Widow
The Secrets of a Viscount
The Widowers of the Aristocracy
The Dream of a Duchess

The Vision of a Viscountess

The Conundrum of a Clerk

The Charity of a Viscount

The Cousins of the Aristocracy

The Promise of a Gentleman

The Pride of a Gentleman

The Holidays of the Aristocracy

The Christmas of a Countess

The Knot of a Knight

The Heirs of the Aristocracy

The Angel of an Astronomer

The Puzzle of a Bastard

The Choice of a Cavalier

The Bargain of a Baroness

The Jewel of an Earl's Heir

The Vixen of a Viscount

The Honor of an Heir

Beyond the Aristocracy

The Pleasure of a Pirate

The Making of a Mistress

The Lyon's Den (Dragonblade Publishing)

The Courage of a Lyon

Stella of Akrotiri

Origins

Deminon

Diana

CHAPTER 1
OH!

March 27, 1839, Norwick House parlor
The argument could be heard throughout the entirety of the Earl of Norwick's Mayfair townhouse. Two young women, frequently at odds, were at it again, each putting voice to some opinion that was the opposite of the other. The rainstorm occurring outside didn't drown their incessant shouts. Rather, the occasional crack of thunder punctuated them.

From the threshold of the parlor in which the argument was taking place, Clarinda, Countess of Norwick, regarded her identical twin daughters with a look of resignation. She did that often given their propensity to vex her.

At least she could tell them apart—most could not. Dahlia Davida bore a slight scar on her neck from when her sister had scratched her, and Diana Dorothea, who preferred to be called Danielle because the man she knew as her father was named Daniel, tended to hold her left hand in a fist as if she needed to punch someone.

"Whatever has you two arguing *now*?" Clarinda asked as her own fists went to her hips. She decided she needed to appear more determined.

More battle-ready.

Girls were trouble.

Twin girls were double the trouble.

Dealing with double the trouble meant girding her loins.

Dahlia and Danielle turned to face her, immediately silenced upon seeing their mother's stance.

"Something important, Mother," Dahlia replied.

"Terribly important," Danielle agreed.

Clarinda blinked. Well, they apparently agreed on something. "Out with it."

"It's about making love," Dahlia stated.

"What's involved, exactly," Danielle added. "I'm quite sure I know, but Davy seems to think otherwise." She directed a glare in Dahlia's direction. "She claims she read all about it in one of Father's books."

"I didn't just *read* about it," Dahlia argued. "I examined all the color plates. They were quite instructive."

Clarinda blinked. So much for battle.

Glancing toward the sideboard, Clarinda had a thought to pour herself a glass of brandy before she dared attempt to answer the girls. Instead, she motioned the twins to take seats near the fireplace and rang for tea.

Perhaps she would merely add some brandy after the maid brought the tea service.

"First, I must ask why you're even discussing this," Clarinda said as she moved to her favorite floral upholstered chair. "Has one of you accepted an offer of marriage without telling me?"

The twins shook their heads in unison. "If love-making involves bending over a library table with my naked bum pressed against some man's bare frontside, then I shall insist Father give me my dowry so I can go on a permanent holiday to Italy," Danielle announced. "I'll have none of that."

Having bent over all manner of furnishings over the years with her naked bum pressed into Daniel Fitzwilliam's groin—she was quite sure it was why she had been blessed with a set twin boys—Clarinda felt a blush rise to color her neck and cheeks. "There are many ways to make love. What you've just described seems awkward, I know, but—"

"Awkward?" Danielle repeated in shock. "I shan't be treated no better than a dog," she huffed, her chin rising with indignation.

"Then you won't bear an heir for your husband," Dahlia argued.

"I won't have to bear one if I'm living an independent life in Italy," Danielle countered.

"*Girls*," Clarinda hissed. "How did this conversation even start?"

For a moment, the two were blessedly silent as they regarded one another before Dahlia, the braver one, lifted her chin and said, "We can hear you."

"What?"

Danielle rolled her eyes. "You and Father."

Straightening in her chair, Clarinda was about to ask what they meant when the maid showed up with the tea tray. "Oh," she said brightly, glad for the interruption.

"Just like that," Dahlia said. "But louder, and more of them."

"Lots more," Danielle chimed in.

Clarinda leaned back as the maid set the silver tray on the low table in front of her, her embarrassment becoming more acute. "More of them?" she asked in confusion.

"The 'oh's, Mother. It's as if you were learning the alphabet and you got stuck on that particular letter," Danielle groused.

Knowing her face was as red as a beet, Clarinda blinked as she waited for the maid to leave the parlor.

Apparently the walls of the mistress suite weren't as thick as she'd thought.

Did she really say, "Oh!" so loudly and repeat it several times whilst Daniel saw to pleasuring her? When they were in the throes of their twice-weekly trysts, him worshipping her body as if she was a goddess, she paid no mind to how she might sound to anyone but her husband. Besides, he took delight in her verbal cues and her occasional commands, and he seemed to use them to coax her to even more intense pleasures before he saw to his own.

The girls probably didn't hear *him*. When he experienced his release, Daniel would hold his breath, and a growl would rumble from deep within him. Anything else he might attempt to say was usually drowned out because his mouth ended up on one of her breasts, or in the pillow next to her head, or against her shoulder.

Even thinking of it now had her wondering if tonight might be one of the nights Daniel planned to visit the mistress suite. If not, she was going to have to pay a call on him in the master suite.

He would like that. At least, he had never turned her away.

Well, there was that one time, on a particularly chilly winter night when he'd had a head cold and was a bit feverish. She had stayed with him the entire night, if only to provide a pillow for his body as she basked in his warmth. She hadn't even minded his rather loud snores since they caused the bed to vibrate in a most pleasant manner. Someone would have to sort how to set off that same sensation but without the accompanying sound effect.

And the head cold.

She caught the head cold, of course, and suffered for the next few days in solitude in the mistress suite. At least the fever kept her warm.

So engrossed in her thoughts was she, Clarinda set about pouring tea without even asking her daughters the usual questions. Her motions were rote until her thoughts turned to how her first husband had made love to her. As a result, the teapot hovered over her own cup, the pot not quite angled enough for any tea to actually pour out.

David's approach to pleasuring her had been far different from Daniel's. She was sure it was because he'd had more experience in carnal matters. He never asked what she wanted, but then, she hadn't known what was available. Even after she'd been married to him for a year, he continued to surprise her in nearly every room of Norwick House.

He had owned a gentlemen's club, after all.

The Elegant Courtesan had employed a number of young women who catered to a variety of tastes, some rather unusual, some downright frightening. The profitable enterprise was shuttered upon her marriage to him, though, partly because she demanded he give it up and partly because he had inherited the Norwick earldom. As an earl, it wasn't seemly for him to make money from a business.

Clarinda inhaled softly at the memory of the club. At the memory of David, who she rarely thought of these days. Although he had died well before their birth, he had fathered the two girls who were now of an age to marry and apparently far too curious about the marriage bed.

The oddest sensation skittered down her spine, and Clarinda gave a start. So did the teapot, which suddenly seemed to have a mind of its own as its liquid filled her cup.

"Oh!" she cried out, sure there had been a guiding hand covering hers for the very briefest of moments.

"Yes, you say it just like that," Dahlia claimed. "As if you're surprised."

Clarinda blinked several times before her gaze darted to one of the parlor windows. In the form of a silhouette, she was sure she saw David. He was leaning against the sideboard, his arms crossed with his elbows held in his hands. One booted foot was crossed over the other, which made him appear rather cavalier. And no older than the day he had died in an awful traffic accident in Oxford Street.

"You cannot deny she has the right of it," David's ghost said with a chuckle. "I certainly lived to hear them. In fact, thoughts of hearing them kept me from dozing overmuch during sessions of Parliament."

Swallowing, Clarinda stared at the apparition. David hadn't made an appearance in over twenty years. "So good of you to join us," she said, not quite sure if she welcomed him. "I could use your help here, darling. It seems your daughters have questions."

David straightened from the sideboard and unfolded his arms. "Oh, no, my sweeting. This is one of those times when your counsel is more astute than mine."

"Then why did you show up *now*? I haven't seen you in—"

"Days, yes I know," he interrupted. "Apologies."

"*Decades*, you mean," Clarinda huffed. "Two of them, in fact. You were always terrible at telling time."

David blinked, his head pulling back on his neck so his chin suddenly doubled. "Hmph," he replied. "How can that be? You're as gorgeous as the day I died," he murmured. "I do hope Danny appreciates it."

The mention of Daniel seemed to conjure Clarinda's current husband into existence, for he stood on the parlor threshold glaring at his late brother. "Of course I know it, you idiot. *I'm* the one who courted her before you took her from me," Daniel accused.

"She was betrothed to *me*," David reminded Daniel. "I was doing my duty taking her to wife. Making her my countess," he added before turning his attention back to Clarinda. "I'm just relieved Torrington was able to arrange it so you two could marry without too much trouble from the church. Or the law." He paused and then his eyes rounded. "I do hope there wasn't any trouble from the church. Or the law?" he asked.

Clarinda and Daniel exchanged quick glances before Daniel moved to stand closer to David. "No trouble," Clarinda replied. Given it had been illegal for her to marry the brother of her first husband, apparently her godfather, Milton Grandby, Earl of Torrington, had done whatever was necessary to see to it an exception had been granted for her marriage to Daniel. With the twin girls already on the way and the twin boys who were born a few years later, Clarinda really didn't want to discover there was a problem with her current marriage. The last thing she needed to learn was that her daughters were illegitimate. Or her sons. The oldest by five minutes, Duncan, named for his paternal grandfather, was the heir to the Norwick earldom.

Since David hadn't sired an heir before his untimely demise, Daniel had simply inherited the Norwick earldom upon his death. Because Daniel was the identical twin to David, those who weren't aware of David's death didn't even notice there had been a change in the identity of the earl when Daniel took his place as the Earl of Norwick.

"Mother, who *are* you talking to?" Dahlia asked before her attention went to the man she knew as her father. She leaned over in her chair and then her eyes rounded. "Oh!" she said, sounding like her mother did when she was in the throes of passion.

Clarinda gave her a quelling glance. "Your father, of course," she replied before she froze.

David, or rather his ghost, if one believed in such things, hadn't made an appearance since before the girls were born. Neither Daniel nor Clarinda had made mention of him, deciding no one would believe them. Far better to think his appearances immediately following his death were merely their minds playing tricks on them.

"Which one?" Danielle asked in awe, her mouth open in a quite unladylike manner.

"The one who looks... younger," Clarinda replied, not quite sure she was glad the girls could see the ghost.

"Younger?" Daniel countered, his attention on his older twin. "Hardly."

"Thinner," Danielle remarked. "Father definitely has a stone or two on this other man."

Daniel scoffed. "I'm the same weight I was when I married your mother," he claimed.

Clarinda furrowed a brow. "Perhaps, dear heart, but I do prefer the way you are now. There's more to hold onto when I'm in the throes of passion, uttering all those 'oh's,' she said drolly.

Daniel lifted his chin and regarded his brother with a grin of satisfaction. When David merely glared at him, Daniel moved in front of the sideboard and poured himself a brandy. "I'd offer you one, but—"

"Oh, please pour me one," Clarinda said as she stood and hurried over to Daniel.

"Awfully early for a drink, is it not?" David asked, his own dark brows furrowed.

"Since you apparently cannot tell time, pretend it's ten o'clock at night," she replied.

"Mother, who *is* this stranger?" Dahlia asked from where she still sat close to the fireplace.

David straightened. "You haven't told them?" he asked.

"If you recall, you only appeared a few moments ago," Clarinda replied.

"But they know I am their father?" David asked, his gaze darting to the twin daughters, his eyes widening in wonder. Clarinda's eyes rounded as David's attention went to Daniel. "They know you're their uncle, do they not?"

Daniel and Clarinda both winced.

The ghost scoffed. "I cannot believe you didn't tell them," David said as his face fell.

"I was married to Clare when they were born," Daniel whispered. "They were raised to believe I am their father. Which I am."

"Mother!" Dahlia called out as she stood. "Danielle and I demand an introduction to this... whatever he is."

"He's a ghost," Daniel stated. "A ghost of my late brother, David. If we ignore him, he'll go away."

"I will not, and you know it," David countered, one of his booted feet making contact with Daniel's shin.

"Ouch!" Daniel complained as he stepped back. His brandy splashed about in his glass, threatening to spill on the Axminster carpet. Although his immediate response was to attempt to kick back at David, Daniel took a calming breath. He knew his attempt would only find air.

"I told you Clare would give birth to twin girls," David said, his attention turning to his daughters. He made his way in their direction, stopping short of the young ladies when fear had them gripping each other's arms. "How do?" he said as he bowed. "David Fitzwilliam, Earl of Norwick, at your service." He reached for Dahlia's hand, but Dahlia and Danielle both stepped back in fear.

"We're so sorry. We'll never ask about sexual intercourse ever again," Danielle vowed.

David jerked back. "Well, now there's a topic I know a good deal about," he claimed. "I used to own the *Elegant Courtesan*." One of his brows arched seductively. "Surely you've heard of it?"

They shook their heads in unison.

"You closed it over twenty-five years ago, David," Clarinda reminded him. "And even if you didn't, they would have no knowledge of it," she said. "They are proper young ladies," she added, even if she didn't believe the claim. She'd been dealing with their antics for over twenty years.

"Hmph," he responded, sounding ever so disappointed. "We employed some well regarded young ladies," he murmured, "although as the proprietor, I did not avail myself of their talents."

"David!" Clarinda scolded.

Ignoring his widow's complaint, David continued his conversation with the twins. "What would you like to know?"

Dahlia and Danielle exchanged quick glances. "Does it hurt?" Danielle asked.

"Never. The opposite, in fact, if you have a considerate lover."

"Even the first time?" Dahlia queried.

Apparently not remembering *his* first time with Clarinda, David turned to regard her a moment. "Sweeting?"

Clarinda rolled her eyes. "The actual act of it was... uncomfortable, although the rest was..." She sighed, aiming an apologetic glance in Daniel's direction.

"Oh!" Danielle said, mimicking what she heard from the mistress suite.

David shook his head. "Not like that," he admonished her. "As I recall, she used the word 'yes' to good effect."

"David!" Clarinda scolded.

"You never say 'yes' with me," Daniel muttered.

"That's because I can't form a coherent word when I'm with you," Clarinda murmured, aiming an elegantly arched brow in his direction.

"Oh," he replied proudly, managing to avoid a quelling glance from one of the twins. They were both staring at the ghost of their real father.

"Why should I be expected to bend over a table?"

David recoiled a bit at hearing the censure in Danielle's voice. "Why, you shouldn't. Unless you find yourself short of time, or you'd like to conceive a baby boy—"

"David!" Clarinda admonished him. "She's not yet *married*."

The ghost blinked. "This is a most improper conversation for a young lady to be having prior to matrimony," he remarked.

"Are you really our father?" Danielle asked meekly. She reached out, but pulled her hand back before it could touch his topcoat sleeve.

"I am. I was. Am still?" He turned to Daniel as if for help in how to respond.

"You're *dead*, David. Which means you have no claim here. On them or on Clare."

"Well, aren't you the killjoy?" David responded.

"In fact, what *are* you doing here?" Daniel asked.

"You tell me. I'm not here because I had any say in the matter," the ghost claimed.

David turned to Clarinda, whose eyes rounded. "I didn't conjure him into existence," she said before he could accuse her of anything. "The girls and I were having a conversation about..." She stopped and inhaled softly. "Perhaps he sensed he should be here to answer their concerns," she whispered. "He *is* their father in the truest sense."

For a moment, Daniel looked as hurt as she'd ever seen him. The poor man had always come second in life, and only because he had emerged from the womb as the second of identical twins.

"I'm so sorry," Clarinda whispered. "I'll make it up to you, I promise."

"I've a mind to take you over a table in the library," Daniel muttered.

"*Oh!*"

"Exactly like that," Dahlia said as she continued to stare at her father's ghost.

"What? When?" David asked, confused.

"When she's in the throes of passion, she says 'oh' just like that."

"Just *you* wait," he replied dryly.

"What?"

"For when you experience such intense pleasure that you will allow a man to do anything to you. Almost anywhere."

Danielle blinked before she gave him a quelling glance. "I doubt that."

"I am a betting man, and I'm willing to wager—"

"*Enough!*" Daniel interrupted.

"More than enough that you will come to learn that I am telling the truth," David went on, ignoring his younger brother.

"Damn you, David. These are *your* daughters. I have tried to ensure they've been raised as proper young ladies. Now you've probably gone and undone over twenty years of careful, deliberate, and expensive education," he accused, his thoughts going to the tuition for Warwick's Grammar and Finishing School and the modiste they employed for their annual wardrobes.

"Nonsense," David replied. "These two are sensible young ladies." He turned to the twins. "You are sensible, are you not?"

They both nodded, although given David's natural tendency to make people do as he pleased, they might have only responded as he expected.

"So what are you looking for in husbands?" David asked as he crossed his arms.

"I want one like Sir Benjamin," Dahlia announced.

David furrowed his bushy brows, which is exactly what his twin was doing. "I don't recall a Sir Benjamin," he whispered.

"Earl of Wadsworth's younger son. Discovered a comet and earned a knighthood as a result," Daniel murmured. "Married Torrington's daughter before this Christmas past."

This bit of news had David's eyes rounding. "Milton Grandby sired a *child*?"

Daniel nodded. "Twins, in fact. His heir has already accepted a writ of acceleration and will be present for this next session of Parliament."

"So one of my daughters could marry the Torrington heir," David announced with a huge grin. "Capital!"

"They cannot," Daniel countered. "He married the Earl of Wellingham's daughter at the same time his twin sister married Sir Benjamin."

David blinked. "Well, what about the Earl of Trenton's son?"

"The oldest—the illegitimate one—married a potter he met at the British Museum, and the youngest is too young to marry," Clarinda commented.

Undaunted, David said, "Morganfield's son, Christopher. He must be a bit long in the tooth by now, but—"

"Married to Alistair Comber's daughter, Juliet."

As if he expected a marquess' son might still be available, he said, "Stephen Slater, Earl of Bellingham. Naval admiral, by now."

"Married to the daughter of the Earl of Greenley,"

Clarinda murmured. "He hasn't been in the Navy for nearly twenty years. And he's living next door to the Earl of Gisborn in Oxfordshire, since Gisborn is married to his sister, Hannah."

"Oh, I wouldn't have suggested Gisborn," David said as he waved a hand. "He's a farmer."

Daniel rolled his eyes, deciding not to mention how rich the earl had become with his invention of a new kind of plow. Either of Gisborn's legitimate sons would make excellent matches except they were the younger than the twins and still in university. Given Gisborn's good health, it was doubtful his heir would inherit in the next decade or so.

"What about Bostwick? He must have a son by now."

"Two. They're away at university," Daniel replied.

"What's wrong with them?"

"They're *younger* than we are, Father," Dahlia said wincing at referring to the ghost as her father. "By more than two or three years."

"In other words, not yet in the market to marry," Danielle clarified.

David seemed to inhale and hold his breath for far too long when he finally said, "Oh, all right then. Everly's son will have to do," he groused.

"Oh, I wish," Danielle breathed at the mention of Alexander Tennison, one hand flapping in front of her face as if she was about to faint.

"Me, too," Dahlia agreed, swooning.

David blinked and then frowned. "So... what's the problem?"

"He's about to marry a jeweler's daughter."

"They're *so* in love," Clarinda sighed happily, which had both David and Daniel giving her quelling glances.

"Well, they are," she argued. "And I'm hoping my daughters will be in love with whomever decides to court them this Season. They deserve no less."

Both daughters said, "Oh!" in unison, which had their mother glaring at them and their fathers chuckling.

"Surely there must be two young men in this town who would suit my daughters," David said when he finally sobered.

"We'll know soon enough. The Season starts next week," Clarinda said on a sigh.

"Then I intend to be at every entertainment," David announced.

Clarinda and Daniel both blinked. "But you won't have invitations to any of them."

David scoffed. "I don't need an invitation," he countered. "I'll just... pop in."

Although Clarinda didn't say anything in response, Daniel's groan was loud enough to be heard by everyone in the parlor.

CHAPTER 2
AN ORAL TEST OF THE GODS

Meanwhile, at Cambridge University
"You are a dunderhead."

The accusation was said with a sort of tired resignation, as if the young man who spoke the words had said them many times in the past.

"I am," Andrew Comber, the spare heir to the Aimsley earldom responded, even though he had never worked in rum production or had even held a cane of sugar in his entire one-and-twenty years. He was watching his older-by-mere-minutes brother regard his reflection in a shaving mirror. The reverse image of the scarlet tapestry waistcoat Anthony wore had him wincing. He looked down at his own plain hunter green waistcoat and audibly sighed. "Unless we wore identical clothes, you taking the test for me was never going to work," he added. "I'm so sorry."

"It would have worked if you'd at least worn the same color waistcoat as I was wearing," Anthony, Viscount Breckinridge, countered. "Now I'm in trouble, too." He rolled his eyes. "Perfect grades for four years and now..." He let the sentence trail off as he sighed.

"I don't own a scarlet waistcoat," Andrew said quietly. He wasn't even sure the two of them possessed waistcoats of the same fabric. Similar colors, perhaps, although they had completely different tastes when it came to the decoration. His brother preferred flamboyant embroidery on his waistcoats—birds, flowers, dragonflies—while he tended to choose more sedate, single-colored fabrics and jewel-toned tapestries.

"Well, needless to say, Professor Smith-Jones wants you in his office now," Anthony stated before he turned around and angled his head to one side. "And I rather imagine we'll be hearing from Father if we don't admit what's happened before he learns of it from the dean, which means we must write a letter."

The feeling of resignation was joined by a combination of dread and fear. Three days of the Lent term left, and Andrew was about to be expelled. He was sure of it. All because he had talked his brother into taking his mythology test in his place.

Professor Smith-Jones wouldn't have even taken notice of his brother except that he had seen Andrew in the courtyard only moments before the start of class. Moments before the final test of the class was administered in his classroom.

The fact that Professor Smith-Jones noticed such things as the color of waistcoats had Andrew realizing the professor had probably been the victim of the same antics by other identical twins in the past. Andrew was almost surprised the man even noticed him at all. The older gentleman wore gold wire-rimmed spectacles and lectured from behind a podium, his baritone voice booming out through the classroom with a sort of authority possessed by kings and tax collectors. He had never thought the man even took notice of his students.

"I'd best go there then," Andrew said quietly. "I'm really sorry this happened. Truly, I am."

Anthony regarded him with a combination of regret and sorrow. "As am I. It's best you not put it off. See what you can salvage, and I'll see to penning a letter to Father."

Nodding, Andrew took his leave of their dormitory room and made his way to Professor Smith-Jones' office. While on his way, a half-dozen possibilities for his future flitted through his mind's eye, not the least of which was his father disowning him and throwing him out of Aimsley House without so much as an allowance. He would never again spend his summers at Pickinghurst in Sussex. Anthony would probably continue their father's edict, ensuring Andrew would be forced to marry for money. Marry some poor young lady in possession of a decent dowry that he might be able to make last for the rest of their lives if he budgeted carefully, and they didn't have too many children.

By the time he knocked on the professor's office door, Andrew had resigned himself to the life of a pauper, holding a tin cup as he begged on some corner near the Bank of England, his hunter green waistcoat threadbare and the soles of his Hobys worn through.

"Comber," Smith-Jones said after Andrew had entered upon hearing the authoritative, "Come," from the other side of the door.

"Sir," Andrew acknowledged. "My brother said you wished to see me."

The professor pushed some papers to the side of his large oak desk and waved to the chair that sat opposite of his own. "Do you know how many sets of identical twins have taken at least one of my classes over the thirty years of my tenure here?" he asked.

Realizing it wasn't a rhetorical question, Andrew shook his head and shrugged his shoulders at the same time. "Ten, sir?" he guessed.

A chuckle rumbled from Smith-Jones's throat. "You and your brother are my first," he replied.

Andrew's eyes rounded. "Sir?"

"I know. I have a colleague who teaches at Oxford. He's had at least five sets over the years. Warned me, he did. So imagine my surprise when neither you nor your brother seemed to have attempted anything untoward for nearly four years."

"You were expecting it, sir?" Andrew asked, his dark brows furrowing.

Chuckling once more, Smith-Jones leaned back in his chair. "Indeed. But... but what has me so surprised is why *now*? You've not done well in this class for the entire semester—"

"I am terrible at taking written exams, sir," Andrew interrupted.

"That's become quite obvious," Smith-Jones stated, his hand indicating several papers Andrew recognized as the other course exams he had nearly failed throughout the term. "And yet, you've never missed a class. I've never caught you sleeping during my lectures."

"I know the material, sir. I remember every last word you said in class." He pointed to the side of his head. "Everything."

Smith-Jones leaned back in his chair. "And yet you're barely passing my class," he countered.

"The words in the tests are jumbled, sir."

Blinking, Smith-Jones regarded his student a

moment before he settled his crossed arms on his desk. "Jumbled?" he repeated.

"I see them. I can read them... sometimes... but it's as if the letters become mixed up. And I get confused. And then I panic and..." He sighed. "It takes me twice as long to sort the question and then write the answer, so I'm never able to finish the exam," he added on a sigh.

Smith-Jones regarded him with skepticism for a moment. "You claim to know the material."

"I do," Andrew affirmed. "I remember everything you've ever said in the lecture hall.

"Apollo's mother was...?"

"Leto."

"And his twin sister?"

"Artemis, goddess of the hunt," Andrew replied.

"Their father was...?"

"Zeus."

Intrigued, Smith-Jones continued to put forth questions, and Andrew answered each and every one correctly. When he was prompted to provide more information, Andrew gave it, his words the exact same words Smith-Jones had used in his lectures.

"Mr. Comber, it is obvious you have been paying attention in my class," Smith-Jones announced. "So I'm going to give you a passing grade."

"You are, sir?" Andrew asked in surprise, his eyes rounding.

"How many other classes are you taking in which you have this... jumbled words issue?"

Andrew shook his head. "Only those that require a good deal of reading, sir," he replied. "Mathematics is not a problem. Numbers seem to stay put on the page. And neither are my art classes."

Smith-Jones regarded him a moment before he asked, "What will you do for your living, Mr. Comber?"

Furrowing his brows, Andrew said, "I am the spare heir, sir, to the Aimsley earldom. Since there aren't any wars at the moment, I hope to spend my days in artistic pursuits. Drawing and painting."

"Well, I already know you're good at drawing," Smith-Jones said, pulling a paper from those in the stack at the edge of his desk.

Andrew winced at seeing the pencil drawing of a scantily clad Professor Smith-Jones in the guise of Neptune. A trident held in one hand and his bushy eyebrows somewhat exaggerated, Neptune appeared ready to send a tidal wave over the entirety of Great Britain. "I wondered what happened to that one," Andrew whispered.

"Fell out of your book after class one day," Smith-Jones replied. "I admit to a moment of seething anger before I realized how good I look as a Roman god."

"You have the voice to go along with the rendering, sir," Andrew stated. "Very god-like. Which is probably why I remember everything you've said in class."

The professor laughed, the booming sound no doubt heard all the way down to the courtyard below. Mere mortals were probably scrambling to take cover lest the stone walls crumbled in its wake. "You're dismissed, Comber. But I'm keeping the drawing," Smith-Jones stated.

"Of course, sir. Thank you, sir."

Andrew stood to leave, but his professor held up a staying hand. "As with any artwork you produce in your future, Comber, you need to sign it," he said, holding out a quill.

Blinking, Andrew took the quill and dipped it in the ink pot at the front of Smith-Jones' desk. He signed his name in the lower right corner of the drawing. "It's my honor, sir," he said as he placed the quill back in its holder and handed the drawing to the professor.

"Now, I trust once you're back in London, you'll find some lovely young woman with a huge dowry who can support you for the rest of your life," Smith-Jones remarked.

"If I'm still alive, sir." At seeing his professor's look of surprise, Andrew added, "My Father will kill me when he learns of this."

Smith-Jones sighed. "I've already informed the dean, but... if you were to send a note to the earl right away, it may help your cause," he suggested. "Better to learn of it from you than from the dean."

Andrew inhaled softly. "Yes, sir."

Feeling a sense of relief combined with dread, Andrew took his leave of the professor's office and made his way to the nearest public house.

If he did marry a young woman for her dowry, at least he wouldn't be forced to live the life of a pauper.

CHAPTER 3
AN EARL FEELS HIS AGE

The following day, Aimsley House, Mayfair
      "So glad *that's* over," Adam Comber, Earl of Aimsley, said as he removed his top hat and handed it to his butler. He'd returned from a political meeting at one of London's many chocolate shops, the varied discussions in preparation for the opening of the next session of Parliament. "I cannot imagine my father ever had the patience to abide the machinations in the House of Lords."

As Hummel helped his master out of his greatcoat, he said, "If it's any consolation, sir, he did not."

The comment did nothing to alleviate Adam's concerns. His father, the sixth Earl of Aimsley, had died the year before. As the heir, Adam had done what Mark Comber had trained him to do these past two decades —take on the responsibilities of the Aimsley earldom and take his seat in the House of Lords. As for the ledgers associated with the earldom, Adam had gladly accepted his wife's offer of assistance. He had decided long ago that the most brilliant moment of his life had been proposing—in a manner of speaking—to a mathematics instructor.

"Is my mother in residence?" Adam asked, referring to the Dowager Countess of Aimsely, Patience Waterford Comber.

Hummel shook his head. "She's at Carlington House, sir. Helping Lady Morganfield with the plans for Saturday's garden party."

Adam stiffened. "And the countess?" he asked, referring to Diana Albright Comber, his wife of two-and-twenty years.

"She's in the classroom upstairs, sir."

Frowning, Adam was about to ask why when his attention went to a pair of children who were descending the hall stairs. The boy, about ten, was dressed smartly in dark breeches and a top coat of superfine while the girl wore a peach frock that made her appear much older than her nine years.

"Well, who do we have here?" he asked as he made his way to the bottom of the stairs, pretending he didn't recognize his nephew and niece by way of his wife's sister, Daisy.

The children's eyes rounded. Daphne performed a perfect curtsy before offering her hand while her brother, James, bowed.

Adam did the honors with regard to Daphne's hand, but he didn't let go after brushing his lips over her knuckles. Instead, he bent down and pulled her into an embrace. "I hardly recognize you," he said with a huge grin, which had his nephew looking ever so relieved.

"Good afternoon, Uncle Adam," James said, letting out an "oof" when Adam pulled him into the same hug.

"Uncle, you're wrinkling my gown," Daphne complained. Her scolding turned to giggles when Adam tickled her. James managed to escape his uncle's hold before Adam could tickle him.

"Whatever are you two doing here today?" Adam asked when he finally released Daphne, grinning at seeing her face light up at his antics. On several occasions, he had warned Daisy and her husband, George, Baron Streater, that he had plans to kidnap the young girl to claim her as his own.

He didn't have a daughter, and they had two.

He did have sons, though. Twins. One-and-twenty and away at Cambridge, which meant the house was mostly quiet these days.

Twenty years ago, he remembered feeling profound relief that his wife had survived the ordeal of their birth. Relief that the babes were both healthy and hearty—their lungs had been proof of that, given how loudly they could wail in the middle of the night. But their birth had left Diana unable to give him more children.

Back then, he hadn't minded one bit.

Now...

"Aunt Diana is tutoring me in arithmetic," James stated.

"Me, too," Daphne chimed in. "I'm learning fractions."

Adam blinked. "How old are you?" he asked in alarm. He had never been good at mathematics. Fractions had been beyond his ken.

Daphne let out an audible sigh. "Uncle, it's not polite to ask young ladies their age," she replied.

"She's nine," James offered, rolling his eyes. "And she's Aunt Diana's favorite."

"Of course she is," Adam replied. "She's my favorite, too," he teased. He regarded his niece and felt a twinge of regret that he didn't have a daughter of his own.

By the gods, what had happened to him over the years? He hadn't even wanted to marry—not really—when Felix, Earl of Fennington, reminded him of a wager that required he be married by the time he was thirty.

That Diana Albright just happened to be walking past White's men's club that afternoon back in 1818 when he and Fennington had been admiring young ladies from the bow window of White's as they passed by... well, it had to have been fate.

That Diana would take umbrage at being admired from said bow window and decide she had to know exactly how she ranked on their scale of one to ten—how did she even know they assigned numbers to young ladies who passed by?—also had to be Fate, for when she stopped in her tracks and then climbed the stairs to the front door of White's, asking to speak with the man in the bow window... well, who was he to question Fate?

He gladly joined her, acting as if he expected her arrival. Walked with her to the corner of St. James and Jermyn Streets and then kissed her in front of the gods and everyone else who took notice of them.

Thank the gods she didn't slap him, for he proposed right then and there.

Well, not really.

He merely announced rather loudly and happily that she had said, "Yes." A smattering of applause followed his antics, and he felt a good deal of satisfaction.

Poor Diana had looked as if she was going to faint.

She was a 'ten' in his estimation, secretly glad Fennington had found her to be only a seven in his.

Fennington was a fool, but then it wasn't long before he was smitten by another young woman who was apparently a 'ten' by his standards.

Adam had never regretted his odd proposal, even when he discovered Diana was an instructor at Warwick's Grammar and Finishing School. There might have been a twinge of hesitancy when he learned she taught mathematics, but even then, he must have known how helpful she would be in the operation of an earldom. How her skills at arithmetic would benefit the Aimsely ledgers.

Then, finally, there had been another twinge upon learning she was the illegitimate daughter of James, Duke of Ariley. Not because she was illegitimate, but because her father was a duke.

Never once had he wondered what might have been had he simply tried the more traditional manner of finding a wife by meeting and courting a young woman. He would have had to attend the annual Season's entertainments on a more regular basis. Dance with eligible young ladies. Ride with them in the park. Converse with them at *soirées*.

If not for Diana, he never would have found a wife for whom he would give up his roguish behavior.

Daphne's giggle had him shaking off his thoughts of the past. "Where are you off to now?" he asked, wincing when he realized his back was twinging from having been bent over for so long. He slowly straightened, a grimace replacing his expression of good humor.

He hated getting old. He could hardly believe he would be one-and-fifty this year.

"Home, sir. Mother is expecting us for tea," James replied.

"Oh, well, be sure to give her my regards. Your father as well," he added, remembering he would be joining George in the House of Lords the following week.

"We will, Uncle Adam," Daphne replied, dipping a perfect curtsy. "We'll be back tomorrow."

"Good-bye, Uncle," James said as he gripped Daphne's hand and pulled her to the vestibule.

Hummel saw to their coats and head coverings before he opened the front door and watched them skip to the town coach parked at the curb.

"I'm going to kidnap Daphne. Adopt her as my own daughter," Adam stated as he crossed his arms and watched the children climb into the coach.

"Very good, sir," Hummel replied, ignoring the earl's claim. "Two letters arrived for you today. I put them on your desk in the study."

Adam blinked, realizing even his own butler had no regard for his plans. He thought of going to his study to see what the post had delivered, but then remembered what the children had said about his wife.

Diana was up in the classroom.

Before he quite knew what he was doing, Adam climbed the stairs, taking some two at a time despite the painful twinges his knees sent out. By the time he made it to the third floor, he had slowed his steps in an attempt to catch his breath. When he made it to the classroom, he paused on the threshold, and his breathing stopped.

The sight of his wife did that sometimes. Dressed in

a poppy colored day gown, she was bent over the small table in the middle of the room, cleaning a slate chalkboard with a linen. When she sensed his presence, she straightened and stared at him. "Is something wrong?" she asked in alarm.

He shook his head as he inhaled deeply. "Not at all," he replied, his mind going back to a time when she had been caught unawares as he found her leaning over a library table. How when she sensed his presence, she hadn't straightened but tucked her elbows beneath her. How she had regarded him with eyes that darkened with desire.

Who was he to consider turning down such an overt invitation?

Adam was fairly sure the twins had been conceived that day in the library.

"Adam?"

Pulled from his brief reverie, Adam gave a start. "The children said you were up here."

She grinned as she joined him at the door. "Daisy asked if I might take on some of their schooling. She's not very impressed with James' tutor, but she's not about to send her son to Eton, either."

"Can't blame her," Adam replied as he gazed down at her. Perhaps it was simply the afternoon light from the window or maybe it was from something else, but he thought her face was glowing. "You're not helping Lady Morganfield plan her garden party?" he asked with an arched brow.

Diana's eyes rounded, surprised he would know of it. "Oh, I wasn't invited," she replied. "Not for the planning, at least. This is only my first year as a countess," she reminded him with a pained expression. "We are going on Saturday, though. It will be good to see everyone again." After a pause, she asked, "Why are you looking at me like that?" She lifted a hand to her cheek. "Do I have chalk all over my face?"

Adam didn't answer. He pulled her into his arms and kissed her quite thoroughly. He'd been about to come up for air when he instead deepened the kiss and groaned before tightening his hold on her.

Then he did break it off, although he didn't pull his face from hers. "If I never told you before, you are a 'ten'," he whispered.

Diana's eyes rounded before a grin touched her lips. "Why, Adam Comber, what are you about?"

"I've absolutely no idea," he replied. "I just... I had to see you."

Blinking, Diana pulled away slightly before her gaze went beyond the door to the one directly across the corridor. "How much of me?" she asked, an eyebrow arching suggestively.

It was Adam's turn to blink. "What did you have in mind?" he asked as his grin matched hers.

Diana didn't respond, but grabbed one of his hands in hers and pulled him into the bedchamber across the hall.

After he was completely in the room and she had shut the door behind him, he scoffed. "I didn't know this was a bedchamber," he said as he glanced around. The velvet drapes were pulled shut, so the room was quite dark.

"It's the only one on this floor," Diana replied as she unbuttoned his top coat, not adding that she was fairly sure it had been the late earl's and his countess' secret love nest. She turned around and presented her back to him. "Well, besides the nursery."

For a moment, Adam simply stared at the soft, dark

curls on the nape of her neck, at how the rest of her long hair was caught up in a large bun at the back of her head. He lowered his head until his nose could push away the curls and he kissed her.

She gave a start at the tickling sensation and inhaled softly. Reaching behind her, she molded a hand over the hardening ridge behind the top of his pantaloons and squeezed.

The move seemed to awaken him from his stupor, his fingers expertly undoing the fastenings down the back of her gown. When he was finished, she turned and undid his waistcoat buttons, her breaths increasing as she pushed his coats from his shoulders.

Adam might have found her enthusiasm amusing, but his need for her had him matching her moves. He had her stripped of her gown and petticoats even as he was attempting to shed the boots from his feet. "I do hope I'm not keeping you from something important," he whispered.

"I cannot imagine what that might be," she replied, pulling the hem of his shirt from his pantaloons. She was about to lift it up when she saw his cravat was still tied. She quickly went to work undoing the knot as he stepped out of his other boot.

"You're so busy these days," he replied, turning her around so he could undo the ties of her corset. "Ever since I inherited. It seems as if I only see you at breakfast and dinner."

Diana turned her head so her chin rested on her shoulder. "There is nothing more important than you," she whispered.

He pulled her corset over her head, leaving her wearing only a silk chemise, and then watched as she hurried to the bed to turn down the counterpane and blankets and linens.

The sight of her bent over the edge of the bed, her bare bottom outlined in the thin chemise, had his manhood at full attention. He stripped the cravat from around his neck as he made his way to stand behind her and then slid a hand beneath the chemise and up between her thighs, cupping her mound.

She inhaled sharply, her back arching as his other arm moved in front of her body, a hand covering a breast and essentially trapping her in place against the front of his body.

In the past, she sometimes fought his hold on her, wriggled around in his arms so she could capture his manhood in her fist. She didn't this time, though, allowing the hand between her thighs to rub her until it was coated with her ambrosia and her womanhood had swelled with her desire.

Adam was about to bring her to ecstasy, to a quick and sharp release, but he had the time to do more.

Pulling his hand from between her thighs—he chuckled at her mewl of disappointment—he had her turned around and up on the edge of the bed and his head between her thighs before her head hit the mattress.

"Oh!" she cried out as his tongue flicked her swollen nubbin.

Adam repeated the move, delighting in hearing her pleas and oh's, in how she squirmed and lifted her knees so her feet hung over his shoulders, a sure sign she was giving up and allowing him whatever he wanted.

If only his back didn't complain so.

Although he wanted to spend more time teasing her before allowing her release, he knew he wouldn't be able to straighten up if he didn't do it now. So he was relieved when her breath caught and her body jerked beneath his hold.

Groaning as he straightened—he might have let out a curse whilst doing so—Adam winced.

"Oh, dear, do come lie on the bed," Diana encouraged, quickly moving to the far side and turning over so she was on her hands and knees.

Adam stared at her, amazed she could experience the throes of passion one moment and speak—and apparently think—coherently the next.

Adam accepted the invitation, although he removed his pantaloons before he climbed onto the bed.

Diana pushed him until he was on his back and then climbed atop him, her knees on either side of his hips. She had his turgid manhood at her opening and then halfway into her as she stripped the chemise from her body.

His eyes rounding at seeing her glorious naked body mounted on his, Adam grinned and groaned. Her breasts, far larger than they had been on their wedding night, were still pert, their nipples hard pebbles at their tips. Her hips were wider, but not by much. And her belly...

She settled all the way onto his manhood and sighed contentedly. "We haven't done it like this in an age," Diana whispered.

Adam swallowed, his gaze going from her belly up to her face. "We can do it like this whenever you'd like," he replied, his hands moving to her hips so he could help with the up and down movements that had his cock straining for its release.

He reveled in watching her breasts bob up and down. Reveled in hearing her inhalations of breath. In feeling her fingernails scrape down his chest and stomach, sending all sorts of strange sensations through his torso. Reveled in how her head fell back and her torso stretched and she held her breath when his thumb rubbed the space where their bodies met.

But mostly he reveled at the reason her face glowed so prettily.

"You're pregnant, aren't you?" he asked in awe, the moment he felt his manhood pulled more deeply into her body. Her waves of pleasure sent him into his own state of ecstasy, and he gasped and sputtered, torn between laughing and moaning, until, breathless, Diana collapsed atop him.

They lay like that for several moments, Adam's arms wrapped around her back and her head resting on one of his shoulders. Although he desperately wanted a nap, he was determined to remain awake, at least until she answered his question.

"Well, *are* you?"

Diana pushed an elbow into the mattress and lifted her head from his shoulder. "Here I'd thought I'd been eating too many biscuits at tea time," she murmured. "But I do prefer your idea much better." She furrowed a brow, though.

"You mean... you don't know?" he asked in dismay.

She sighed, apparently trying to determine if she should share his enthusiasm or weep at the alternative. "I am five-and-forty years old," she said. "I've not felt sick at all these past few months. Remember, the physician claimed I wouldn't be able to have more children after the boys were born, but I suppose my womb could have healed enough after all this time." She paused and winced. "I thought... well, when I wasn't having my monthly courses, I just thought I was..." She let the sentence trail off, not sure he would know about the change in life that happened to women when they grew older.

"Too old?" he prompted. "My sweet, you're far younger than when Mother stopped having her monthly courses," he claimed.

Diana's eyes rounded. "You *knew* about that?" she asked in surprise.

"The entire household knew," he replied on a huff. "Don't you remember when Father suffered the worst of her behavior? He left for Haymarket to watch horse racing for nearly two months. I think even the readers of *The Tattler* knew, she was so mean-spirited," he added, referring to the gossip rag his mother had edited for over two decades.

Patience had sold the publication to another party upon the death of her husband, claiming it was time someone else oversaw London's gossip, and then she had promptly used the money to go to Europe on a shopping spree. She had returned to London only the week before, bringing with her a half-dozen trunks filled with gowns and all manner of fripperies and even some statuary.

Adam turned on his side, which had Diana rolling off his body and straightening on the bed. He had a hand on her belly before she had completely settled, his gaze following how he smoothed it over the slight mound. He reached down and kissed her belly. "Trust me, my sweet, you're with child," he said with a huge grin. He moved his lips to her nipples and kissed each one in turn. "And I could not be happier."

Diana placed a hand over his. "I should see my physician before you get your hopes up," she warned.

"Your sister is going to be thrilled, too," Adam said, ignoring her comment.

"Daisy? Why?"

"I've been plotting how I was going to kidnap Daphne and adopt her as my own," he replied, his lips quirked.

Startled by his admission, Diana regarded him warily. "I didn't realize you wanted a daughter," she said. "In fact, I remember a time when you said you were glad we *didn't* have a girl—"

"I know, I know," he interrupted. "I didn't want to have to set aside blunt for a dowry, or pay for new wardrobes every Season, or challenge young bucks who had a mind to court her," he admitted. "But... now I've changed my mind."

Diana blinked and then ran her fingers through his silvering hair, reminded that when they had married, he'd only been gray at the temples. The strands of hair felt like the finest silk.

"You haven't read your correspondence yet today, have you?" she asked in a whisper. When he'd come to the classroom, she was sure it was because he wished to discuss their current sons, not speak of future children. Having received a letter of her own from their younger son, Andrew, and seeing the seal embossed in the wax of the other that sat upon her husband's desk—clearly that of Cambridge University—she was fairly certain Andrew's future didn't include a final Easter term.

"Haven't been in my study all day," Adam said on a happy sigh. "Whatever it is, it can wait."

Diana moved her fingers to the back of his neck and pulled him down for a kiss, deciding she wouldn't share what she knew. Now was not the time.

When a cracking sound emanated from Adam's

back, he winced and chuckled. "I am getting old," he whispered.

"You're only one-and-fifty," she argued, but her eyes rounded slightly, as if she had realized something. "You think a child will help you feel young again?" she accused.

He grimaced but then finally nodded. "Either that, or it will be the death of me," he replied with a grin.

Diana gave him a quelling glance but reached up to kiss him again. "Well then, let's hope I am with child and that it does indeed youthen you," she said. Diana was about to add that he couldn't die before said child had grown up and left the nest, but she thought better of it.

She watched as he rolled onto his back, the grin still lighting his face as he fell asleep. Wide awake, Diana stared at the ceiling and contemplated their possible new future.

CHAPTER 4
MOTHERS OF TWINS CONFER

*T*he *following day, March 29, 1939, Norwick House parlor*

An incessant drizzle had begun sometime early that morning, which had the ringlets at Clarinda's temples wilting. She might have had her lady's maid touch them up before she accepted any callers, but she was so surprised when the butler, Belvedere, found her in her salon writing letters, she told him to take Lady Aimsley to the parlor. "Deliver a tea tray, won't you? I'll be right there."

"Of course, my lady," Belvedere replied before he nodded and disappeared down the corridor.

Clarinda met Diana only a moment after she'd been seated in one of the upholstered chairs near the fireplace. Diana quickly stood.

"I know you weren't expecting me today—"

"But I'm so glad you've come," Clarinda said as she reached out her hands and took Diana's in hers. She gave them a squeeze. "Tea is on the way. Whatever has brought you out in this awful weather?"

"Oh, Clare, I'm in a quandary, and I'm hoping you can set my mind at ease."

Clarinda's eyes widened. "Whatever is wrong?" She took a seat opposite of Diana. A number of possibilities flitted through her mind—a problem with a servant, a philandering husband, recalcitrant twins—so she was entirely unprepared when Diana replied.

"I've just come from my physician."

Clarinda blinked. "Oh?" she responded, immediately imagining the worst.

"I am with child."

Blinking again, Clarinda straightened in her chair and a brilliant smile lifted her face. "Why, that's wonderful!" At the same moment, the gray beyond the parlor windows was replaced with sunshine.

It was Diana's turn to blink. "How did you do that?" she asked, her gaze going to the only window she could see from her vantage.

Her attention going to the window directly behind Diana, Clarinda's breath hitched when she saw that David's ghost was leaning against the wall. He merely shrugged, as if he were the one responsible for the sudden change in weather. "Oh, Diana, you must be thrilled," she replied, ignoring her friend's query.

"Aimsley certainly is," Diana offered. "He's over the moon with the thought of having a daughter," she added. "Me? I'm not so sure."

Clarinda leaned forward, her face taking on a look of concern. "What's wrong?"

"I'm five-and-forty."

Waiting, as if she expected Diana to say more, Clarinda finally gave her head a shake. "I'm nine-and-forty." She finally furrowed a brow. "Are you frightened? Of childbirth?"

Diana inhaled softly. "I'm more frightened of having to go through everything all over again," she replied. "Not just the delivery, but..." She sighed. "Everything that follows. Tutors. Schooling. Introductions to Society. All alone, should my husband not live that long." She didn't add what she had since learned about her boys. That they had been expelled from university and would be home later that day or the next.

Swallowing, Clarinda settled into her chair. "Do you have reason to expect Aimsely—" She still had issues calling Adam Comber by his new title—"will *die* anytime soon? His father lived to be—"

"Nine-and-sixty, yes, I know," Diana said with a nod, relaxing a bit at the reminder. "Which Adam has in his favor. As well as his enthusiasm at the possibility that I'm carrying a girl. He wants a daughter. Desperately."

Clarinda angled her head to one side, wondering if her own husband was in want of more children. Daniel had never said, apparently satisfied with two of each. Although they enjoyed a spirited round of lovemaking at least a couple of times a week, she had never found herself with child after the birth of her second set of twins. She simply assumed her body had experienced enough of bearing children and was no longer capable of the feat.

Her gaze went briefly to David, who simply arched a brow. Then she remembered the times he had appeared in the past—after his death and before the birth of his daughters—and her hand went to her own belly. She did a quick calculation, attempting to remember when she had last experienced her monthly courses.

"Clare, what's wrong?" Diana asked, her gaze going to the window behind her. Her hostess' gaze had been on that very spot for the past few moments, and she wondered what she saw through the window. Only blue sky was apparent beyond the glass.

"I think I may be with child as well," Clarinda murmured.

"You do?" Diana asked, taken aback by the comment. Her eyes widened.

"Oh, my dear Diana. I perfectly understand your predicament," Clarinda wailed, grimacing when she noticed David's expression of delight. He had his head thrown back, as if he was laughing hysterically.

Bastard.

"You do?" Diana repeated, her alarm still evident.

Clarinda nodded, her attention still on David. "Don't you find it rather odd that about the time our children have reached the age to marry, we find ourselves with child again?"

"I do," Diana agreed, her head nodding. "Especially after what Adam learned about our twins this morning." She winced, rather glad he hadn't gone to his study the day before. His general good mood throughout dinner and their time together in his bedchamber later that night wouldn't have happened if he had read the letters from Andrew and the Dean of Academics at the university.

Now that he had, he was livid. Only her reminder that she was off to see her physician had him settling down a bit.

A maid appeared on the threshold, a tea tray held in front of her. She hurried to the low table between the ladies and set it down. "Would you like me to serve, m'lady?"

"I'll see to it," Clarinda replied, deciding she didn't want any servants learning of her pregnancy. At least, not yet. She leaned forward to prepare the cups and pour the tea. She waited until the maid had curtsied and left the parlor before she furrowed her brows. "Pray tell, what did he learn about the boys?" She knew Anthony and Andrew quite well. Her daughters were about the same age, and their circle of friends included the boys. She knew that Andrew, the spare heir of the twin, had held a candle for Danielle since they were young children.

"It doesn't matter," Diana replied with a shake of her head as she accepted a cup of tea. She expected that after a few days of circumspection, Adam would change his mind and relent on his demand that the boys return home, court, and take wives before he would resume their allowances. "Well, except that he's quite insistent the boys get married."

Clarinda furrowed a brow, wondering what had the former rogue deciding such a thing. Perhaps he remembered his behavior far too well and didn't want his sons following in his footsteps. "Well, if it's any consolation, my twins are rebelling against the idea of marriage," Clarinda stated as she offered the plate of biscuits. "Take two or three," she ordered when Diana meekly took only one. "Dahlia found the books about sexual congress in the library. Now they have a fear of the marriage bed," she said with a roll of her eyes. She helped herself to two of the lemon biscuits. "They want... proof, I suppose, of a man's ability to make marriage... worth it. Proof they won't have to put up with a philandering husband." She sighed. "I thought I had done everything right whilst raising them," she added on a sigh. Clarinda's gaze once again went to the window behind Diana, but she gave a start when she realized David was no longer there.

Bastard.

She bit into a lemon biscuit, determined she would eat all of them if Diana didn't help herself to more.

"I'm quite sure my sons were counting on a Grand Tour of Europe," Diana countered, lifting a finger to brush a crumb from the edge of her mouth. "At least, Andrew certainly was. He's talked about it since he was a young boy."

"Danielle claimed she wants to use her inheritance to go to Italy. Maybe even live there," Clarinda groused.

Lady Aimsley chuckled. "My boys were counting on a few more years of attending the entertainments before taking wives," she said with a wince. Although she was fairly sure they weren't about to live the lives of rogues, much like their father had done before marrying her, she wasn't sure what might have happened to change them during their time at university. For all she knew, they might be tupping serving wenches at every public house or paying prostitutes for quick tumbles. The thought had a shudder of revulsion passing through her. She finished off the biscuit and started on another.

"Have they any young ladies in mind to court?" Clarinda asked, sharing her friend's concern. "The current crop of debutantes are just so..." She rolled her eyes as she ate another biscuit.

"Insipid," Diana said.

"Exactly."

"Far too young to be marrying."

"Far too young to be having babies," Clarinda put in, helping herself to another biscuit. She couldn't understand what had her feeling so hungry all of a sudden.

"Which means they really need to be looking to marry young ladies closer to their age," Diana stated, starting on another biscuit.

Clarinda blinked. "How old are they?"

"Nearly one-and-twenty."

A slow smile appeared to brighten Clarinda's face. "Oh, but the solution is so perfect, Diana," she murmured.

"Solution?"

"Of course. My girls are two-and-twenty. They need to marry your boys," Clarinda stated. "They already know them. They've been socializing with them since they were children," she reasoned. "And I do believe your Andrew has his eye on Danielle."

Clarinda knew from her conversations with Dahlia that her oldest twin had always found that Anthony's mannerisms made him seem older than he was, but she respected his position as heir to an earldom. As for Andrew, Dahlia thought of him as the perfect younger brother, one she could boss about, while Danielle deferred to whatever Anthony said while she and Andrew behaved as if they were the best of friends.

"Problem solved," Clarinda stated. She blinked when she realized David had reappeared next to the window, giving her a nod of satisfaction.

Bastard.

Diana blinked. "Oh, it makes sense, of course," she agreed. For her sons to be wed to the daughters of the Norwick earldom did make perfect sense.

Never mind that Anthony found Dahlia too opinionated or Danielle too demure. That Andrew thought of Dahlia more as his older sister or Danielle his best friend or perhaps more. Between the four of them, they should be able to determine the perfect couplings.

"How do we make this happen?" Diana asked.

Clarinda furrowed a brow, but her attention went to David, who had settled against the wall, his arms crossed and his face displaying a self-satisfied sort of expression. "Perhaps we don't have to *do* anything," she replied, arching an elegant brow.

David's expression changed to one of alarm.

"Let's let fate intervene, shall we?" Clarinda added, rather enjoying how the ghost of her late husband seemed to slide down the wall until his bottom hit the floor.

"Well, if you're sure," Diana replied uncertainly.

Clarinda grinned. "I'm quite sure," she said, one hand going to her belly.

She could only hope she wasn't carrying another set of twins.

CHAPTER 5

HOMECOMING AND AN
ULTIMATUM

*M*eanwhile, at Aimsley House in Mayfair
Dusty and mud-splattered, its springs squeaking in protest, the ancient traveling coach of the Aimsley earldom pulled up to the curb in front of Aimsley House and stopped. The four horses that pulled it neighed and snorted, adding their own protest to the noisy arrival.

Hummel had the front door opened and two footmen dispatched to see to luggage even before the driver had the coach door opened. The twin boys emerged, although Hummel straightened slightly at seeing they were no longer boys but young men.

He hadn't noticed so much when they had been home for a few days at Christmastide. Their spirited antics and general happy countenances had enlivened Aimsley House during the holiday, and when they had departed for the Lent term at Cambridge, they had taken that lively spirit with them.

From their dour expressions and business-like manner now, he realized they had left their lively spirits behind at university. Or perhaps it had been drummed out of them by humorless professors.

"Welcome home," Hummel said as the two stepped over the threshold and gave up their greatcoats into his waiting arms.

"Good to see you, Hummel," Andrew said. He sighed. "Is Father in residence?"

About to answer, Hummel found he didn't need to when the earl emerged from his study. He acknowledged him with a nod and then waved the twins into the room before shutting the door—rather loudly.

The two footmen passed him, a trunk suspended between them. "We'll come down for the second one as soon as we finished delivering this one."

Hummel frowned. Usually the twins brought only their valises when they returned home between terms—not their entire trunks.

It was at that moment when all three servants froze, for the word, "Expelled?" could be heard from inside the study. Even behind the closed door, the master's shout was loud. The anger behind it was just as clear.

Adam Comber, Earl of Aimsely, was not happy.

"I passed the test, Father. I got all the questions right, once the professor asked them verbally," Andrew explained in a plaintive voice. "But I knew I wouldn't pass the written exam. It takes me far too long to read the questions—"

"I don't care," Adam interrupted. "I mean... I do, but the manner in which you went about it was entirely *wrong*. Don't you two know they were just waiting for you to attempt something like this? To exchange places in class?" he asked.

Andrew and Anthony dared glances at one another, their mirror-image reflections making it appear to their father as if they were staring into a looking glass. "We've never done it before," Anthony claimed.

"I don't care. They were watching for it. And you've been caught." He'd been pacing in front of his desk as he yelled at his sons, and now he moved to stand behind it. He wasn't sure if his sudden exhaustion was because of what he and Diana had been doing all night or because of the anger he had been experiencing since reading his correspondence, but he had to admit he was glad he had waited.

Had he opened the letters the day before, when Hummel first informed him he had two letters, he never would have joined Diana in the classroom. Never would have been seduced by her. Wouldn't yet know that she was with child and possibly carrying his daughter.

That realization had led to their afternoon in bed. An intimate dinner. An evening of rediscovery. An entire night of lovemaking and laughter, teasing and titters, kissing and caressing.

He'd awoken that morning feeling happy and young and... yes, a bit sore, but not as much as usual. Enjoyed a shower bath and a shave. A hearty breakfast.

And then he had made the mistake of reading the damned letters.

The subjects of those letters now sat before him, their backs ramrod straight in the ridiculous floral print chairs his mother had insisted be installed back when his father still lived.

Both looked as guilty as they were.

Although even Adam could hardly tell them apart, Anthony had always taken the lead, exerting his right as the first-born when answering questions or making decisions. Even now, he spoke up for the both of them. "What punishment do you have in mind for us, Father?"

Adam blinked. He had briefly discussed it with Diana only the hour before, half-expecting she would advocate on their behalf and ask that he go easy on the boys.

But she hadn't.

What punishment do you have in mind for the boys? she had asked.

When he'd told her of his plan, she had scoffed and said, *Well, you'll not hear an argument from me. Every mother wants to see her sons wed. The sooner, the better. Although...*

She hadn't finished her last thought, so Adam wasn't sure what had her dark brows furrowing before she stood on tiptoe and kissed his cheek.

He remembered blinking. Remembered feeling empowered. Remembered thanking his lucky stars he had such a wise woman as his countess.

But he was also having some second thoughts. That "although..." sounded more ominous by the moment. He made a mental note to ask her about it later that afternoon.

Seating himself in the large leather chair behind his desk, Adam leaned back and exhaled. "Your allowances are hereby forfeit. There will be no Grand Tours for either of you. You want your allowances resumed, you'll have to secure a promise of marriage and then be married."

Anthony and Andrew regarded one another in shock before returning their startled gazes on their father. "Mm...m... married?"

Adam was quite sure he had never heard his oldest son stutter before. He was also quite sure the young man had never passed out, either, but the way his face paled and his eyes glazed over, Adam decided there was a first for everything.

"May we wed who we wish?" Andrew asked, apparently taking the news far better than his brother.

Blinking, Adam allowed a shrug. "Well, I would hope you have your sights set on an appropriate young woman," he replied. "A daughter of the *ton* or.... a well-to-do merchant's daughter," he hedged.

"Oh, I've already secured a promise of marriage from an earl's daughter," Andrew replied.

This had Anthony recovering his faculties as well as the use of his eyebrows, for they both lifted in alarm. "Since when?"

Andrew shrugged. "I was... eight, I think."

His father scoffed. "You remember when you were eight years old? Because *she* probably doesn't."

His eyes darting between his father and his brother, Andrew said, "Of course. And I'm sure she does. Don't you?" When he saw Anthony's usual expression of boredom when he spoke of their past, he added, "I remember everything I've ever heard spoken, sir, which is how I learned at university. And Eton before."

Adam frowned. "You're not joking?"

Anthony held up a staying hand. "He speaks the truth, Father. Since he has such trouble seeing letters correctly or in the right order—he's rot at reading—he's learned to memorize everything that's said during his lectures—"

"Not just lectures."

"—and anything else he hears. He'd make an excellent spy if the Crown still employed any," Anthony finished on a sigh.

"I'm fairly sure they still do," Andrew said, his expression looking as if he were a bit worried the Crown might have given up on surreptitious intelligence gathering.

"Well, you're not going to become a spy for the Crown," Adam stated. "But I'm sure your skill could come in handy at some point. Now, although you think you have a promise of marriage, I suggest you secure an updated promise and a definitive date."

"I will, Father. And when I do—"

"*If* you do..."

"May I take her to Italy and Greece for our wedding trip?"

Anthony scoffed. "You're determined to take your Grand Tour, even with a wife in tow?" The way his brows were knit together at the base of his forehead, Andrew knew his brother didn't agree with the plan.

Andrew sent a grimace in his brother's direction. "I am, and I think escorting a young woman about Europe could be rather scintillating."

"You can do whatever you want with your allowance once you're wed," Adam stated, ignoring their discussion. He had taken their mother to Rome soon after they were wed, which was probably why there were twin sons sitting across from him right now. Although they had gone to see the sights, he had spent a good deal of the time enjoying the sight of Diana, naked in their hotel room, doing a perfect imitation of the Roman goddess of love.

Adam had to erase the memory of those early days of his marriage when his cock threatened to take up every available inch of space in his pantaloons, not that there was much extra space there. In fact, if Diana hadn't gone off to see her physician, Adam might have taken his leave of the study and resumed what they were doing a few hours ago.

"Lady Morganfield's garden party is tomorrow, and Lord Weatherstone's ball is Tuesday night," Adam stated. "I suggest you wrangle some invitations." He inhaled softly and then added, "Dismissed."

His two boys dared glances at one another before they slowly got to their feet and filed out of the study.

Leaning back in his chair, Adam's thoughts once again went to his wife and their future child. His sour mood quickly dissipated, and he grinned as he stared at the correspondence that had arrived that morning.

He might not have bothered opening any of the bright white missives, but given it was nearly the Season, he knew most of them would be invitations to balls and *soirées*.

Except for one short note from the Earl of Norwick, all of them were invitations. As for the note, he reread it several times before he gave his head a shake and set it aside.

Was the man mad?

CHAPTER 6

A CALLER'S CURIOUS
REQUEST

An hour later, Norwick House, Mayfair
Ensconced in the parlor with an embroidery hoop and a steaming cup of tea, Danielle Fitzwilliam was about to take her first stitch in the stretched pristine white muslin in the middle of the hoop when Hummel cleared his throat.

"You have a caller, my lady," he announced from the doorway.

Surprised at the interruption, Danielle nearly dropped the needle. Her gaze went to the clock on the mantel.

Eleven o'clock in the morning.

Who paid calls at this time of the day?

She supposed she shouldn't be too surprised. Lady Aimsley had left her mother's company only a few moments ago, the two engaged in what appeared to be a serious conversation. Although she had tried to listen in from beyond the parlor door, she had been unable to make out their words. She had noticed her father—the ghost of her real father—casually leaning near the opposite window from the door. He was obviously near enough to overhear everything the two countesses were saying, but his position in the room kept him out of sight from Lady Aimsley.

Danielle hadn't yet decided what she thought of the ghost. He wasn't frightening in the least, but then he hadn't attempted to speak with her directly. She had a thought to engage him in a conversation about her desire to live an independent life. Perhaps he would encourage her uncle to let her have her inheritance early.

Her short reverie was interrupted when the butler inhaled and said, "Lord Andrew Comber."

Had Hummel overheard her thoughts?

"He apologizes for the early call but said he knows you're usually up and about by this time."

Oh, does he now? Danielle almost replied. But another part of her thrilled at the thought that one of her contemporaries—one she hadn't seen since he was home for the Christmastide—would think to pay a call on her. Especially today, given her sister was in the middle of her riding lesson with the Norwick House groom. Although Danielle could ride and did so on occasion, Dahlia enjoyed it far more and insisted she be allowed to ride a few times a week.

"I'll be right down," Danielle replied, setting the hoop atop her sewing basket.

She was halfway to the door when she stutter-stepped, remembering the date.

Why ever would Andrew Comber be in London in March? She wouldn't have expected him home from Cambridge until he finished his studies. Unless he had to return to London for some sort of emergency.

Some sort of family issue.

Resuming her quick steps, Danielle descended the stairs much like she would have as a child, holding her skirts up well above her ankles. Deciding she would appear much too anxious if she didn't slow down, she deliberately paused at the bottom of the stairs to shake out her skirts and take a slow breath.

Andrew was admiring a painting in the vestibule, his profile angled up slightly. A top hat was tucked under one arm, but he wasn't wearing a great coat.

"Andrew?" she said quietly, not sure if she should expect sorrow or happiness. Sometimes, when they were with their group of friends—fellow heirs and daughters of peers—she would greet him as friends did in France, kissing him on both his cheeks as he did the same to her.

They were alone now, though, and she dared not attempt it if he was the bearer of bad news.

Andrew turned and regarded her a moment before he bowed. "Lady Danielle," he murmured as he took her hand in his and brushed his lips over the back of it. "So good of you to receive me," he added. "I know it's early for me to be calling." He didn't immediately let go of her hand, but held onto it.

"Is everything all right?" Danielle asked, her gaze taking in his dark hair and sapphire eyes. He looked much like his father, and if he'd been grinning, there would have been a hint of mischief in his handsome features. Although he bore a pleasant expression, he definitely wasn't smiling.

"As well as can be expected," he answered, a wince crossing his features.

Alarm had Danielle furrowing a dark brow. "Would you like to come have tea with me in the parlor?" She glanced around. "I can send for my lady's maid—"

"Will you come for a walk with me instead? In the park? We won't go far." He still held onto her hand, and gripped it tighter as he practically begged for her company.

Danielle blinked and then glanced down at her day gown, about to say she would need a few minutes to change into a walking gown and half boots.

"You needn't change your clothes. We won't go far," he repeated on a sigh. When she glanced down at the hand that held hers, he suddenly let go as if he'd been burned. "The rain has stopped, and the sun is out. It's quite a brilliant day."

"All right," she finally acquiesced, reaching for her redingote. The navy blue superfine didn't exactly match the cobalt of her day gown, but something in Andrew's manner had her deciding it wasn't important. He helped her into the redingote and then placed the only hat he found on the shelf atop her head.

"You look especially fetching today," he remarked.

Danielle's eyes rounded. "Oh, dear. Now I know something *is* wrong," she replied. She gave a quick glance in a framed mirror near the front door, adjusting the hat so it sat at more of an angle before she pulled out and slid its hat pin into place. "Whatever are you doing in London?"

"I'll explain everything after we're outside," Andrew said, holding the door for her.

Glancing back into the hall, thinking she should tell someone she was leaving the house, Danielle instead accepted Andrew's offer of an arm and they took their leave of Norwick House.

"How did you get here?" Danielle asked, when she noticed the lack of equipage in front of Norwick House.

"I walked," he replied. "I've spent most of the morning in the traveling coach—we left Cambridge before dawn—and I needed to stretch my legs."

The two walked in silence until they had crossed Park Lane and were making their way to the Stanhope Gate, their steps uneven given the puddles they had to avoid along the way.

"Aren't you supposed to be at university?" Danielle finally asked when they stepped onto a crushed granite path. There would usually be dozens of children with their nurses scattered about the Hyde Park lawn, but the morning's rain had the grass too wet for them to be playing out of doors.

"I am," Andrew replied. "I've been... expelled. For the rest of the academic year."

Danielle gasped. "Whatever happened?" she asked, trying to imagine Andrew defacing a statue or skipping classes. Neither matched his personality. He wasn't a troublemaker nor a rogue or a rake. Not like his father had been at that age. Adam Comber, Earl of Aimsley, had attended Oxford, but Danielle doubted he had ever graduated.

"I got caught cheating," Andrew replied, his gaze directed toward the gate.

Danielle inhaled softly. "But you weren't, not really. Were you?" she countered, secretly shocked at his words.

He sighed. "I asked my brother to take my Greek mythology exam for me. He agreed, but the professor had seen me in the courtyard and remembered I was wearing a green waistcoat, and Anthony was wearing—"

"Oh, dear," Danielle breathed, knowing immediately that Anthony Comber would have been wearing a much more audacious waistcoat, one featuring elaborate embroidery. "One quite unlike yours," she finished for him. She grimaced. "As I recall, you know Greek mythology. Why ever would you—?"

"I still cannot read well," he uttered. "You know I'm rot at it. The professor verbally asked me the exam questions, and I answered all of them correctly, but he had already spoken with the dean about our changing places, and, well, I passed the class but both Anthony and I were expelled."

Danielle dipped her head, unsure of what to say. There was only one positive thing she could think of at that moment. "Then you'll be able to attend all the Season's entertainments with us," she blurted.

Despite his mood, Andrew barked a laugh and paused beneath the gate. "Of course *you* would be the one to find the silver lining in my cloud," he murmured before he resumed their walk along the crushed granite path leading west.

"When were you planning to leave for Europe on your Grand Tour?" she asked, secretly hoping he would put off the trip until the summer—or later. With so many of her friends having wed or off at school, life in London hadn't been the same since Christmas.

"Father has decided we won't be going."

"Not now, I understand, but later of course," she countered.

"Um... not exactly."

It was Danielle's turn to halt, which forced Andrew to spin around and face her. She had gripped his forearm that hard. "Are you saying you'll *never* be allowed to go to Europe?"

He swallowed. "I must be married when I do so," he replied.

The response was so unexpected, Danielle let go her hold on him and stepped back. "You'll have to wait five or ten *years?*" She knew neither one of the Comber heirs intended to wed until they'd had a chance to sow their wild oats and engage in all manner of irresponsible behavior. At least, that's what they had claimed upon learning that their friends, the Grandby twins, had married last autumn and left for the Kingdom of the Two Sicilies on their wedding trips.

Danielle wasn't so sure Andrew was capable of behaving poorly. He'd always been upright and responsible in his younger years. She didn't think his mother would have allowed anything less. As for Anthony, she wasn't so sure. As the heir-apparent to the Aimsely earldom, he seemed more determined to have fun before duty required him to behave.

"Well, not exactly," he hedged, in answer to her mention of five or ten years. "Father is understandably upset with us."

"Go on."

"He has directed that we must marry," Andrew stated.

Her eyes rounding at his comment—Danielle had never heard of anyone having to marry after being expelled from university—Danielle stared up at him before she glanced around. "Well, then I suppose it's a good thing you'll be able to attend all the entertainments. It sounds as if you'll need to be courting, and the Season will offer the best opportunity for you to do so."

"I suppose," he hedged, pulling her hand back onto his arm so they could resume their walk. "I'm not quite one-and-twenty, though," he murmured.

"George Grandby is only one-and-twenty," Danielle

countered, referring to Viscount Hexham, the heir to the Torrington earldom. "He and Anne are over the moon happy, though. They recently returned from their wedding trip. George has accepted a writ of acceleration and will take his father's place in Parliament, and Anne, Lady Hexham, has taken over running Worthington House. Perhaps you should speak with him. Discover what you can about marrying at your age."

Andrew furrowed a brow. "I'm really not too concerned about it. Taking a wife, I mean." He paused. "Seeing as how I already secured a promise of marriage some time ago."

Danielle glanced up at him, a huge grin lighting her face. "Oh?" She glanced around. "Do I know the lucky lady?"

His face lighting at hearing 'lucky lady', Andrew stared at her. "Of course you do." He leaned down, his lips capturing hers in a tentative kiss, one that had her eyes rounding while his closed. He didn't linger, though, awareness of someone nearby skittering across his back. He slowly straightened, prepared to apologize for taking liberties.

At that moment, though, Danielle's attention went to a man standing next to a nearby hedgerow, smoke from a cheroot he held curling up in the spring air. He was watching them, and Danielle recognized him.

Her real father. Or his ghost, rather.

Apparently her father had decided to act as her chaperone.

"I do?" she asked, returning her attention to Andrew and acting as if he hadn't kissed her.

"It's... you."

"*Me?*" Danielle blinked and then furrowed her

brows, as if she were trying to remember the occasion when she might have agreed to such an arrangement.

"You said you would marry me. You were about ten at the time," he claimed. "Danielle, I remember everything you've ever said to me."

Danielle opened her mouth to respond but closed it and swallowed. "Oh," she replied, wincing at the recollection of the conversation she and Dahlia had had with their mother only a few days ago. It seemed 'oh' was an appropriate response for any number of situations. Her gaze darted to her father's ghost, seeing his pleasant expression had been replaced with one of worry.

Returning her attention to Andrew, she said, "Actually, I've decided I wish to remain unmarried. As soon as I'm five-and-twenty, I'm going to take my inheritance and go to Italy and Greece."

Crestfallen, Andrew looked as if he'd lost his best friend. "What? When... when will that happen?"

"About three years from now," she replied. "Unless I can talk..." She was about to say 'Father' but wondered if she should say 'Uncle' instead. How many people in the *ton* knew that the man she had always thought of as her father was really her uncle? A quick glance at the hedgerow showed her father was still standing there, although he was no longer smoking. His arms were crossed, though, much as they had been in the parlor a few days ago. "If I can talk my parents into giving me my inheritance early, then I'll leave as soon as arrangements can be made."

"*Alone?*" Andrew asked in alarm.

Her gaze once again darted to her father. "Well, I'll have to have a traveling companion, of course."

"You'll take me, then. Or... or I'll take you," he stammered.

Danielle tittered. "I'm afraid that won't be possible, Andrew," she replied. "What would people think?"

"That we were married," he replied, almost too quickly.

Torn between what she had decided for her future and Andrew's version of it, Danielle reached up and kissed him on the cheek. "May I have a few days to think about it?"

He nodded. "Of course," he replied. "Will I see you at Lady Morganfield's garden party tomorrow?"

"You will."

"And may I have two dances at Lord Weatherstone's ball?"

Danielle chuckled. "Of course, Andrew." She sighed. "I'm going back to the house now. I don't require an escort, though," she added, noting her father's ghost was still hanging about. "I'll see you tomorrow." She dipped a curtsy and hurried off toward the east, leaving Andrew struggling to breathe.

CHAPTER 7
A RIDING LESSON
GOES AWRY

Meanwhile, in Rotten Row, Hyde Park, Mayfair

Mounted in a sidesaddle and sitting as straight as she could manage, Lady Dahlia Davida Norwick took up the reins of the bay upon which she sat and was about to use her crop on her right side when Winston, the Norwick House groom, held out a hand and shook his head.

"This one doesn't require the crop, my lady," Winston warned. "Not like the mare you rode last week."

"Oh," Dahlia replied, wincing when she heard the word come out of her mouth. After the talk they'd had with their mother a few days ago, she and Danielle had begun to tease one another about how often they said the word in response to comments from others. "If not the crop, then how do I make it known I wish for him to move?"

"Your left boot, my lady. Just give it a slight kick inward and the beastie will begin walking. He'll take verbal commands as well, so if you'd like him to quicken his pace, you can urge him on. Just do be careful. He loves a good run."

The groom was mounted on the mare Dahlia had ridden to the park, and now they had switched horses so she could have the experience of riding the newest horse in the Norwick stables. The Thoroughbred, Vindication, was muscular but slight in build. He was also older, his time as a race horse long over. Daniel had purchased the bay at the urging of the groom, claiming he would make a good stud and an excellent riding horse. He hadn't mentioned from whose stables the race horse had originated.

Dahlia grinned in delight as the horse began an easy walk. "Why, he's got a perfect gait," she said happily.

"You'll find he's a very smooth ride, even when he's running," Winston remarked. "I wasn't planning to run him. Thought it would be too muddy, but the road seems firm enough. If you'd like, you can give him the rein, but you'll probably end up with mud all over your riding habit," he warned.

Scoffing, Dahlia said, "It wouldn't be the first time." Curious as to who else might be using the King's Private Road, she glanced around, surprised to find there were no other riders ahead of them and only one well behind them. That morning's rain had obviously deterred any who might have otherwise ridden at noon, or they were waiting until later in the afternoon for their exercise.

"Does he trot?" she asked.

"Oh, yes. He's been trained for all manner of riding. Probably even hunting, too," Winston replied. "Best horse the earl has ever purchased."

"Do I use the crop to make him run?"

"Won't need to, not if you allow him to build up his speed," the groom replied. "Just—"

"Dig my heel in a bit more?"

"Aye." Winston grinned. His own mount was caught unawares as the Thoroughbred quickened his walk to a trot and then to a run. The groom urged the mare to follow suit, although he knew there was no way he could catch up to Vindication.

Another horse was certainly giving it a go, though. One that seemed to come out of nowhere. Ridden by a gentleman sporting a short top hat and leather riding breeches, the Irish walker intercepted the Thoroughbred just beyond the last turn of the road.

Alarm had Winston digging his heels into the mare. Something was happening, and he was too far back to do anything about it.

CHAPTER 8

A FATHER'S ADVICE IS
UNBELIEVABLE

*M*eanwhile, *in another part of Hyde Park*
    "Damn girls don't know their own minds sometimes."

Lord Andrew gave a start, turning to discover a gentleman standing next to him. He hadn't heard the man's approach, so he was taken by surprise. "Sir?"

"I'm her father," David Fitzsimmons stated on a sigh. "I couldn't help but overhear your odd proposal. Odd, but memorable."

"Sir?" Andrew repeated, his brows furrowed at seeing a man who looked very much as he remembered the Earl of Norwick to look, although considerably younger. "Have you taken the waters in Bath? You look as if you've youthened, sir."

"As a matter of fact, I have," David replied with a grin. "Now, did my Danielle agree to wed you?"

Andrew dipped his head, his face reddening with embarrassment. "I planned to pay a call on you later today, my lord. To ask your permission to court her," he said, not wanting to admit what had happened. He was still smarting over Danielle's surprising response. Not quite a rejection, it still left him smarting.

"Oh, you have it," David said with a wave of a gloved hand. "You had it back when you proposed to her when she was nine or ten," he added as he crossed his arms. "So, did she agree to marry you now?"

Despair had Andrew frowning. "She did not... although she asked for a few days to think about it," he added on a sigh.

"Oh, dear. That's never good. But the alternative— her not marrying? Taking her inheritance and living an independent life? That won't do."

"It won't, sir?"

"Of course not. Which means you must take matters in hand."

Andrew angled his head to one side. "You've an idea, sir?"

"Of course I do," David replied with a nod. "You're going to kidnap her."

Andrew boggled. "Sir?"

"Kidnap her."

He scoffed. "I can't do that, sir. It's... it's illegal. And I'm already in trouble for cheating at Cambridge."

"Nonsense. It's not illegal if *I'm* the one telling you to do it," David argued. "I'll explain everything to Clarinda—she'll be so relieved to learn you wish to wed her daughter, she'll help as best she can—so there won't be any issue on our part."

"But..." Andrew furrowed his brows. "Where would I take her? And what sort of ransom would I be demanding?"

David straightened, pretending to think on the query. "Take her to the empty townhouse where your grandfather used to keep his mistress. The one in

Bruton Street," he advised. "The ransom will be her agreement to marry you."

Andrew blinked. "Pardon, sir, but I really don't think incessant begging is going to have your daughter agreeing to wed me."

"Then don't beg." David's brow arched suggestively. "Ruin her."

"Sir?" Andrew scoffed and glanced around, as if to ensure no one could hear the earl's directives.

"Her damned sister read a few of the books in my library. The ones detailing sexual acts," David explained with a wave. "She examined the color plates."

"Oh, dear," Andrew murmured, his eyes widening. "But those aren't even..." He stopped speaking. "I mean, normal people don't really engage in *those* sorts of acts. The ones in those French books, I mean," he stammered.

David seemed to think on this comment for a moment. "I used to own the *Elegant Courtesan*," he countered. "I assure you, the clients there engaged in all sorts of—"

"Yes, well, they weren't doing it with their *wives*," Andrew interrupted, his face reddening with embarrassment.

"True," David replied with a nod. "But what Dahlia saw cannot be unseen, and what she's described to Danielle has left them both a bit afraid of the marriage bed, and *that* is why they are claiming they have no intention of marrying."

Andrew considered the explanation, not about to admit he'd had similar reactions to what he'd seen in those books. His own experience with sexual congress was quite limited—a few tumbles with a tavern maid in

Cambridge. "What do you suggest I do, sir? To... to change her mind?"

"Ruin her. Pleasure her. Make love to her. Prove to her she cannot live without you. Gain her agreement to wed, and then marry her."

As much as Andrew had thought the earl was testing him—teasing him in an effort to trap him in some sort of tawdry scam to prove he was unworthy to be Lady Diana Dorothea's husband—he now realized the man was serious.

"All right. Tomorrow. I'll whisk her away during the garden party. That will give me tomorrow night and all day Sunday and Monday... part of Tuesday—"

"Gads, son, it shouldn't take you more than an hour to prove yourself," David said.

Andrew relaxed some. "Of course, sir," he replied, not exactly sure he could accomplish what the earl was suggesting. Especially in only an hour.

David furrowed his bushy brows. "You *do* know how to pleasure a woman, I hope? Learned something of the Roman arts?"

Andrew blinked before he scratched his brow. "I'm sure I can manage, sir," making a mental note to pay a visit to the Aimsley House library. He was fairly sure he could find a few books on the topic.

"Then make the arrangements for the use of the townhouse," David ordered before he paused, one finger lifted in the air. "In fact, you should let your father know you intend to *live* there when you're wed. Extra incentive. Danielle having her own household and all."

His eyes widening in understanding, Andrew said, "Yes, sir. I'll see to it right away." He gave a bow and turned to go. After a few steps, though, he thought to ask if David knew what Danielle's favorite flower might be. A bouquet delivered from a hot-house florist could only help his cause. He spun around and stood, befuddled.

The earl was no where to be found.

CHAPTER 9

AN HEIR MAKES A
BOLD MOVE

A half-hour ago, back at Norwick House
Anthony Comber, Viscount Breckinridge, watched from atop his horse as his brother and Lady Danielle made their way toward the Stanhope Gate to Hyde Park. He had to give Andrew credit—his twin hadn't wasted any time in taking the necessary steps to re-secure her promise of marriage. Andrew might have remembered Danielle agreeing to marry him when she was ten years old, but she very well might have forgotten by now.

Their father's edict had Anthony experiencing a number of emotions in the last hour. The pre-dawn rain had contributed to his poor mood upon leaving his dormitory early that morning. Now anger and disappointment warred with resentment as to which would prevail. He was exhausted, though, tired from their pre-dawn travel from Cambridge and weary from the 'what-ifs' that had him wishing he could set Time's clock backwards in an effort to set things right.

Even when he imagined what he might have done —or not done—with respect to changing places with his brother two days ago, he realized he still would have done it.

He would have worn a different waistcoat, though, and insisted his brother stay in their dormitory until he had returned from taking the exam.

The thought surprised him. The right thing to have done was refuse his brother's request outright.

He had taken pity on his brother, though. Always would, for the malady that prevented Andrew from being able to read as easily as Anthony had kept his slightly younger brother from doing as well in school as Anthony did. As for Andrew's ability to remember everything he had ever heard... well, although it might come in handy for him, Anthony didn't think he would find it particularly useful.

He glanced at Norwick House, wondering if his future wife was somewhere inside. Of all the girls they had befriended in their youth—daughters of the *ton* who were about their same age—Andrew had always favored Danielle. He wasn't surprised his brother would pursue her for marriage. The dunderhead was probably in love with her. Probably had been since he proposed marriage when he was eight years old.

As for Lady Dahlia, Anthony still wasn't convinced he should settle for her to be his eventual countess.

Settle.

The thought had him wincing.

Is that what he'd be doing should he decide to propose marriage to her?

Settling for her rather than trying to find someone he might eventually love?

He had only decided on her in the last hour because of all the young women he knew in London, he had known her the longest. They had attended the same entertainments. Their mothers were good friends. They were about the same age.

Dahlia was perfectly suited to be a countess. She was confident and self-assured. Mayhap a bit opinionated, but only because she knew her own mind. She already knew how to help run an earldom. How to host balls and *soirées*. How to keep her name out of *The Tattler*. 'Duty' could have been one of her middle names.

Anthony chuckled at the thought.

Dahlia Davida Dutiful Fitzsimmons.

He quickly sobered. They would have a marriage of convenience. Nothing more.

Except the wedding needed to happen sooner rather than later. Although he had set aside some of his allowance from prior years, it wasn't enough to last him through the entire Season. He didn't have the luxury of courting anyone else, not that he was interested in any of the young women who were his age. Dahlia had nearly two years on him.

A stable boy ran up to him before he could dismount. "I can hold him for you, sir, if you've come to pay a call."

"I have," Anthony replied, handing the reins to the young boy. "Might you know if Lady Dahlia is in residence?"

The stable boy's eyes widened. "She ain't, sir. She's having her riding lesson with Mr. Winston."

Anthony glanced toward the park, seeing only his brother and Lady Danielle disappearing through the trees on their way toward the Serpentine. "Where do they ride?"

"Over in Rotten Row, sir. They took the new 'orse," he said proudly.

"Oh? What nag might that be?" Anthony asked, amused by the boy's comment.

"A right Thoroughbred, sir. Vindication. He was a winner at the track. Lord Norwick wanted him here as a stud."

Anthony gave a start, recognizing the name. Although he had only attended a few horse races during his lifetime, he had seen Vindication in action. "One of Hunt's horses, wasn't he?" he asked, referring to the Duke of Huntington. The man had an impressive racing stables, mostly due to his duchess, who had a knack for matching mares to studs to create horses with both stamina and speed. "I think I'd like to see him in action," Anthony said as he remounted his horse.

In reality, he wanted to see Lady Dahlia on the horse. He knew she could ride—he'd even accompanied her and her sister for an occasional afternoon parade in Hyde Park—but she'd always been on Irish walkers or Welsh ponies.

He gave the boy a farthing. "Thanks for the information."

The stable boy grinned. "You're welcome, sir."

Anthony rode off to the Hyde Park Gate, daring a glance through the Stanhope Gate in the event he might be able to see his brother and Dahlia's sister. They were apparently too far into the park, though, so he urged his horse into a run to the south.

When he turned his mount into the Hyde Park Corner gate and passed under the Triumphal Arch, he wondered at how empty the park seemed. The earlier rain must have kept midday riders from their mounts, for when he arrived at the King's Private Road, he found it almost empty of riders.

Almost, because there were two riders halfway down the road. Even from his vantage, he could see Lady Dahlia. A caramel bay sporting white stockings, Dahlia's mount exhibited a gait in keeping with his history as a race horse. Dressed in a sapphire blue riding habit and a rather tall hat decorated with peacock feathers, Dahlia looked like a perfect countess. Her posture was straight, her hold on the reins assured.

Next to her was apparently the Norwick House groom. He was riding a calm black mare, which seemed odd for this time of the year. Perhaps the horse was already carrying a foal.

Anthony kept his own mount mostly reined in, preventing the Irish walker from more than a fast trot, even though it wanted to join his brethren. He was nearly within shouting distance on the northern leg of the King's Private Road when something changed up ahead. The race horse increased his speed from a walk to a trot to a full run.

Meanwhile, the groom kept his mount to a trot.

Alarmed, Anthony dug his heels into his horse, which sent the Irish walker into a run. Although Dahlia's horse had a decided lead on him, Anthony made sure to move to the inside curve of the road, hoping he could gain distance on the racer as it went around the sharp turn to the left.

He glanced over at Dahlia, sure her eyes were wide with fear when she dared a glance back. He spurred his mount, heartened when the walker increased his speed in an attempt to come alongside the Thoroughbred.

Dahlia's mount ran on the outer most lane of the curve, which allowed Anthony to urge his mount so it was slightly ahead of Dahlia's as they came around the last of the curve. He angled his mount so the two horses were eventually running alongside one another.

"I've got you!" he called out.

Dahlia glanced over at him, apparently recognizing him for the first time.

"What?"

When the two horses were nose to nose, he reached over and captured Dahlia around her waist.

Sensing he was about to be run off the road, the race horse slowed and Anthony was able to pull Dahlia off her horse and onto his walker, her riding habit's mud-splattered skirts billowing so they wrapped around his back.

"I've got you!" he repeated, his pulse pounding in his ears. He pulled back on the reins with his left hand as he pulled her closer to him with his right arm around her waist. The walker finally slowed to a trot and Anthony took a breath for the first time in several seconds.

"Are you all right?" he asked between labored breaths.

"Breckinridge?" Dahlia asked in disbelief. "Whatever do you think you're *doing*?"

"Saving you," he replied as he pulled the Irish walker to a halt. "Are you hurt?"

Dahlia scoffed. "I'm quite fine, no thanks to you," she replied, her tone indignant. "What do you think you're doing?" she asked again, ceasing her struggles. If Anthony released her, she would end up falling to the muddied track below.

Anthony lowered her until her feet were on the

ground, and then he quickly dismounted. He pulled her into an embrace. "I've never been so worried in my entire life," he said, catching a whiff of her perfume and then inhaling deeply. He kissed her cheek and then her forehead. He tightened his hold on her even as she struggled in his arms.

When he let go, she pushed back on his shoulders and nearly tripped on the skirts of her riding habit as she stepped backward. "Let *go* of me," she demanded. A gloved hand sailed through the air and impacted his cheek.

"Davy," he breathed, confused by her reaction. He lifted a gloved hand to his cheek, his expression displaying his confusion.

She straightened and regarded him a moment as she caught her breath. Then she glanced around, showing relief when she saw that the groom had Vindication's reins in hand. "I was having the ride of my life," she said on a sigh, "until *you* came along." She took a deep breath and then furrowed her dark brows. "What ever are you doing in London?"

Anthony blinked. "Saving you, I thought," he replied in confusion.

"Oh, Breckinridge. I didn't need saving," she said on a sigh.

"I'm so sorry," he replied, not sure what else to say. "You were going so fast—"

"Well, he *is* a race horse," Dahlia said as she placed her hands on her hips. "But perfect for riding. I never once felt as if I would be unseated."

Anthony winced at both her words as well as her stance. For some reason, her reaction had his body responding in a most unexpected manner. His cock suddenly hardened, and he knew his riding coat wasn't up to the task of hiding it. "You were glorious," he said, stepping towards her.

"What?"

"Glorious. You looked *glorious* on that horse."

Dahlia blinked, her gaze darting to the Thoroughbred. "He's an excellent ride," she replied, sure her face was bright red from exertion.

Anthony took another step toward her. "Is he?"

Blinking again, Dahlia furrowed a brow. "I said he was."

"*I* want that honor," he stated, once again wrapping an arm around her waist to pull her hard against him.

"*What...?*"

Her response was cut off when he captured her lips with his, kissing her quite thoroughly. He continued to do so, until he felt her body finally soften, her rigid stance weakening against the front of his body. When he was sure she had given up fighting his hold, he pulled his lips from hers. "Marry me, Dahlia. Be my viscountess. My eventual countess," he whispered.

Her body once again stiffened in his arms, and he winced.

Dahlia pulled away enough to gaze at him in horror. "Are you *drunk*?"

It was Anthony's turn to blink. "What? No!" he replied. "How can you ask me that?"

Staring at him as if he had grown horns and a trident for a tail, Dahlia huffed. "How *old* are you?"

Anthony inhaled softly, surprised by the query. "Almost one-and-twenty," he replied.

"Whatever are you thinking to propose marriage at your age?" she asked in despair.

He stared at her a moment before exhaustion had him sinking to the ground, his knees on the track as he sat back on his haunches. "If I wait until I am older to ask, some other young buck will have claimed you as his wife," he replied. "I cannot let that happen."

Dahlia rolled her eyes. "I can assure you, that will *never* happen," she replied. "I have decided I won't be marrying anyone."

Anthony stared up at her. "What?"

She rolled her eyes again. "I have decided I have no intention of bending over a library table in order to bear someone's heir," she said, with all the indignation she could muster.

His eyes darting to one side, Anthony tried to make sense of her response and quickly came to his feet. "What are talking about?"

Dahlia scoffed. "Sexual intercourse, of course," she replied in a whisper.

He blinked. "Over a library table?" he asked in confusion.

She seemed to lose some of her resolve, but she still lifted her chin in defiance. "I've heard it's done that way. In order to ensure a boy is conceived."

At a loss for words, Anthony scoffed. "My lady, I would never treat you so," he whispered. "I would only ever make love to you in a soft bed. After I've pleasured you to within an inch of your life," he murmured.

This last had Dahlia wavering slightly. He reached out to steady her with a hand on her shoulder. "We belong together, Dahlia. We've known it since we were children," he murmured, sounding as if he were resigned to the idea.

Her brows furrowing, Dahlia shook her head. "You don't love me," she whispered.

Anthony winced. "Perhaps... perhaps not yet," he admitted. "But it won't be long." He might not have felt affection for her, but his body's reaction to holding hers had certainly been a surprise. Despite how tired he felt, he wanted nothing more than to kiss her senseless. Strip her bare and make mad, passionate love to her.

He even glanced down at the road, an image of them, naked, rolling about on her velvet riding habit, forming in his mind's eye as his cock hardened even more.

At that moment, the groom stepped up with both horses. "My lady? Is this man bothering you?"

Dahlia tore her gaze from Anthony. "No, Winston. Lord Breckinridge is leaving now," she replied. She took the reins of the Thoroughbred, and the groom quickly knelt and formed his gloved hands into a step onto which she placed one of her booted feet. She lifted herself onto the sidesaddle and then arranged her skirts over the back of the horse, wincing at seeing clods of dirt and mud streaking the velvet.

"Lord Breckinridge," she said with a nod.

Anthony stared up at her and swallowed, realizing she was dismissing him. "Will I see you at Lady Morganfield's garden party tomorrow?" he asked.

Dahlia afforded him one last glance. "I suppose," she replied. She hit her left heel into the horse, and he surged forward into an immediate trot.

Watching her go, Anthony sighed before turning his attention to the groom. "Keep her safe," he said.

Winston gave a start. "Of course, sir," he replied.

Mounting his walker, Anthony directed one last look at Lady Dahlia before he urged his horse toward the exit of Hyde Park. Given the speed at which the walker had been forced to run, even if only briefly, his gait was sluggish at first before it evened into a slow walk.

He might have made it all the way to the southeast gate but for the man who stood in the middle of the road, just under the Triumphal Arch.

CHAPTER 10
STATING A CASE FOR A CAUSE

An hour later, Aimsley House

"You want to do *what?*" Adam Comber, Earl of Aimsley, asked as he stared at his spare heir. He had been leaning back in the leather chair in his study when Andrew found him a few minutes before, pondering which invitations to accept for the following week's entertainments.

"I'd like to live in my own townhouse," Andrew repeated. "With Lady Danielle, once we're wed."

Adam blinked. "Your own townhouse? Are you quite sure?" He leaned to one side. "Hummel? Are you there?"

The butler appeared on the threshold of the study, his arms behind his back. "Yes, sir?"

"Is my countess about?"

"She's in the classroom, sir. Should I have her join you?"

Adam shook his head. "That won't be necessary." He regarded his son with a questioning look. "Did you already propose to Lady Danielle?"

Andrew winced. "I did. In the park. She... she asked for a few days to think about it, but I'll see her tomorrow at Lady Morganfield's garden party, and I'd like to take her to the townhouse, to show it to her."

"To help your cause?" Adam guessed.

A grimace forming at the reminder of what Danielle's father had suggested he do, Andrew nodded. "It was Lord Norwick's idea, actually."

"You already spoke with him, too?" Adam asked in surprise.

Andrew nodded. "He was quite helpful. Had a number of suggestions. He wants to see his daughter married as much as I wish to marry her, even though she claims she wants to live an independent life. He's also going to speak with Lady Norwick. Engage her help in the matter."

Grinning, Adam said, "Well, the idea of you in your own townhouse is an excellent idea." He interlaced his fingers as he regarded his son. "I have to admit to a bit of surprise at how quickly you're seeing to your future."

"Lady Danielle wishes to go to the Kingdom of the Two Sicilies and to Greece for the wedding trip," Andrew blurted.

Adam rolled his eyes. "Ah, so this is your way of taking a Grand Tour despite the circumstances?"

Andrew could feel the heat of embarrassment coloring his neck and cheeks. "I suppose so, sir. Besides, if she doesn't marry me, she claims she'll use her inheritance and go there on her own."

His brows furrowing, Adam shook his head. "Well, we can't have that now, can we? She can't go alone!"

"I volunteered to be her traveling companion,"

Andrew said with a shrug. "But I would rather go as her husband."

Once again leaning back in his chair, Adam sighed. "Well, then, let's hope some convincing at a garden party changes her mind."

Andrew winced, deciding it best he not share Lord Norwick's other suggestions for what he should do after the garden party. He didn't wish to be in any more trouble than he already was.

CHAPTER 11
A FATHER'S ADVICE IS INCONCEIVABLE

*M*eanwhile, back in Hyde Park near Hyde Park Corner

His attention on his mind's eye and his disappointment at Lady Dahlia's apparent refusal of his marriage proposal, Anthony pulled back on the reins of his Irish walker, startled by the sudden appearance of a rather tall man standing under the Triumphal Arch, directly in his path.

The gentleman wasn't on horseback, but Anthony hadn't seen him approach from any of the nearby roads.

How had he missed seeing the man before he was right in front of him?

"Pardon, sir," Anthony apologized. His eyes suddenly rounded when he recognized the gentleman. "Lord Norwick?"

"I am," the ghost of David Fitzsimmons replied as he tipped his hat. "Am I to understand Lady Dahlia denied your proposal?"

Glancing back to where Dahlia and her groom had resumed riding, Anthony wondered how her father had already learned of his failed proposal. "She did, sir," Anthony acknowledged. "I, of course, intended to ask your permission to court her, but when I found her here today, I thought to broach the subject. Discover her thoughts on the matter." He dismounted as a matter of courtesy, and the two shook hands.

"Take heart that she didn't reject you as much as she did the marriage bed," David replied.

"Sir?"

David rolled his eyes. "She managed to find some books in the Norwick House library on the subject of sexual congress," he explained. "The French ones," he added dramatically.

Anthony considered this bit of news and he suddenly understood. "The ones with color plates?" he guessed, his manner guarded.

David lifted a gloved finger. "The very ones. Now she's decided she doesn't want to have anything to do with, well, *marriage*," he explained.

Furrowing a brow, Anthony gave his head a shake. "Hard to believe, given she's always seemed so duty-oriented," he said. "Which is why I thought of her first. To be my viscountess," he added. "The eventual Countess of Aimsely."

David regarded him with suspicion. "You seem rather young to *have* to take a wife. Your father is in fine form and will live for another two decades," he remarked, as he if knew Lord Aimsley's future. "Your brother, I can understand. He's heels over head in love with Lady Danielle and is determined to snag her before some other young buck can convince her to wed, but you—"

"Require a wife if I'm to continue receiving an allowance," Anthony stated, curious if his brother had already paid a call on Lord Norwick to ask permission to court Lady Danielle.

"Ah," David replied, his head lifting in understanding. "Got caught cheating at university, did you?"

Anthony gave a start, wondering if the earl had spoken with his father that morning. "I attempted to take a test on Andrew's behalf. He has difficulties when reading, sir."

"But he remembers everything he's ever heard," David remarked. "A skill which will come in handy for the rest of his days."

"No doubt," Anthony replied, once again furrowing his brows. "Regarding your oldest twin, do you suppose there's a chance she might change her mind? About marriage... the marriage bed, I mean?"

David shrugged. "Eventually. But in the meantime, might I suggest you amend your proposal of marriage?"

"Amend it, sir?" Anthony asked, suspicious.

"Indeed. Offer her a marriage of convenience. Demand a quick wedding. In exchange, she retains her virtue but enjoys the benefits of a married lady in the *ton*."

Anthony blinked. "Benefits, sir?" He winced, realizing he was sounding much like a parrot.

David nodded. "Her standing in the *ton*. You're a viscount, are you not?"

"I have the courtesy title of Viscount Breckenridge," he acknowledged.

"So, she would be Viscountess Breckenridge. Eventually, she will be Countess of Aimsley, should you outlive your scoundrel of a father—"

"Scoundrel, sir?" Anthony interrupted, never having thought of his father in that light. He winced again, realizing he had once again repeated something the earl said.

David blinked. "At some point, you really must learn more about Adam Comber. What he was like before he married your mother," he said on a sigh. "I suppose she hasn't even told you how she met your father?"

It was Anthony's turn to blink. "Well, she's a duke's daughter, so I assume at some ball or *soirée*—"

The earl scoffed. "Wrong," he interrupted, his hands lifting to flutter as if in exasperation. "Now, back to my daughter, Dahlia. As a viscountess, she will enjoy invitations to card parties—which are quite the thing among the married ladies—as well as invitations to parlors and parties for which she isn't currently on the guest list," he explained. "She will find herself on an elevated plane compared to her current status.

"Sell her on that plan, secure her agreement to wed, and then, once all those married women who have experienced the marriage bed have convinced her of how wonderful it is, she'll beg you to take her virtue."

Anthony stared at his possible father-in-law. "And you think this will occur in my lifetime, sir?"

David opened his mouth to respond and then frowned. "Within a fortnight, more like," he said. "Once her sister has apprised her of how much she's enjoying the marriage bed, Dahlia will demand your presence in her bedchamber. Mark my words."

His brows arching in shock, Anthony asked, "Lady Danielle has already wed?" He felt a momentary wave of disappointment on behalf of his brother, for he knew Andrew had held a candle for the younger Norwick twin his entire life.

"Well, she will be after your brother thoroughly ruins her. After tomorrow's garden party."

"*What*?!" Anthony took a step back, as if he'd been punched in the face.

The earl shrugged. "You needn't act so surprised. He proposed to Lady Danielle earlier today. I just came from that part of the park," David explained as he waved a gloved hand in the direction of the Serpentine. "If it's any consolation, Danielle is as afraid of the marriage bed as Dahlia, but we've a plan to overcome her hesitation."

"By ruining her at a garden party?" Anthony asked in dismay, throwing up his hands as if in defeat.

"*After* the garden party," David clarified. "Once Danielle has seen the townhouse your brother has arranged for them to live in, she'll beg him to bed her."

"Townhouse?" Anthony repeated, deciding he really was sounding like a parrot. "*What* townhouse?"

"Never mind the townhouse," David said. "Focus on your proposal of a marriage of convenience with Dahlia. Get her alone during the garden party, off by one of the tall hedgerows, and secure her promise of marriage," he encouraged. "Can you do that?"

Anthony placed a hand on the neck of his Irish walker in attempt to calm the impatient beast. They had been standing in the middle of the road for some time, although no other riders or carriages had attempted to access the King's Private Road. "I will, sir," he replied, his gaze turning back to discover that Lady Dahlia and the Norwick House groom were headed in his direction. In another minute, the two would be within speaking distance.

Realizing he didn't wish to say anything else to the young lady—at least not until he'd had a chance to rehearse an amended marriage proposal—he turned to say his farewell to the Earl of Norwick and boggled.

The man had disappeared.

Furrowing his brows in confusion, Anthony first looked left and then right before quickly mounting the walker. Without a look back, he urged the horse into a gallop and headed out of the park, his plan for the following day forming in his mind's eye.

CHAPTER 12
CONFUSED SERVANTS

*M*eanwhile, at Norwick House

Even before Danielle stepped into Norwick House, the front door held open by Belvedere, tears had begun to form in the corners of her eyes. By the time the butler had her redingote in his arms, they had begun to drip down her cheeks, and she sniffled. She fished for a hanky in her pockets, finally lifting a square of embroidered linen to her cheeks.

"My lady?" Belvedere asked in alarm. He moved back to the door and looked out, as if he thought to discover who had Lady Danielle so upset. "Whatever is wrong?"

"Nothing. Nothing at all," she replied as she pulled the pin from her hat and handed it to the servant. "Well, not nothing. Just a poorly done marriage proposal." She hurried through the hall and up the stairs, sniffling as she went.

Belvedere blinked and then rolled his eyes. He was about to return to the butler's pantry when he heard a commotion out front and returned to the door.

Opening it, he gave a start at seeing Lady Dahlia dismounting Norwick House's newest addition to its equine collection. The Thoroughbred was snorting, its breathing labored.

Riding one of the mares, the head groom, Mr. Winston, was still several yards from the house, although his mount was doing her best to catch up to the Thoroughbred.

Dahlia stomped into the house, belatedly gathering the hem of her mud-splattered riding habit into the crook of an arm before she sailed past the butler and up the stairs.

Sensing the Thoroughbred might bolt—the stable boy hadn't yet appeared—Belvedere hurried out the door and stepped up to the horse. He grabbed the reins, glancing about nervously until the stable boy came running from the back of the house.

"Whatever has happened?" he asked when the groom halted the mare and dismounted.

Mr. Winston rolled his eyes and took the reins from the butler. "A misunderstanding is all. Some young buck thought her ladyship was in need of saving," he said before he huffed. "He showed some damn good riding skills, though. Managed to get an Irish walker to run as fast as Vindication here and then pulled her ladyship onto his mount."

Belvedere's eyes rounded. "Was she hurt?"

The groom shook his head. "Not a mark on her, other than her pride," he murmured. He seemed to consider something a moment before he added, "I think the young man proposed marriage to her."

Glancing back into the house, just to ensure Lady Dahlia hadn't returned to the front door, Belvedere furrowed a bushy gray brow. "And why would her pride have suffered if she gained a marriage proposal out of it?" Remembering what Lady Danielle had said upon her arrival, he wondered what it was about today that had young men proposing marriage to the Fitzwilliam twins.

Chuckling, the groom said, "Well, she was having the ride of her life on Vindication here, only to have it interrupted," he explained.

"And the young man? Who was he?"

At this point, Mr. Winston inhaled to respond but seemed at a loss for words. "He looked like Lord Breckenridge, or it could his brother, Andrew," he finally said. "But I'm quite sure they are both away at university."

"Hmph. They might have returned to London for Easter," the butler reasoned. When he noticed that Winston seemed even more perplexed, Belvedere added, "What is it?"

Winston shook his head. "You'll think him mad, but... well, after he got up from kneeling on the road, the young man got on his horse and rode off like he was going to leave the park. Then all of a sudden like, he halts and dismounts under the arch. Stands there like he's talking to someone, but there's no one else in sight. And just as we're close enough to hail him, he remounts and rides off."

Belvedere furrowed both of his brows. "What do you suppose he was doing?"

Winston shrugged. "Rehearsing, mayhap? For when he tries again with her ladyship," he suggested. "It's just... I really think Lady Dahlia had changed her mind, seein' as how she was looking all moon-eyed at him. Seemed like she was going to speak with him, so when she was about to call out to him, he looks back, sees we're close, and then he rides off at full tilt, like he's being chased by the devil himself."

Rolling his eyes, Belvedere countered with, "Well, wouldn't you, if some lady refused your proposal?"

Taken aback, the groom seemed to give this some thought before he said, "Well, I don't rightly know, seeing as how I would never propose marriage unless I knew the young lady was going to say yes."

Belvedere grimaced and huffed. About to return to the house, he paused and said, "Well, at least Lady Dahlia wasn't crying like her sister was when she arrived a few minutes ago."

The groom shook his head. "What happened to her?"

"A poorly done marriage proposal," Belvedere replied, deciding he would know more before dinner. The twins would no doubt be sharing their news with their mother at tea time, and he intended to be near the parlor when they did so.

CHAPTER 13
CHAOS IN THE CLASSROOM

Meanwhile, at Aimsley House
Hat in hand and a look of dismay aging him several years, Andrew made his way into Aimsley House. He handed his hat to Hummel. "Is Mother back in residence?"

The butler nodded. "She has returned. I believe she is in the classroom, although her students haven't yet arrived."

Andrew gave a start. "Students?"

"Your cousins, sir. The Baroness Streater has arranged for Lady Aimsley's help in their education."

The younger Comber twin acknowledged this information with a nod. He wasn't surprised—his mother had tutored him in arithmetic before he left for school —and hurried up the three flights of stairs to the classroom.

Andrew found his mother sitting in a rocking chair, her attention on an open book.

"Good morning, Mother," he said, and then

wondered if it was the afternoon. He'd been awake for so long that day, it felt as if it was time for dinner.

Diana Albright Comber lifted her gaze from the book and gave him a brilliant smile. "Andrew!" she said as she stood and rushed to him. Despite the fact that he had several inches on her, she pulled him into an embrace. When she stepped back, she sobered and sighed.

"I received your letter," she said.

Andrew dipped his head. "All those years, and Anthony and I never once switched places in class," he murmured. "And then the one time we do it..." He sighed. "I suppose you received my letter. Did Father speak with you?"

Diana gave him a quelling glance. "He did, but what's done is done, and you'll simply make the best of it by attending all the Season's entertainments," she replied, arching a dark brow in an attempt to tease him.

"Did he also tell you about... about the marriage requirement?"

Diana pretended ignorance and blinked. "What?" She stepped back, as if she'd been slapped.

"The marriage requirement," a slightly different voice said from behind Andrew.

The younger twin stepped aside to reveal Anthony, breathless from having climbed the stairs in a hurry. "Hello, Mother."

"Anthony!" Diana repeated what she had done with Andrew, but she locked gazes with the younger twin a moment to indicate he needed to remain right where he was.

When she stepped back, she pointed to the chairs her students used during their time in the classroom. "Take a seat, you two. I want to know all about this marriage requirement. Right now," she ordered, wondering if what their father had told them matched what he had told her that morning.

The twins exchanged quick glances before they folded themselves into the small chairs, their knees ending up at the level of their chests while their mother continued to stand. She started with her fists on her hips, but soon crossed her arms. "Out with it."

As was usual for Anthony, he took the lead and explained what had happened and then what their father had directed they do if they wanted their allowances resumed.

"Well, I can't say I'm in agreement with his edict," she murmured, wincing when she remembered she had agreed with her husband's decision earlier that morning. Back then, she had felt excitement at the thought that their sons would take wives and sire grandchildren. "I hardly think it's right that marriage should be some sort of punishment."

"It's hardly a reward," Anthony countered on a sigh.

"I don't mind," Andrew stated. "I mean, I won't if Lady Danielle agrees to wed me."

Before his mother could react to this revelation, Anthony said, "Lord Norwick mentioned Father was a scoundrel. Said I should ask you how you came to be married to him."

Their mother blinked, her face coloring with a blush. She couldn't imagine Daniel, Earl of Norwick, mentioning such a thing to her son. Daniel was fifteen years older than Adam, and the two hadn't been much more than acquaintances back when Adam was forced to marry in order to win a wager.

She would have to have a word with Norwick the next time she saw him.

"Your father was... well, yes, he was a bit of a scoundrel. Before we wed," she acknowledged. She had heard Adam Comber referred to by a number of monikers, including flirt, rake, and libertine. She sighed and then pulled a chair—a chair sized for an adult—to the table and settled onto it. She had to suppress a grin at how she was still an inch or two higher than her boys.

"How did you two meet?" the boys asked in unison. They glanced at each other, scoffed, and rolled their eyes.

Diana furrowed a brow. "At White's." When the two who were staring at her boggled, she huffed and added, "More formally at the corner of St. James and Jermyn Streets."

"White's?"

Realizing she would have to tell them the whole sordid tale, she said, "While I was walking in front of White's, I saw a man in the bow window watching me. I had heard that gentlemen do that and then rate the women who walk by with numbers, and I decided I wanted to know how I ranked, and so I marched up the steps to the front door—"

"You didn't!" Anthony whispered in awe.

"Mother!" Andrew chimed in.

"I was... incensed. Angry. I asked to see whoever it was in the window, and the butler disappeared and your father came to the door with his coat and hat and acted as if he was expecting me. Called me 'my sweeting' and apologized to me for losing track of time."

"What?" The twins exchanged curious glances.

"Exactly my reaction," Diana countered, glad she wasn't alone in her shock. "I'd never seen him before, but... well, he was the most handsome man I'd ever seen in my entire life. He escorts me down the street—"

"What was your number?"

Diana blinked. "What?"

"What was the number Father assigned to you?" Andrew asked, his features displaying his humor.

"He claimed ignorance of the practice," she replied with a shrug. "But he has since said I am a ten."

The twins displayed their disappointment with furrowed brows. "So then what happened?" Andrew asked.

Diana once again blushed. "Once he learned I wasn't married or otherwise betrothed, he kissed me."

Staring at her as if they expected she would continue with the story, Diana realized the comment about kissing didn't seem as scandalous to them as it had been for her.

Well, it had been over two decades ago.

"He kissed me at the corner of St. James and Jermyn Streets," she stated. "In front of everyone and the gods. And then, when he comes up for air, he calls out 'She said *yes*!' as if he'd proposed marriage to me. Which he hadn't."

Although Andrew seemed thoroughly entertained by the story and chuckled at the last comment, Anthony's brows had furrowed, and he seemed deep in thought.

"Oh, dear. What ever are you scheming?" Diana asked of her oldest son.

Anthony gave a start. "I was thinking that perhaps I should have made sure there were crowds of people about when I kissed Lady Dahlia on the lips. When I proposed," he whispered. "Except there wasn't anyone there but the Norwick House groom. At least, I didn't think there was."

His mother brightened. "You asked Lady Dahlia for her hand? Why, you must have done so whilst I was paying a call at Norwick House."

Andrew glanced over at Anthony. "When did *you* propose to Dahlia?"

His brother rolled his eyes. "Right after you proposed to Danielle, at least, according to Lord Norwick."

His eyes rounding in shock, Andrew stared at his brother a moment. "If you only just asked Lady Dahlia a few minutes ago—?"

"It's been mayhap a half-hour," Anthony corrected.

"Mayhap forty minutes for me," Andrew countered, his mouth left open in shock. "How did he get to you so quickly? He didn't have a horse with him. At least, I didn't see one."

Anthony considered his brother's query and then scoffed. "He wasn't on horseback when he stopped me under the arch," he replied. "Maybe he has a twin," he murmured.

Diana gave a start at hearing this last and then shook her head. Her dark brows furrowed, though, as her mouth dropped open. "I only just returned from speaking with Lady Norwick about a half-hour ago," she murmured.

"So?" Anthony asked.

"Well, Lord Norwick was in his study. He saw me as I was taking my leave," she said before she placed a hand over her middle.

Had she imagined the earl saying his greetings to her as she passed by the open door to his study? Perhaps the baby had her seeing things. She straightened on her chair and lifted her chin. "Now, you two didn't come all the way up here to learn the story of how I met your father, so... besides letting me know you were home, why did you?"

The twins exchanged quick glances again before Andrew took the lead this time. "I came because... well, when Lord Norwick knew that Danielle had turned me down—"

"What?"

"I know. It's hard to believe, given she accepted my proposal when I was eight years old. She's been the only girl for me since we were in leading strings, but she did say that she would think about it. But Lord Norwick was suddenly there. Told me what to do to secure her hand, and although I think I can... do what he says, I mean, I'll be acting no better than a rake."

Diana gasped. "Whatever are you supposed to do?"

Andrew cleared his throat. "Kidnap her."

"That's a far sight better than what he told *me* to do with Lady Dahlia," Anthony complained before his mother could put voice to a protest.

"What did he tell *you* to do?" she asked.

"Secure her agreement to a marriage of convenience. One that affords her my name, title, and protection and assurances that I won't attempt to bed her until she falls in love with me."

"That could be never," Andrew said on a scoff. "You require an heir. Surely Norwick knows that."

"He claims it won't be long before she's amenable," Anthony countered, his gaze going to his mother. He had to suppress a grin at seeing her horrified expression. "You look as if you've seen a ghost," he accused.

A shiver passed through Diana Comber just then,

which had her hands rubbing up and down her upper arms. "Perhaps I have," she whispered.

"Mother?" Andrew leaned over the table and reached out a hand to capture one of hers. "Are you all right?"

She blinked. "I am not," she stated.

The twins exchanged worried glances. "We don't have to marry the Norwick girls," Andrew offered. "If you had someone else in mind—"

"*That's* not the issue. Your choices are commendable. Clarinda will be thrilled that you've proposed to her daughters. Truly," she said. "I think she feared they might end up spinsters."

"Didn't she know of my regard for Lady Danielle?" Andrew asked, his brows furrowed.

"Yes, of course. But it was her daughters who claimed they wanted to live independent lives," their mother explained. "And now that she is with child, and I am with child, I cannot bear to think of us having to go through this all over again in twenty years."

Andrew blinked.

Anthony blinked.

And Adam, who had just arrived at the door in the company of his niece and nephew, grinned broadly. If he had seemed old earlier that morning, he certainly didn't now. "Oh, my sweeting, we'll manage just fine," he claimed as he urged Daphne and James into the room. "In the meantime, your sister sent word we can keep Daphne if we'd like. Daisy says she'd rather give her to us than have me kidnap her."

Andrew and Anthony, struggling to stand from the low chairs to greet their younger cousins, both stared at their father in alarm.

"Kidnap her?" they repeated in unison. They

exchanged quick glances, their expressions suggesting they thought their father mad.

Daphne stepped forward and stood on tiptoe. "He's teasing," she said, managing a wink with one of her large blue-gray eyes. "He merely wants to practice having a daughter in case Aunt Diana gives birth to a girl baby."

Still reeling from the news that their mother was with child, the twins considered this bit of news before taking turns lifting Daphne's hand to their lips in greeting.

"We'd be honored to have you as a temporary sister," Andrew offered with a grin. He reached over to his nephew and ruffled the blond hair on his head. "Lucky you," he added with a wink of his own.

James grinned. "Uncle Adam says you have to get married," he said. "Unlucky you."

Both twins scoffed, their eyes rounding in shock at hearing the boy's assessment. "Just you wait, Cousin James," Andrew stated. "One day you'll be heels over head in love with a young lady, and I'll remember this day," he warned.

"Well, whatever you do, please don't kidnap Lady Danielle," his mother pleaded.

"What's this now?" Adam asked, rather enjoying the chaos in the classroom. For the first time since the early morning hours he'd spent with Diana, he felt happy. He was still curious as to what she was about to say before she took her leave of his study, but he had decided he could bring up the matter again when they were alone.

"If Lady Danielle agrees to marry me when I ask her again at the garden party, then I won't have a need to kidnap her," Andrew replied with a shrug.

"And although I have decided I would much rather

marry Lady Dahlia without any strings attached, I shall do as Lord Norwick suggested," Anthony said. "A marriage of convenience is better than no marriage at this point." He aimed a glare in his father's direction.

His mother quickly stood and crossed her arms, which had all the males in the room falling silent and freezing in place. She inhaled as if to speak, managed to say something about marriage being a punishment, even as her eyes rolled up and her legs crumpled beneath her.

Adam was able to get to her in time, though, catching her in his arms before her head hit the carpeted floorboards.

Meanwhile, whilst all the males in the room boggled at the sight of Lady Aimsley fainting, Daphne merely grinned in delight.

Men were so easily duped, she thought.

CHAPTER 14

SECOND THOUGHTS ARE A
GIRL'S PREROGATIVE

A few minutes later, Lady Norwick's salon, Norwick House

Tears still dripping down her cheeks, Lady Danielle Fitzwilliam rushed into her mother's salon and sniffled. "I think I made a mistake," she wailed.

A quill loaded with ink was held aloft above a sheet of Lady Clarinda Fitzwilliam's favorite writing paper, the countess about to begin a letter. She regarded her daughter with a grimace before she quickly returned the pen to the ink pot. Unfortunately, a drop of ink managed to escape, gravity leading it to the middle of the sheet of stationery, where it landed with a *plop* and created a splash that radiated in all directions.

If only there was a punctuation mark that matched the round dot surrounded by what appeared to be fur.

A catastrophe, she thought with some amusement.

"Really, Danielle, must you be so melodramatic?" Clarinda asked in dismay. "What did you do? Turn down an offer of marriage?"

Danielle's keening increased in volume, and a new

round of tears erupted. "I don't know... I don't understand why... why I'm even... even crying," she stammered between sobs. "I don't *want* to marry."

Clarinda gave a start, her eyes rounding. "Oh, dear.
So you really *did* turn down some poor gentleman's
offer of marriage?"

She had barely finished the question when her other
daughter, Dahlia Davida, rushed in, breathless, and
seemed to suddenly swallow whatever it was she was
about to say.

"Let me guess," Clarinda said upon Dahlia's arrival.
"You've made a terrible mistake." Her eyes narrowed
when she noticed the mud-splattered riding habit. "Oh,
dear," she added. "What in the world happened to
you?"

Dahlia huffed in an attempt to catch her breath.
"Lord Breckinridge and Vindication," she replied with a
grimace. "He's an excellent ride," she quickly added.

Both Danielle's and Clarinda's eyes rounded at this
pronouncement. "Oh, is he now?" her mother asked.
"You've no doubt agreed to marry him, I should hope?"

Dahlia furrowed her dark brows. "Mother, I'm not
going to marry a *horse*," she stated. Realizing what she
had said and how it had been interpreted, her own eyes
rounded as her face took on a decidedly reddish cast.
"Nor will I marry Lord Breckinridge, especially after
what he did to me in the park." When she realized how
this last comment sounded, she scoffed and displayed
an even darker blush.

Danielle and Clarinda exchanged quick glances.
Neither put forth a query, deciding it best to remain
quiet.

"He bodily removed me from Vindication. While
the horse was running at full speed," Dahlia claimed in

a hoarse whisper. She was fairly sure Hummel was somewhere nearby, and she didn't want the servants learning of the incident.

"Oh, how romantic," Danielle breathed as she clasped her hands together, failing to swallow a sob as she hiccuped. "He *saved* you. From certain death, did he not?"

Dahlia's mouth dropped open. "He did no such thing. I was having the ride of my life. Why, Vindication is an excellent runner. He would never unseat me. I wasn't in any danger at all!"

Attempting to hide her disappointment at learning Dahlia didn't appreciate Anthony's derring-do, Clarinda angled her head to one side. "I know you're upset, darling, but can't you see it from his perspective? The woman he wants to wed, atop a horse he thinks is out of control? What would you expect him to do?"

Dahlia narrowed her eyes. "How did you know he proposed marriage?"

"Oh, I didn't," Clarinda countered, a self-satisfied grin touching her lips. "However, apparently every matron in the *ton* has known he would eventually propose to you," she remarked. "I have to admit, it's a bit sooner than I would have thought, but that's all the better for you."

"How is that better?" Dahlia asked, scoffing.

"He could have waited until he was nearly thirty, like most of them do," her mother replied. "After you had settled comfortably into your life of lonely spinster-hood," she teased. She sobered. "Now, you have some room to... negotiate."

The twin girls exchanged glances, their dark brows furrowing in question. "What are you saying?"

Clarinda motioned for them to take seats on the sofa beneath the window. Given the small size of the salon, the sofa she used when reading was the only other piece of furniture besides her escritoire and the chair in which she was seated. "I know you both claim you don't wish to wed, but... there are certain advantages you could enjoy if you did so, and you wouldn't necessarily have to live with your husbands. At least, not at first."

Dahlia dared a glance at her sister, who was blushing. "Why are *you* blushing?"

Danielle turned to stare at her. "I don't know that I am," she replied before turning her attention back to her mother. "What advantages, Mother?"

"In Dahlia's case, a title. Viscountess Breckinridge to start with and eventually that of the Countess of Aimsley," Clarinda replied.

"Go on," Dahlia urged.

"Protection."

"We have that," Danielle stated. "With Father... or Uncle Daniel, I suppose I should say."

"Daniel will not live forever," Clarinda replied, a wince appearing when she realized she could easily outlive him. He was considerably older than she was, as was her brother, the Earl of Heath. "And you'll not have children, at least not legitimate children," she went on, hoping there wouldn't be illegitimate children in their futures. The earldom wasn't in possession of a seaside cottage in which the girls could reside whilst raising a bastard.

"That's because having a child would require at least one trip to the marriage bed," Dahlia replied.

"Would it really be so bad, do you suppose?" Danielle whispered. "What if you had a contract with

Anthony that limited the positions in which you're willing to be bedded?"

Dahlia stared at her sister as if she were a traitor. "Who have you been speaking with?"

Danielle shrugged. "Mother, I suppose," she replied in a whisper. "All the 'ohs' weren't because she was appalled," she reasoned. "And why are we whispering?"

Clarinda rolled her eyes. "I cannot help what comes out of my mouth whilst your uncle pleasures me," she stated in a loud voice.

"Ssh!" Dahlia said as she lifted a finger to her lips. She pointed with the other hand to the door. "Hummel," she mouthed silently.

Clarinda scoffed and moved to shut the door. She faced the two girls, her hands on her hips. "I'm of a mind to find the Comber twins at the garden party tomorrow and tell them they can have their ways with you. Ruin you thoroughly so that you have to marry them."

"Too late," a male voice said from the corner.

All three women shrieked in unison before Clarinda rolled her eyes. "David!" she scolded. "How long have you been standing there?"

"Since you invoked my name," he replied as he unfolded his arms from his chest and plunged his hands into his pockets. "I'll have you know it's all under control," he added, a grin of satisfaction lifting his lips. "Whilst you and Lady Aimsley were discussing your pregnancies, I was seeing to our daughters."

Dahlia and Danielle both gasped. "Mother?" they said in unison. "You're having a baby?"

"David!" Clarinda scolded again. "I haven't yet told Daniel," she wailed.

"Or us!"

She gave her daughters a quelling glance. "I haven't even confirmed it with a physician," she added. "I only suspected it this morning, when Lady Aimsley paid a call."

The girls turned their attentions on their father. "Is she?" they asked, as if they trusted his answer.

"Yes, but it's another boy," he said as he waved a hand in dismissal.

"Thank the gods," Clarinda murmured.

The girls sighed in disappointment. "It would be nice to have a sister."

Before Clarinda could stop him, David piped up with, "But you already do."

Their startled gazes going to their mother, the twins both said, "What?" at the same time.

"Don't look at me," Clarinda said. She lifted her chin in David's direction. "He's the one who had an *affaire* with my late Aunt Arabella," she added on a huff.

"Before she married the Earl of Craythorne," David put in, not about to admit to an illicit *affaire*. "Whilst I was still a young buck in university."

The girls looked as if they were going to faint. "Cousin Isabella?" Danielle ventured. "The Duchess of Huntington is really our... our *sister*?" she whispered in awe.

"Half-sister," Clarinda stated.

"Does *she* know?" Dahlia asked in shock.

"She knows," Clarinda replied. "As does Octavius, the duke," she added, deciding that would be their next query.

"In my defense, your Aunt Arabella was the spitting image of your mother," David stated. "Gorgeous."

"I was two-and-twenty when she died," Clarinda countered on a huff.

"Hummel must be about to burst," Dahlia whispered to her sister.

"*I'm* about to burst," Danielle replied. "Our sister is a *duchess* with four of the most beautiful children on the planet. I once wondered what it might be like to marry Lord Tiberius," she admitted, referring to the heir to the Huntington dukedom. She grimaced. "And now I learn he's my... my *nephew*?" she wailed.

"I had my eye on Lord Augustus," Dahlia countered, a glare going to the ghost of her father as she realized Tiberius' younger brother was also her nephew. "*Eww.*"

"I would have put a stop to any hint of courtship," Clarinda said on a sigh. "But I'm quite sure Huntington would have beaten me to it."

"For many years, he was the only one who knew," David murmured. "He kept Isabella at Huntinghurst as his ward, completely unaware she was seeing to restoring his stables to their former glory."

Dahlia suddenly straightened. "Vindication," she murmured. "Mr. Winston said he came from the Huntington stables."

"He did indeed," David acknowledged. "You have your older sister to thank for his perfect breeding. For why it was you didn't need saving when you let him have the rein this afternoon." He sighed. "But I must admit to a moment of exhilaration when Lord Breckinridge rode up next to you, with no regard for his own life, and wrapped his arm around your waist, and pulled you onto his brave Irish walker," he said on a sigh. "Such a display of gallantry. Chivalry—"

"Stupidity," Dahlia whispered. "I was fine!" she said

in a louder voice, Hummel be damned. "I didn't need saving."

"But *he* didn't know that," Clarinda said as she knelt before her daughter. "He could have died doing what he did, Dahlia. Does that count for nothing with you?"

Dahlia blinked. She swallowed. She blinked again and allowed a long sigh. "It was rather exhilarating," she admitted after a time. "And he smelled so good. Like limes and sandalwood."

"Andrew smells like that," Danielle said on a sigh. "And he tastes like..." She stopped, well aware there were three sets of eyes suddenly fixed on her. "What?"

Clarinda grinned. "So, he kissed you," she said as her brows waggled. "Did you... enjoy it?" she asked, her happy countenance quiet at odds with what a mother should be displaying upon learning her daughter had been kissed.

Danielle opened her mouth to reply, but David stepped forward and said, "I think she did, but she was so surprised and so determined not to be moved by Andrew's advances, she refused to consider how much she might appreciate having him as a husband."

Scoffing, Danielle was about to put voice to a protest but instead only sighed. "What of it?"

"What did you tell him?" Clarinda asked, still kneeling before her daughters.

Danielle furrowed her brows. "I told him I would think about it, even as I had already decided I wouldn't. That I would eventually turn him down."

"But why?" David asked in surprise, a hint of anger in his query. "He has loved you his entire life. He's only ever thought of *you* to be his wife. He wants to take you to Europe on your wedding trip. When I learned that particular bit of information, I gave him permission to kidnap you."

Blinking several times, Danielle seemed to melt into the loveseat. "Marrying him would be like marrying my brother," she whispered, not about to react to his comment about kidnapping.

Andrew wouldn't do such a thing.

Dahlia made a sound of disgust. "Would not," she countered. "It would be like marrying your best friend."

Danielle angled her head to one side. "Agreed." She furrowed a dark brow. "Isn't that... wrong?"

Sighing, Clarinda struggled to her feet, glancing up at David when he hurried to assist her. "Sometimes marrying your best friend is the very best you can do in life," she whispered.

Tears once again streamed from Danielle's eyes. "You say that as if you were best friends," she accused, her gaze darting between her mother and the ghost.

"Oh, we weren't," Clarinda replied. "I was referring to... to Graham Wellingham and Hannah, Baroness Harrington, who I think shall finally be marrying despite two decades of separation," she said on a happy sigh.

"Emily Grandby and James Burroughs," David put in, referring to the youngest daughter of Gregory Grandby and the oldest surviving son of Lord Andrew Burroughs. When three sets of rounding eyes settled on him, he added, "I know things."

"The Torringtons," Clarinda said on a happy sigh. "Milton Grandby and Adele Slater knew each other from the time they were children, and they finally wed after Adele was widowed."

"That's because Milton was a coward," David whispered.

Clarinda gave him a quelling glance. "But he managed to father children who have been raised with an appreciation for doing their duty."

Dahlia and Danielle, friends with the Grandby twins, both rolled their eyes at this comment. "We were *there*, Mother," they said in unison, referring to the night William Grandby, Viscount Hexham, had proposed to Anne Wellingham, only daughter of the Earl of Trenton, and Angelica Grandby had accepted an offer of marriage from Sir Benjamin Fulton, probable heir to the Wadsworth earldom.

"I do *like* him," Danielle admitted after a quiet moment. "Andrew, I mean."

"He has my permission to court you," David stated.

Clarinda's eyes rounded. "You didn't," she said in shock.

David's eyes darted to the side. "Didn't do what?" he countered.

Struggling to respond, Clarinda said, "Show yourself to him."

"I did indeed," he replied, rising to his full six-foot height. "As I did to Anthony... I mean Lord Breckinridge," he quickly corrected. Anthony hadn't even been born when David was alive. He directed his gaze onto Dahlia. "He has my permission to court you, although he does understand it might be some time before he can expect you to spend the night with him."

Clarinda looked as if she might faint. "Oh, dear. Oh dear, oh dear, oh dear."

"Oh, my," Dahlia whispered, wanting nothing more than to pummel the ghost of her father.

Danielle secretly smiled. She could hardly wait to be kidnapped.

CHAPTER 15
REQUESTS ARE MADE

The following day, Saturday, March 30, 1839, Aimsley House

Knowing his mother usually wrote her correspondence in the early morning hours before breakfast, Anthony rose early and dressed. He allowed his father's valet to shave him and then made his way to her small salon on the second floor.

Not wanting to startle the countess, he tapped the dark wood door with the back of his knuckles.

Diana glanced up, a smile lighting her face when she realized it was Anthony who stood in the open doorway and not the butler. "Do come in. You're saving me from having to respond to yet another invitation," she said as she indicated a pile of open notes on a silver salver.

"Thank you, Mother," he said as he nodded and then stood with his hands clasped behind his back. Inhaling to speak, he didn't when her eyes suddenly rounded.

"Oh, dear. Whatever has you looking as if you're about to be executed?" Diana asked in a hoarse whisper.

Anthony's eyes darted sideways. "Although I don't believe entering into a marriage is quite so odious, I probably do appear apprehensive." He rolled his eyes. "I feel apprehensive."

Diana stared at him. "Did you propose to Lady Dahlia again?"

Dipping his head, Anthony said, "I will try again during the garden party today. I fear I may have bungled my chance with her yesterday, but that's not why I'm here."

Reeling from learning he had already proposed, Diana motioned him to the only other chair in the salon. "Tell me," she ordered.

"It's more of a request, really. I wondered... if I do marry, I understand I should probably continue living here at Aimsley House—"

"Of course, you will," Diana agreed. "You'll move into the late earl's apartments here on the second floor," she added.

Anthony gave a start. "What about grandmama?"

Diana inhaled softly. "Patience has informed me that she's moving to the townhouse in Brighton—"

"Brighton?"

She nodded. "She has friends there. Other widows who apparently enjoy the sea air and who like the entertainments offered at the palace. I think she also likes that it's so much closer to France." Pausing a moment, Diana chuckled. "I really don't expect her to stay long in any one place. Ever since she gave up *The Tattler*, she's at loose ends. I'm of the opinion she might start a gossip rag down there, in fact. For something to do."

"Oh, dear," Anthony murmured, failing to hide his humor. One good thing about being related to the gossip maven of Mayfair meant his name never appeared in *The Tattler* other than in a complimentary manner, but now that she wasn't its secret editor, he would be as vulnerable as any other member of the *ton* when it came to the subjects of the gossip rag's weekly articles.

"You're welcome to move into the apartments as soon as you'd like," Diana said. "In fact, you should invite Lady Dahlia for dinner tonight. Take her on a tour. Although she won't have the household to run on her own until after I'm gone, at least she can be sure she'll have some rooms of her own. Privacy. We can even see to a lady's maid for her if she doesn't have one."

Anthony stared at his mother for several seconds, stunned at how quickly she had provided a solution to his concern. "She may turn me down," he warned, not adding 'again,' although he was tempted. If he'd been entirely sane, he would give up his quest of Dahlia and turn his attentions to other more willing young ladies.

Diana winced. "She cannot," she replied. "She must marry you."

Anthony grinned at hearing her comment. "I know you hold me in high regard—you have to because you're my mother—but I'm not yet sure about Davy's feelings on the matter."

"She *will* marry you," his mother insisted. "If she doesn't, you'll end up with some insipid miss you'll regret for the rest of your life, father an heir and a spare, and then take a mistress so you don't have to listen to your wife complain about the cook and the house-keeper while she tups the footman."

Anthony reared back at hearing her possible future for him. "Mother," he scolded softly.

"Oh, don't you 'mother' me," she warned.

He stared at her. "That didn't happen to you and father," he countered, remembering how she had described their original meeting. For as long as he could remember, his parents had always been a loving couple. But perhaps something had happened while he and Andrew were away at school. "Did it?"

"Of course not," Diana stated, obviously offended he would think such a thing. "But it has happened to others. Your grandmama wrote those very words in *The Tattler* more times than I can count."

Feeling profound relief, Anthony patted a hand on his chest. "Apologies," he murmured.

Diana regarded him with a wistful smile for a moment. "You could just ruin her," she whispered. "Her mother wouldn't mind a bit."

"*Mother!*"

Angling her head to one side, Diana was about to scold him again but instead said, "Bring her to dinner tonight. Show her the apartments. I'll be sure to have them looking their absolute best." She gave a one-shouldered shrug. "Have her stay as long as she'd like," she added as she waggled her brows.

When his expression of shock warned he was about to reply with another '*mother*,' she quickly held up a finger. "It's time for breakfast. And do be sure to speak with your father about the tenant cottages. The issue of their maintenance has come up again with the foreman," she added with a grimace.

"All right," he replied. "But I have to stop at my bedchamber on the way. I'll see you down there."

• • •

*M*eanwhile, at the other end of the house
Blurry-eyed from a restless night featuring dreams about Danielle Fitzwilliam and nightmares about Greek gods, Andrew emerged from his bedchamber and stopped short in the corridor. His cousin, Daphne, already dressed in a pink gown with a white pinafore and white stockings, stood in front of the adjacent bedchamber's door staring at him. The girl's hair was done up in a riot of curls, and from the way she stood in her black half-boots staring at him, she looked as if she owned the place.

"For a moment, I was going to ask you if you'd lost your sheep," Andrew murmured. "You look like Little Bo Peep."

Daphne's fists went to her hips as she gave a huff, apparently offended by the comparison. "And you look as if you're three sheets to the wind."

Andrew blinked and wondered how a nine-year-old would know of such a thing. He glanced down at his wrinkled nightshirt, but then he noticed her gaze had landed somewhere higher. He gingerly felt his head and groaned at how his hair shot off in all directions. "Only my hair does," he replied. "I didn't even have anything to drink last night."

Well, except for the port after dinner, but she didn't need to know about that.

He wished he'd had a glass or two of brandy. There were times he was sure Lord Norwick was in his bedchamber, giving him ludicrous instructions on how to kidnap Lady Danielle to secure her hand in marriage.

He much preferred the nightmares. At least in those

there was a chance some minor god would take pity on him and save him from his fate.

"Well, I've no idea who you were talking to in your sleep, but you really should learn to keep it down," Daphne complained. "You woke me up at least twice last night."

Raising a finger as if he was about to counter her accusation, Andrew instead furrowed a brow. "I was talking in my sleep?"

Daphne's expression showed a hint of fear. "Well, if it wasn't you, then who else would it have been?" she countered.

Deciding to put the blame squarely where it belonged, Andrew said, "Oh, that was the ghost of Lord Norwick. He's been haunting me of late." Struggling to keep a straight face when Daphne's eyes rounded in horror, he headed for the bathing chamber he and his brother shared. "See you at breakfast."

He took great delight in how Daphne shrieked and rushed past him, a blur of pink and white. She disappeared down the stairs.

"You're incorrigible," Anthony said from where he stood outside his bedchamber door, already dressed in Nankeen breeches and a navy top coat of superfine. His waistcoat, scarlet and embroidered with flowers, was more sedate than most he wore. His eyes widened upon seeing Andrew's state of dishabille. "Good God, you really do look as if you've seen a ghost."

Andrew gave his brother a quelling glance. "Just you wait until it's *your* turn," he warned before disappearing into the bathing chamber.

Furrowing his brows, Anthony wondered at his twin's parting comment before he made his way down the steps and into the breakfast parlor.

. . .

*B*reakfast had been over for nearly a half-hour when Andrew approached his father's study. He would have done so immediately after the morning meal, but Anthony had joined the earl in a discussion about tenant cottages that started in the breakfast parlor and continued into the study.

Andrew had never been so glad he wasn't the heir. If the issue of tenant cottage maintenance fell under his responsibility, he would have ordered completely new ones be built. The current ones were obviously a source of ceaseless problems.

Once Anthony had disappeared up the stairs, presumably to return to his bedchamber, Andrew ducked into the study and closed the door.

"I must mark this date on my calendar," Adam said with a quirked brow. "Both of my sons coming into the study of their own accord—"

"I wish to make a request, Father," Andrew interrupted, his anxiousness apparent.

Adam angled his head to one side. "As I told your brother, if you're requesting a stay regarding the marriage edict—"

"I am not."

"Or you're taking exception to your cousin Daphne's having joined us for a few months—"

"I do not, although I believe she takes exception to her bedchamber being next to mine. Apparently I talk in my sleep."

Adam straightened in his chair. "She said there was a ghost in your bedchamber," he commented. "Took your mother a few minutes to settle her down before she would eat her breakfast this morning. Diana is going to see to it she's moved into a different bedchamber."

Barely suppressing a grin of amusement, Andrew merely shrugged. "Probably for the best."

Adam furrowed a brow and waved a hand to the chair in front of his desk. "Well, if it's not about marriage and it's not about Daphne, what have you in mind?"

"The townhouse we spoke of yesterday. It's in Bruton Street. I'd like to live there."

Blinking, Adam regarded a rather large leather-bound ledger that held a special place on one corner of the mahogany desk. He didn't usually pay the tome any mind—as the household's best resident in mathematics, his wife saw to the earldom's ledger—but Adam wondered what property his son might be talking about. "Uh, Bruton Street," he repeated, flipping through the pages of the ledger in search of an entry that might have the property listed. "Truth be told, I'm not recalling that we own a townhouse in Bruton—"

"Grandfather housed his mistress there. A long time ago," Andrew stated.

Closing the ledger a bit harder than he intended, Adam regarded his son with confusion. "You know this how?"

About to answer, Andrew realized he couldn't mention the late Earl of Norwick. He would sound like a fool quoting a ghost. "I learned of it from a relative of Lady Danielle's. When he discovered I intended to ask for her hand. He's the one who thought I should have a house to offer her ladyship," he explained. "A place to live. Once Anthony inherits, his wife will be the lady of this household," he added with a shrug. "I don't think there's enough room here for two couples and their children."

His father regarded him with raised brows. "You've given this a good deal of thought," he said in awe. He lifted a folded note from his desktop. "As has the man to whom you refer," he added, waggling a brow.

"Sir?" Andrew replied, his attention going to the bright white missive.

"It seems Lord Norwick wants you to marry his daughter, one Lady Diana?"

Andrew gave his father a curt nod. "That's Danielle," he replied, chuffed at learning Lord Norwick had sent word that he wanted Andrew as a son-in-law. "I love Lady Danielle. Whilst I'm waiting for an answer to my marriage proposal, I thought to... sweeten the pot, so to speak."

Leaning back in his chair, Adam's eyes widened slightly. "Well, then. I suppose I should discover more about this property," he murmured. In a louder voice, he shouted, "Hummel!"

The butler opened the door to the study only a few seconds later. "Sir?"

"Let Lady Aimsley know I'm in need of her," he said.

Hummel's eyes darted sideways.

"Not like that," Adam said in dismay, which had Andrew's eyes rounding.

"Right away, sir," Hummel said before disappearing.

"Father," Andrew whispered with an embarrassed grin.

When the servant was gone, Adam turned his attention back to his son. "Just you wait. You'll be doing the same thing with your Lady Danielle. Mark my words. Middle of the day, when you're supposed to be tending to matters of estate, you'll find yourself horny, wanting nothing more than to tup her over a library table," he said at the exact moment his countess, Diana, appeared on the threshold.

"Adam!" she scolded.

Both men jumped to their feet, Andrew having a hard time hiding his humor while his father sobered and hurried over to greet his wife with a kiss on the cheek and the back of her hand.

"Apologies, my lady. Seems your son is in love and determined to find a home for him and his future bride."

Diana lifted a brow and regarded Andrew with a wan grin. "So... a townhouse?" she guessed.

"Yes," he replied.

"Well, there's the one in Bruton Street—"

"There is?" Adam interrupted, his mouth dropping open. "How is it *I* don't know about it?"

Diana gave him a prim grin. "If you think I was going to remind you about your father's love nest from when he was too young to know better, so that you could house a mistress there—"

"I would *never!*" Adam countered. "But it would have been good to know about it." When he noted her quelling glance, he added in a hoarse whisper, "For *our* secret love nest."

"Bounder," she accused with a grin. She turned her gaze on Andrew. "The address is number twenty-five, and Parker is the name of the butler in residence there," she said. "I'll send word to him you're to be expected."

"So... I can have it?" Andrew asked, turning his attention back on his father.

Adam and Diana exchanged quick glances. "Not that we're in a hurry to see you off on your own, but your little brother or sister will require a bedchamber at some point," his mother commented, patting her middle.

Wincing, Andrew nodded. "Of course. I couldn't help but notice Cousin Daphne already has her own bedchamber, here," he said.

"Only for the nights she stays here with us," Diana assured him. "Once the babe is born, it will go back to being a guest bedchamber."

Noting how his father beamed in delight at the mention of the baby, Andrew rolled his eyes.

"Oh, don't you roll your eyes at me, son. If you and Lady Danielle do tie the knot soon, you'll have one of your own not long after."

Andrew had a moment when he couldn't seem to breathe. "I suppose so," he whispered. He glanced over at his mother, who was regarding him with a wistful expression.

"You needn't look so shocked, darling," she said as she placed a hand on his arm. "First you'll have to marry her," she reminded him.

"Then we'll be off to the Continent," he said, his face brightening. "I can't imagine we'll have a baby before we return to England, though."

Diana and Adam exchanged amused glances. "Then you might want to schedule Rome as the last place you visit," his mother said in a quiet voice.

Color suffused Andrew's face. "Noted." He was about to take his leave of the study but turned and said, "Might I make a suggestion regarding the tenant cottages that seem to have you so vexed?"

His parents glanced at one another in surprise. "I'm all ears," his father replied.

"Just build new ones. Modern cottages. It will probably cost you far less in the long run than what it's costing you now for all these maintenance issues you and Anthony keep complaining about," he stated. He nodded to his mother and left the study. He had a certain earl to call on and a garden party for which to dress.

*M*eanwhile, in the study, Diana and Adam regarded one another with expressions of awe. "Did our youngest twin just say what I think he said?" Adam asked in a quiet voice.

Diana gave her husband a prim grin. "He's smarter than you think, darling. He remembers everything he's ever heard. And he has a good point. Build new cottages. You can have your foreman turn the old ones into loafing sheds or barns for the smaller animals."

Adam's eyes widened. "Why, that's a capital idea, my sweet," he replied happily, kissing her on the forehead.

"And don't forget, we have a garden party to attend soon. I need to change clothes and have my maid redo my hair."

Slowly sobering as his eyes darkened, Adam glanced around the study. His attention settled on the desk.

"Oh, if you think you're going to tup me over that desk, think again, you bounder," Diana said as she crossed her arms. Her gaze turned to the sofa. "However..."

She was prevented from saying more when her husband lifted her into his arms, took her to the sofa, and had his way with her.

CHAPTER 16
PREPARING FOR A PARTY

eanwhile, over at Norwick House
"What are you going to wear to the garden party?" Dahlia asked as she leaned against the door jamb of Danielle's bedchamber.

Danielle turned in her dressing table chair, which had her lady's maid, Peterman, stepping to the side as she held a curling iron aloft. A lock of Danielle's dark hair was wound around the cylinder, and Danielle feared her hair might burn at any moment. "Let's not dress alike," she suggested.

Dahlia sighed. "Not up for a bit of fun with the Comber twins?"

Her eyes rounding in shock, Danielle gasped and considered what Dahlia might have in mind—her posing as Danielle whilst Danielle pretended to be Dahlia. "You wouldn't," she said.

"Not interested in becoming a viscountess?" Dahlia countered, making it sound as if the position of Viscountess Breckinridge was Danielle's for the taking.

"Although I like Lord Breckinridge—I truly do—I

cannot imagine being married to him," Danielle replied. "Anyway, neither one of us is interested in marrying, so it's moot."

Dahlia's eyes narrowed. "Father made a good point, though. The one about... about a title and protection should I agree to marry Anthony. It would no doubt come with an allowance, too, and an apartment of my own in Aimsley House."

Danielle breathed a sigh of relief when a ringlet appeared from the curling iron, her lock still intact despite the odor of burnt hair hovering in the air. The lady's maid moved onto a different section of her hair. "You wouldn't be in charge of your own household until..." She paused a moment. "Well, until Lady Aimsley died or... or moved to a dowager cottage some-where," she said, more of a reminder rather than a recommendation that Dahlia marry Anthony Comber.

Shrugging, as if she didn't want the responsibility, Dahlia countered, "Whereas you will no doubt have an entire house to oversee whenever you do marry. Or even if you don't."

"I wouldn't mind," Danielle said. "Especially if the housekeeper is particularly good." The thought of having her own household to run appealed to her. Whether or not she was married.

"Will you do me a favor?"

Danielle stiffened, her eyes turning up to watch another ringlet fall from the curling iron. This one was as tight as the last, and her hair didn't suffer the conse-quences of the heat. "What favor is that?"

"Wear a matching dress. The peach frock with the floral motifs along the hemline. Pretend you're me, and I'll pretend I'm you."

Scoffing, Danielle said, "We'll never get away with

it. You have that scar and—"

"I can hide it."

Furrowing her brows in suspicion, Danielle stared at her sister's reflection in the mirror above the dressing table. "Are you asking because you want *Andrew* to kiss you behind a hedgerow?" For some reason, the thought of Andrew doing such a thing had a hint of the Green Monster forming inside her.

She had replayed the kiss he had bestowed on her in the park the day before over and over as she had attempted to fall asleep the night before. When she had awakened that morning, the kiss was her first thought. She had felt a stab of disappointment when she realized she was alone. That Andrew wasn't there to continue what he had started in the park.

"No," Dahlia replied. "I'm asking because I'm curious as to if Lord Breckinridge will attempt another proposal. With all those conditions Father's ghost mentioned."

Her eyes rounding once again—this time at the mention of the ghost—Danielle dared a glance at her lady's maid's reflection and winced.

"Ghost, milady?" Peterman whispered, Danielle's hair forgotten. The poor girl appeared paler than milk.

Danielle took hold of her lady's maid's hand and managed to pull the iron from her hair without burning her fingers. "It's just an expression we use when... when Father's *attention* isn't all there," she stammered. "His mind is always on other matters these days."

Peterman seemed to relax and moved to reheat the iron in the fireplace whilst Danielle gave Dahlia a quelling glance. "If I do pretend to be you and Lord Breckinridge does propose, what am I to say?"

Dahlia shrugged. "What do you want to say?"

Danielle scoffed again. "Well, *no*, of course."

"Why?"

Reeling as if her sister had slapped her across the face, Danielle gave her head a shake, sending a half-dozen ringlets in all directions. "He thinks me... ridiculous," she replied. "Besides, Anthony is far too serious for me. And now that he *has* to marry, I cannot help but think he would hold me in contempt for that very reason."

"Now you know exactly how I feel," Dahlia huffed as she crossed her arms. She rested the back of her head against the door jamb as she stared up at the ceiling.

"You don't have to marry him," Danielle murmured.

"No, I don't," Dahlia agreed.

Danielle couldn't help but think her sister was about to say more, and when she didn't, Danielle considered her own jealousy at the thought of Andrew kissing her sister. "If you don't marry him—"

"I won't."

"—and you see him with another young lady—one of our friends, or... or someone fresh from the schoolroom—what then? Will you feel jealousy? Will you be angry with yourself for not having accepted his offer when you had the chance?" she asked in concern. "Dahlia, I shouldn't want you to have regrets."

Dahlia merely shrugged.

"What if... what if while we've changed places, Andrew proposes to *you*? What then?"

A wan grin settled over Dahlia's features. "Should I say yes?"

Frowning, Danielle shook her head. "You just want him to kiss you," she accused.

"I do not."

"Then why change places at all?"

Dahlia shrugged again. "I suppose I'd like to know if we could get away with it. At our ages." They had managed on several occasions to change places—without even trying—which made for confusion during dinner conversations. When it happened like that, it was merely a source of amusement.

"*They* didn't get away with it," Danielle reminded her, referring to the Comber twins, a hint of warning in her voice.

"They weren't dressed alike."

"How do you know that?"

"Are they ever?" Dahlia countered. "Anthony wears decorative waistcoats whilst Andrew's are always far simpler. More sedate. Boring."

"I think I could tell them apart, even if they wore the same waistcoat," Danielle claimed.

"How?"

"Anthony always walks about as if he's already an earl. More... upright. Taller," Danielle claimed. She sighed when she recalled how Andrew had looked at her the day before. He adored her, even if he only did so as a best friend. Anthony didn't gaze at her like that, with longing in his eyes. "How does Anthony look at you?" she asked in a quiet voice.

Dahlia furrowed a brow and moved into the room. She lifted a hip and settled on the edge of the bed as she considered the query. "What do you mean?"

"Does he gaze at you as if he wants to kiss you?"

Her expression not changing, Dahlia considered the question for a long time. "He did yesterday," she admitted. "At least, I think he did."

"You would deprive yourself of the opportunity to *be kissed* by him today?"

Dahlia's eyes widened. "What makes you think he'll kiss me today?" The reminder of a kiss had her remembering how it had felt to have Anthony's lips pressed against hers. At how the solidity of his body had felt as he pulled her close, his arm at her back like steel, the scent of him so fresh and citrusy. She'd been too shocked and angered to consider if she might like it to happen again.

"He proposed marriage," Danielle reasoned. "You may think he rode away with his tale betwixt his legs yesterday, but he's had a night to consider his next move. To consider Father's words," she added, daring a glance at Peterman. The lady's maid was obviously listening to their conversation, for the curling iron was nearly glowing red in the flames. "Peterman!" she scolded.

The lady's maid jumped and pulled the iron from the fire, her eyes wide in horror. "I'm so sorry, milady."

"You're not coming anywhere near me with that until it's cooled down some," Danielle warned.

"Yes, milady."

Danielle turned her attention back to Dahlia. "Let's wear the peach colored gowns," she suggested. "And you'll need to have your lady's maid do your hair to match mine."

Dahlia's eyes widened. "I will," she agreed, a grin lifting the corners of her lips. "You won't regret this," she said as she hurried to the door.

Danielle turned around in her chair and glanced at her sister's retreating back in the mirror. "I'd better not," she replied.

CHAPTER 17
TWO BROTHERS CONFER

*M*eanwhile, in the library at Aimsley House
"Here you are," Anthony said as he glanced down one of the rows of books in the large library of Aimsley House. Although their father had never been a voracious reader, their grandfather and the earl before him had been. They had seen to adding hundreds of volumes of leather-bound books on topics ranging from animal husbandry to farming techniques as well as a number of gothic novels and books that looked as if their spines had never been bent.

Andrew quickly closed the book he'd had open on his arm, the *thump* filling the otherwise quiet room. "Been here for the last half-hour," he replied, sliding the book back onto the shelf and pulling out another.

"We should leave for Carlington House soon," Anthony suggested. "We don't want to arrive too late, or Mother will blister our ears."

"Oh, of course," Andrew said as he put the book back and pulled the bottom edges of his top coat down. "How do I look?"

Anthony winced. "Like you always do," he chided. "Could you just once wear a waistcoat befitting the occasion? It's a garden party, not a meeting of the Royal Society."

Andrew glanced down at his green waistcoat. It was void of decoration. No embroidery. No fancy buttons. He'd worn it to Norwick House when he paid a call on the Earl of Norwick to formally ask if he could offer for Lady Danielle's hand. He hadn't expected the earl to react with so much excitement, and to behave as if they hadn't discussed the matter only the day before in the park. From Daniel Fitzwilliam's reaction, Andrew realized the earl believed his youngest twin daughter would be left a spinster. "But... it's silk, and it's green," Andrew argued. "Isn't that appropriate for a garden party?"

Anthony sighed and rolled his eyes. "Come. Let's get you into something more festive," he said as he motioned for Andrew to join him.

The two took their leave of the library and headed up the stairs. "Are you going to propose to Lady Dahlia again?" Andrew asked as they turned on the landing and headed up the next flight of stairs.

"I haven't yet decided," Anthony replied, even though he was still plotting how he and Lady Dahlia might leave the garden party so he could discuss the matter with her. "Not sure I wish to experience her rejection of me yet again."

Andrew sighed. "She didn't reject *you*, exactly," he murmured.

His older-by-a-few-minutes brother gave him a quelling glance. "If not me, then who?"

"Not who. *What*," Andrew stated. "The idea of marriage. I do believe Lord Norwick had the right of it. We just have to help the Norwick twins overcome their fears. Give them assurances that we won't treat them like... like animals," he whispered. "That we'll hold them in high regard. Honor their wishes and worship the very ground they walk on."

"You say that as if they're goddesses," Anthony remarked on a huff.

"Danielle is," Andrew claimed.

Anthony gave his brother a quelling glance before he led them down the corridor to his bedchamber. "Norwick's suggestion did have merit," he agreed. "The idea that I could offer for Dahlia's hand and agree to conditions seems reasonable." He gave his head a shake as he opened a wardrobe filled with waistcoats. He pulled one out, frowned, and put it back before pulling out another. Holding it up, he said, "What about this one?"

Andrew frowned. "It looks exactly like the one you're wearing," he complained, noting not only the bright peach satin but the elaborate embroidery featuring flowers and bumblebees.

"Good, except mine has dragonflies instead of bees," Anthony explained, undoing the buttons of his brother's top coat and waistcoat. "Don't think me mad, but I have an idea."

Wincing as he removed his top coat and waistcoat, Andrew regarded his brother with suspicion. "Do I want to know?"

"Let's switch places."

Andrew blinked. "Are you mad?" he replied on a huff. Then his brows furrowed. "Why?" He pulled on the waistcoat and began buttoning it up. "You *do* remember how it didn't work a few days ago."

"I wish to discover Lady Dahlia's response when *you* propose marriage."

Unbuttoning all the buttons he had already fastened, Andrew shook his head. "No. No. No. Absolutely not," he said, pulling the garment from his shoulders. "I have no desire to propose to Lady Dahlia. I want *Danielle*. In fact, I've already secured the earl's permission," he added, glad he'd taken the time to meet with the man.

Why, Daniel Fitzwilliam, Earl of Norwick, had been so glad at hearing his news that someone wished to marry Danielle—and quickly—, he blurted out an enormous sum for a dowry and assured Andrew the details would be sent to Aimsley House in only a couple of days.

"Drew! Think about it," Anthony argued, pulling the waistcoat back onto his brother's shoulders. "Dahlia won't be saying aye or nay to *you*. She'll think you are me."

"So why don't *you* do the proposing?"

Anthony buttoned the waistcoat. "I wish to discover if Dahlia can tell the difference betwixt us," he admitted. "And if she can, does she prefer you over me?"

Andrew scoffed. "To what end?"

Anthony took a deep breath. "Truth be told, I think I may hold her in higher regard than I thought," he admitted, wincing even as he put voice to the admission. "Should I have to hear her deny me again..." He winced. "I cannot face her."

Giving a start, Andrew stepped back. "What if she says yes?" he asked in alarm. "She'll expect me to kiss her," he claimed.

Anthony considered this a moment. "So, kiss her," he said, even as he displayed a grimace. "But not too passionately. Not like you would Lady Danielle."

"What will *you* be doing?"

A shrug lifting his shoulders, Anthony said, "Watching from behind a hedgerow."

"Coward," Andrew accused.

"Mayhap."

"I have plans," Andrew murmured. "To ask Danielle if she's made up her mind."

"I'll do it," Anthony stated.

Shaking his head, Andrew said, "You cannot."

"Why not?" He furrowed his brows before his eyes widened. "Oh, because you're supposed to kidnap her if she turns you down?" The query came out in a teasing tone, but Anthony quickly sobered when he heard his brother's response.

"Exactly," Andrew replied.

"Where... where were you planning to take her?"

"I'm not telling."

Anthony rolled his eyes. "Oh, all right. If she turns me down, I'll find you and let you know of her decision, and then you can kidnap her."

"I'm going to require the town coach."

Scoffing, Anthony asked, "How am I supposed to get home?"

"Ask Lady Dahlia for a ride," Andrew answered, waggling his eyebrows. "Lady Norwick can act as her chaperone."

About to scoff again, Anthony seemed to think on this suggestion a moment before his face lightened in understanding. "That's a brilliant plan. If Dahlia turns you down, I can mention to Lady Norwick how sorry I am that her daughter rebuffed my marriage proposal."

"Oh, Dahlia will not be happy if you say that in front of her mother," Andrew warned.

Anthony considered the comment for a moment.

"No, she won't. But her mother will side with me, which means I'll have both her father *and* her mother in my court," he reasoned.

"Whatever happens, you cannot tell them that I've kidnapped Lady Danielle," Andrew stated. "I mean, if she hasn't made up her mind."

"I won't," Anthony agreed. He reached into his waistcoat pocket and pulled out his chronometer. "If we don't leave right now, we may miss our chances," he warned. "Some other young bucks may already have their minds set on kissing our girls behind the hedgerows."

Andrew dared a glance in Anthony's looking glass, wincing at the sight of the waistcoat. "I look like a popinjay," he murmured.

"A handsome popinjay," Anthony countered, giving him a grin. "Come. Let's go."

"What about Mother?"

"She and Father and Daphne left on his phaeton a few minutes ago. Whilst you were in the library," he said as they headed down the stairs. "Mother and Father were acting like they used to when we were younger," he added, rolling his eyes much like his father did when he heard something unbelievable.

"You mean, like they're in love?"

Anthony gave his twin a quelling glance. "Exactly."

Wincing at his brother's callous comment, Andrew paused at the bottom of the stairs, even as his brother was making his way to the front door. "If you were in love with Lady Dahlia, you would act that way with her," he stated.

Turning on his heel, Anthony regarded his brother with a look of shock. "I rather doubt that," he replied, even though his expression faltered. "I certainly wouldn't do it so others could pay witness," he added, lifting his chin defiantly.

"I want *everyone* to know I love Lady Danielle," Andrew announced. "Always."

Retracing his steps to join his brother at the bottom of the stairs, Anthony scoffed and gave his head a shake. "What are you about?"

"Father does it with Mother all the time. Haven't you noticed?" Andrew asked in a quiet voice. "He doesn't want her thinking he's taking her for granted. Doesn't want her taking a lover because she thinks he's grown complacent, or because he has his eye on hiring a mistress," he explained.

"Father would never hire a mistress," Anthony claimed. "Everyone in Mayfair knows he's heels over head in love with Mother."

"*Exactly*," Andrew replied, one of his brows arching to emphasize his point.

About to argue, Anthony realized his brother had a good point. Perhaps he did need to make his regard for Lady Dahlia more apparent—to her and to everyone else. "Noted," he said on a sigh as they resumed their walk to the vestibule. "By the way, what were you reading when I interrupted you up in the library?"

Andrew struggled to keep a blush from coloring his face. "A book on animal husbandry," he replied. "Breeding."

Anthony aimed a grimace in his direction as they hurried out the door.

CHAPTER 18
RECONSIDERING A
REFERENDUM

*M*eanwhile, *on the Aimsley phaeton heading toward Carlington House*

"If I didn't already tell you, you look rather fetching in that frock," Adam Comber said as he pulled back on the reins of his matched grays. A young boy was chasing a small dog down Park Lane, the canine dodging back and forth through the traffic. "As well as out of it," he added in a voice low enough it couldn't be overheard by their niece. Daphne was perched on the small seat behind theirs, facing the other direction. Although she gripped the sides of the bench as if her life depended on it—and it probably did—she seemed to be having fun.

"Why, thank you," Diana replied, beaming in delight. Her face was still flushed from their earlier encounter in the study, and she turned a brilliant smile on her husband. "Bounder," she added.

Adam chuckled. "You've always made me a very happy man."

"Are you flirting with me?" she asked with a giggle. She spun the handle of her parasol between her thumb and forefinger, which had the lacy border flinging out much like a ballgown during a waltz. The weather was especially fine, and with nary a cloud in the sky, Lady Morganfield's garden party would probably go on all afternoon.

"I may have to pull you behind a hedgerow and kiss you senseless," Adam warned as he had the horses maneuvering past the boy.

Diana grinned. "I have reason to believe those hedgerows are going to be quite crowded today."

"Oh? What have you heard?"

"Well, it is the first entertainment of the Season, and Adeline is expecting a rather large turnout. She learned from Agnes, the Countess of Weatherstone, that her son Sebastian is back in town, and he's planning to attend."

"Viscount Cougham is back in London?" Adam asked in surprise, referring to the heir to the Weatherstone earldom. "Where has he been all this time?"

"In northern Italy. The Alps. Recovering from some sort of accident," Diana explained. "She claims he's reformed. That he's no longer interested in performing feats of derring-do," she added with a quick glance at her husband. She was quite sure that he had been much like Sebastian at one time. Back when he was known as a scoundrel.

Adam scoffed. "He still holds the record for driving a coach-and-four the fastest in Richmond," he stated. "Took that honor from me," he added on a sigh. "Probably wants to go out on top."

It was Diana's turn to scoff. "You used to drive a

coach-and-four at breakneck speeds?" she asked in alarm.

"I was a member of the Four-in-Hand Club," he acknowledged proudly.

"Do you miss it?"

Adam seemed surprised by the query. "Not a bit," he replied after a moment of introspection. "I suppose I value my life too much now," he added as his brows furrowed.

"Well, if you have a need for speed, you could drive a bit faster," Diana suggested.

Shocked by her words, Adam regarded her a moment. "What's this now?"

"I could do with a bit more invigoration," she replied. "Add some more color to my cheeks. This is a high-perch phaeton, is it not?"

"It is," he acknowledged, understanding her meaning. "Hang on, Daphne," he called out. "Your aunt wishes for me to drive faster."

"About time, Uncle," Daphne replied with a giggle.

Adam grinned and used the crop to urge the horses into a faster trot. After a moment, he had the matched pair running, and Diana's shriek of excitement and Daphne's laughter could be heard by those on the pavement.

"Tell me something, my sweet," Adam shouted over the sound of the horses and spinning wheels. "What were you trying to say yesterday when you fainted?" He had wanted to ask during dinner and then again when they had met in her bedchamber, but other matters had occupied his mind at the time.

Diana's look of joy sobered slightly. "I reconsidered my opinion of forcing the boys to marry," she replied.

"Why?" he asked in a shout. He slowed the horses

as they approached Carlington House. There were a number of carriages and coaches already pulled up in front of the mansion, their brightly garbed occupants spilling out onto the half-circle drive.

"I don't want our sons thinking of marriage as some sort of punishment," she explained. "I would hate for them to take it out on their wives. To resent them for a decision they were forced to make in the name of money. At an age far too young to be considering marriage."

Adam's surprise at hearing her assessment had him halting the phaeton more quickly than he intended, which had the both of them pitching forward. He had an arm in front of her waist, though, which kept her on the bench seat. "That isn't quite what I intended when I gave them the edict," he replied.

"Then what had you thinking they needed to *marry*?" she countered. "If not as a punishment for changing places?"

Adam inhaled to answer but seemed to think better of his reasoning. "I just... I wanted them to learn responsibility, I suppose," he muttered.

"Have you ever thought Anthony *wasn't* a responsible young man?"

He regarded his wife for a moment and sighed. "No," he replied. "You're right. He's entirely too responsible for his age, at least when he's in my presence," he added. "But I cannot help but think that when he is not, he's out getting away with rakish behavior. Sowing his wild oats and gambling and driving coach-and-fours in the middle of the night."

Diana scoffed. "What makes you say such a thing?"

He dipped his head. "Because that's how *I* was

when I was his age. Had my father bamboozled. Mother... not so much."

Staring at her husband in disbelief, Diana wondered if Anthony really was how his father imagined him. With him having been away at university for these past few years, she really didn't know how he behaved. "Perhaps you should have a talk with him. After the garden party."

"Don't you mean have a talk with both of them?" Adam asked.

Diana shook her head. "Just him. Andrew... Andrew isn't like Anthony," she replied. "I believe he truly wants to wed Danielle." She remembered her earlier conversation with Anthony. "Oh, I did tell Anthony to invite Lady Dahlia to dinner tonight," she said. "Especially if she agrees to marry him today. And I told him to move into the other apartments on the second floor."

Adam considered her comments and finally nodded. "You have the right of it," he replied as a stable boy hurried up to take the reins. He tossed the boy a coin before descending to the pavement below. Then he walked around to the other side of the phaeton and lifted Diana down from the bench, wincing when his shoulders threatened to give way.

"Oh, do be careful, darling," Diana warned.

"I hate getting old," Adam murmured as he moved to help Daphne down from her seat. She shook out her skirts before placing a gloved hand on his arm.

Diana's prim grin had him doing a double-take. "Wot?"

She giggled. "You certainly didn't seem old earlier today," she teased, her brows waggling.

Straightening to his full height before offering his

other arm to her, he smiled. "Let's hope I never feel too old to make love to you," he murmured. "Or life won't be worth living."

She gave him a quelling glance and then pasted a brilliant smile on her face.

It was time to face the *ton* for another Season of entertainments.

CHAPTER 19
A GARDEN PARTY

A half-hour later, the back gardens of Carlington House, Mayfair

Under a rare bright sky, a growing number of the peerage and a few of their children assembled on the green lawn behind Carlington House. Their brightly colored gowns and waistcoats were almost more festive than the early spring flowers which decorated Lady Morganfield's gardens. Almost, because due to that year's rather wet weather and lack of sunshine, Adeline Carlington, Marchioness of Morganfield, had arranged for her gardener to plant blooming flowers she had acquired from a hothouse in Chiswick.

She wasn't about to have her party moved indoors due to a lack of foliage out-of-doors.

Her peach gown vying with a clump of tulips for attention, Danielle Fitzwilliam was watching a pair of viscounts spy on some young ladies seated at the wrought iron tables directly behind the house. She grinned when she recognized the Earl and Countess of Aimsley seated at one such table, apparently enjoying lemonade alongside a young girl. Curious as to the identity of the pink-clad blonde—the earl seemed especially interested in whatever she had to say—Danielle was about to make her way to the tables when a footman approached.

"Lady Danielle?" he asked in a quiet voice. He held out a silver salver filled with champagne glasses. Given the number of bubbles still rising from the bottom of the glasses, it was apparent the champagne had recently been poured.

"Yes?" She helped herself to a glass and was startled when she realized she was holding more than just the glass when the servant went on to a nearby couple.

Danielle stared at the paper the footman had surreptitiously slid into her gloved hand. Glancing about to see if anyone was looking in her direction, she finally moved to stand next to a marble statue while she opened the folded parchment.

Lady D,
I wish to have a word in private. Please join me in
the library.
A.

Scoffing, Danielle once again surveyed those who strolled about the grounds, determined to discover if someone was trying to play a trick on her. *Words in private? In the library?* What if someone was setting her up? What if she was caught—unchaperoned—with...?

She glanced at the paper again.

A.

Andrew, she thought with a sigh of disappointment.

He was no doubt anxious to learn her decision regarding his marriage proposal.

Or perhaps he had changed his mind. Perhaps he'd had second thoughts and wished to withdraw his offer.

Danielle downed the glass of champagne in just a few gulps and then wished she had taken smaller sips. Her knees would be jelly before long.

Nodding to those she passed on her way into the house—the back doors to Lady Morganfield's conservatory were wide open—she made her way through Carlington House and to the main stairs. Her slippers barely made a sound as she climbed the marble steps. The library wasn't hard to find, but she hesitated before she entered the darkened room.

She inhaled softly at the familiar scents of vellum and vanilla, leather and mildew. Carpet covered the floor and seemed to swallow up any sounds. Although there were windows along the back wall, there were freestanding shelves filled with books that blocked most of the light.

"Thank you for coming."

Danielle gave a start at hearing the familiar voice and turned to discover a young man she thought was Andrew Comber regarding her from where he stood near a library sofa. He'd obviously been seated and was now standing. Upon her approach, he bowed and then reached for her hand. The scents of limes and sandalwood wafted past her nose.

Dipping a curtsy, Danielle waited until he had straightened before she said, "Your note was rather cryptic." Her eyes narrowed when she noted his manner of dress, and they narrowed even more when she stepped back to regard him with suspicion. "Lord Breckinridge?" she said in disbelief.

Anthony scoffed. "How did you know it was *me*?"

Tipsy from the champagne, Danielle tittered. "Oh, please. I've known you since we were in leading strings," she scolded. Her eyes suddenly widened when she thought the footman might have made a mistake when he gave *her* the note. It was no doubt meant for her sister. "Oh, dear."

"What is it?"

She blinked and angled her head to one side. "Who do you think *I* am?"

Anthony inhaled and held the breath a moment. "The fact that you came suggests that you are Lady Danielle," he replied. "I told the footman to give it to you, since I rather doubt your sister wishes to speak with me."

Danielle furrowed a brow. "So, the note *was* meant for me."

He nodded. *So much for switching places.* "Indeed. I thought to..." He displayed a grimace, realizing he had to change tactics. "Learn what I might. Surely you have your sister's ear."

Sighing, Danielle moved to sit on the sofa. Her knees were buzzing from the champagne more than her head was. Not sure where to start, she said, "Dahlia is not angry with you. If anything, I think she's a bit upset with herself at having dismissed you so quickly yesterday." Danielle dipped her head. "Apparently as quickly as I dismissed your brother." Wincing, she motioned for him to join her on the sofa. The champagne had her speaking far more easily than usual.

"I must admit, I was surprised you didn't give him an answer right away," Anthony murmured as he moved to the end of the sofa. Only a few minutes ago, he had paid witness to Clarinda Brotherton Fitzwilliam,

Countess of Norwick, engaged in a lively conversation about Danielle and Andrew with the other matrons of the *ton*. For them, the union seemed inevitable. "Andrew was under the impression you had already agreed to marry him." He took a seat but left a good deal of space between them.

"Mayhap when I was ten years old," Danielle responded. After a pause, she sighed and added, "I adore him. I do, Breckinridge. We've always been the best of friends."

Frowning, Anthony regarded her a moment before he asked, "Is that not a good enough basis upon which to marry?"

Danielle allowed a wan smile. "A week ago, I would have said yes to his proposal," she said. "Without hesitation."

Anthony gave a start and then frowned. "What happened to change your good opinion of him?" Even as he put voice to the query, the reminder that they had been expelled from university crossed his mind, and he had to swallow a curse.

She shook her head. "It was nothing *he* did, I assure you."

Staring at her in confusion, Anthony gave his head a shake. "So... his being expelled—?"

"Had nothing to do with me leaving him in the park yesterday," she finished for him.

Instead of prompting her, Anthony waited. When she huffed in dismay, he asked, "What? What is it?"

"My sister showed me a book she found in our father's library." She rolled her eyes. "Uncle's library, I suppose I should say."

Anthony's expression made his confusion apparent. "I wasn't aware you had an uncle here in London."

Once again wincing, Danielle glanced toward the library table. A copy of *deBrett's* lay open, and she quickly stood and retrieved the book and returned to the sofa, almost before Anthony had a chance to stand.

"You may not be aware, but the current Earl of Norwick is actually my uncle. My father..." She paused and glanced about the library, wondering if invoking his name would have his ghost making an appearance. "My father died in a traffic accident before my sister and I were born, and Mother married his twin brother." When Anthony lifted a finger, as if to put voice to a protest, she quickly added, "Yes, it was entirely improper and probably even illegal for them to marry, but Lord Torrington—he was my mother's godfather— he made it possible somehow."

Anthony seemed to take this bit of news in stride. "Well, there is certainly historical precedence for such a situation," he commented, watching as she opened the book, *deBrett's Peerage & Barontage*. She flipped through the pages as he spoke and now presented the Norwick page for him to review.

Anthony looked as if he might be on the verge of a headache as he studied the latest entries. "So... your brothers are really your half-brothers, *and* your... your nephews?" he asked in a whisper.

Danielle blinked. "Oh, my. I never thought of them like that." When he arched a brow, she added, "I've only just been reminded of this a few days ago. I've grown up thinking of Daniel as if he were my father."

Anthony's finger moved to the listings for her and her sister. "Dahlia Davida and... who is Diana Dorothea?" he asked in alarm.

"Oh, that's me," Danielle said.

He looked up, once again confused.

"I asked people to call me Danielle because Dahlia used to go by Davida in honor of our real father—"

"Danny and Davy," he interrupted. "I remember. We teased you about having boys' names."

Danielle grinned. "After all this time, Danielle seems to have stuck, but Davida, not so much."

"My mother's name is Diana," Anthony said in a quiet voice.

"I know."

Anthony studied her a moment. "So... this is the book your sister showed you?" he asked, motioning to the copy of *deBrett's*.

Straightening on the sofa, Danielle shook her head. "Oh, I wish," she replied. "Although there might be some scandalous situations hidden in *deBrett's*, it's not about to have one rethinking their entire future."

He angled his head to one side. "What book had you rethinking your *future*?"

Danielle grimaced as she felt her face heat with her embarrassment.

Why did one have to blush when blending into the background would be preferential?

"It was a book about... *sexual congress*." She whispered the last two words as her face flushed in a bright pink. "Which wouldn't have been so alarming, except that it had... it had *illustrations*. Color plates. With quite vivid drawings."

Anthony stared at her a moment before a grin touched his lips. "French, no doubt," he murmured.

"Indeed. You know of it?" she asked, her eyes rounding.

He inhaled to answer and then dipped his head. "I rather imagine most libraries in Mayfair have a copy," he said, his own face reddening. "If not of that one, then another, similar..." He stopped speaking and took a deep breath. "Might you share what you found particularly... alarming?"

Danielle glanced over at the library table. "Davy showed me a color plate of a woman bent over a..." she pointed toward the table... "a library table, and a man was behind her—"

Anthony cleared his throat. "You needn't say anything more," he stated.

"It's why we've decided we'd rather not marry," Danielle blurted.

"What?"

Danielle thrust out her chin. "I'll not be subjected to such an indignity," she stated.

"Nor would you be," he replied. When Danielle regarded him with surprise, he added, "Those... *positions* aren't meant for respectable husbands to be employing on their genteel wives. They're..." He stopped and swallowed, suddenly aware they were no longer alone in the library. "We really shouldn't be speaking of such things."

Danielle frowned. "If not married couples, then who would be doing it?"

Anthony didn't respond, his worried gaze directed at the rather tall man who was leaning against the end of one of the library shelves, his arms crossed over his chest. From the expression David Fitzwilliam displayed, Anthony wondered if he would be meeting the man at dawn in Wimbledon Common. "My apologies, my lord." Anthony moved to stand, sure he was about to suffer the consequences of being found with Danielle without a chaperone in sight.

David straightened and waved at Anthony to remain seated. "Oh, you've nothing for which to apologize, Breckinridge. I'm well aware of the issue regarding my daughters' discovery. You would think with my having owned a rather lucrative gentlemen's club featuring only the finest courtesans, that my daughters would be better—"

"Father!" Danielle admonished him.

Anthony furrowed both brows and then glanced over at Danielle. "I thought you said your father was dead?"

She glanced over at David's ghost. "He is," she replied.

His eyes widening in alarm, Anthony stared at David. "For a dead man, you look rather well, my lord."

David dipped his head. "Thank you. I think so, too."

"So... you... you're a *ghost?*" Anthony stammered. Then he remembered that morning, when Andrew had told Daphne he was haunted by a ghost.

David rolled his eyes. "Yes, I suppose I am."

"You spoke with me in the park yesterday." Anthony's voice was calm despite his growing sense of dread.

The late earl nodded. "I did."

Anthony stared at David before turning his attention on Danielle. "Well, this certainly explains much," he said.

"It does?" Danielle countered.

"Yesterday. In the park. How he could be in two places almost at the same time." He turned back to David. "You were almost in two places at once, were you not, my lord?"

"Amazing, isn't it?" David remarked proudly, straightening. Then he sobered. "So why is it *you're* sitting there with Diana and not with Dahlia? You could be kissing my eldest in the gardens," he accused. Then his eyes narrowed. "Already changed your mind, have you?"

Anthony's eyes rounded in fear. "I... I, uh, merely wished to—"

"Breckinridge merely wished to know if Davy has changed her mind regarding marriage," Danielle put in. "And as for kissing anyone in Lady Morganfield's gardens, well, there's really nowhere to do it without being caught," she claimed. When her father directed a raised brow in her direction, she blinked. "Not that I would have first-hand knowledge, of course," she quickly added.

David pulled his chin into his neck, which had him displaying a double chin and a frown that was most frightening. "Why not just ask the lady directly?" he queried, his attention back on the viscount. "Do what I suggested in the park yesterday?"

Anthony cleared his throat. "I don't wish to annoy her, my lord," he replied. "Further anger her... if indeed Lady Dahlia is still angered by what happened in the park."

"Coward," David said under his breath.

"Father," Danielle said in a scold. "I rather appreciate Lord Breckinridge taking me into his confidence." She had a brief thought that perhaps Andrew was doing the same with her sister. If so, what was Dahlia saying about her?

"You have always been a true friend, my lady," Anthony murmured, his gaze settling on her for perhaps a moment too long.

"Well, don't be long," David said suddenly.

Anthony tore his attention from Danielle to look in the direction of the late earl, but discovered he was no longer leaning against the end of the shelf. A quick glance around the library showed the ghost had disappeared. When Anthony turned his look of shock onto Danielle, she merely shrugged. "He does that," she said. "Just pops in and out."

Blinking a few times, Anthony finally relaxed into the sofa. "How long has he been... popping in and out?"

Danielle remembered what her mother and Daniel had said in the parlor when David had shown up a few days ago. "He's just returned after having stayed gone for more than two decades," she replied. "Apparently, something Dahlia said regarding the fact that she didn't wish to marry had him appearing again."

"You don't seem bothered," Anthony remarked, still unsettled by the sudden appearance—and disappearance—of the late earl's ghost.

"Oh, I was a few days ago," she assured him. "When he first appeared. But when Mother and Uncle Daniel spoke with him... or scolded him, rather, I decided I had nothing to fear from him. He is my real father. He merely wishes to see to it we're suitably settled, I suppose."

Anthony regarded her for a moment, as if he were seeing her in an entirely new light. "For many years, I thought of you as merely a friend. Almost a younger sister." At seeing her arched brow, he quickly added, "I know you're a bit older than I am, but hear me out."

"All right," she agreed, intrigued.

"I admit, I do not really wish to marry. At least, not yet."

Danielle regarded him a moment before she nodded. "I cannot blame you," she responded. "So... why did you ask for my sister's hand?"

Anthony inhaled to reply and then scoffed. "I actually proposed, but seeing as how angry I made Dahlia with my attempt to rescue her from what I thought was a runaway horse—"

"It was rather thoughtful of you," Danielle interrupted. "Rather brave, in my opinion."

"Thank you," he acknowledged, once again giving her an assessing glance. "But my father's edict—that I marry in order so he will resume my allowance—leaves me little choice."

Danielle gave a start at hearing this last bit. "Requiring marriage doesn't seem like an appropriate punishment for being expelled from university," she murmured. "Is that why...?" Her mouth dropped open. "Is that why Andrew proposed to *me*? Because his allowance has been cut off? And he needs to be married for it to resume?" A look of astonishment coupled with disgust passed over her face.

Anthony winced. "He didn't tell you?" Danielle's face fell, and he watched as she visibly swallowed.

"He was so excited about the prospect of us going to Greece and the Kingdom of the Two Sicilies on a wedding trip, he didn't mention *that* particular tidbit," she explained. Her eyes rounded. "Was Dahlia the first girl *you* thought to ask? When you learned you had to marry?"

He furrowed a brow and allowed a one-shouldered shrug. "Who else would I wed?" he asked.

"You mean, because Angelica and Anne are already married?" she countered.

He winced. "I was never going to have the opportunity to wed either one of them," he claimed, referring to Angelica Grandby and Anne Wellingham, now Lady Fulton and Lady Hexham. "They have both been good friends, of course, and I hope they will continue to be so for the rest of our lives, but even I knew that neither would still be available when it was finally time for me to wed."

Danielle nodded. Girls always seem to wed at ages far younger than their male counterparts.

"So your next thought was Dahlia?"

He shook his head. "She was my *first* thought, actually. She always has been."

Danielle's gaze softened, her opinion of Anthony having risen a notch. "And now? If we cannot change her mind? Who will you pursue?"

It was his turn to swallow. "I suppose that depends on the answer you give my brother."

Staring at the viscount for a moment, Danielle struggled to reconcile his comment. Her eyes rounded. "Do you mean to say that you intend to court *me* if my sister doesn't accept your suit?"

Anthony rolled his eyes. "Must you make it sound so... so awful?"

Danielle opened her mouth to respond and quickly shut it. She sighed. "I apologize. That's not what I meant," she stammered. "It would not be. Awful, I mean."

Anthony arched a brow. "So... you would not turn me down outright?"

She inhaled softly. "Anthony," she whispered. "I haven't yet given Andrew an answer."

He gave a start. She had never called him by his given name before. She had always addressed him as Breckinridge, at least from the time his father had inherited the earldom. "I need a lifeline, Danielle."

Tears pricked the corners of her eyes. "I would know for the rest of my life I was your second choice," she whispered, not about to give him a straight answer.

He nodded. "So help me gain your sister's hand."

Danielle gave a start. "You're still going to pursue her?" she asked in alarm.

"Well, of course."

"But... why?"

Settling into the sofa, he crossed his arms. "I think we both know your sister and I have always been destined to marry," he replied. "With a bit of cajoling, some coaxing..." He inhaled and added, "Your father provided a recommendation that I will put forth to Dahlia if we cannot convince her."

Danielle gave a start. "Oh, dear. I don't think I want to know what *he* recommended," she said before glancing over at the library table. "You might have to ruin her," she whispered.

"Wot?" He straightened on the sofa.

"You heard me. She's convinced she won't like the marriage bed—"

"You said she doesn't wish to be tupped over a table," he interrupted. "Surely I can convince her I wouldn't expect her to do that."

"She is curious," Danielle murmured thoughtfully. "Perhaps you could... get her alone somewhere. Kiss her senseless. Get her into a bed and ruin her."

He stared at her in disbelief. "Danny! I am an honorable man," he argued.

She shrugged. "Sometimes honorable men must perform dishonorable acts," she countered. At seeing his look of distress, she rolled her eyes. "Oh, all right. I'll help convince her," she said.

The look of relief Anthony displayed was almost comical. "Thank you. I will be forever grateful. And I'll be your very best brother, should she marry me," he replied.

Danielle gave him a quelling glance. "Just what I need. Another brother." Her eyes suddenly rounded. "Do you have a sister?"

Giving a start, Anthony shook his head. "Not that I'm aware of?"

"Then who is the Little Bo Peep sitting next to your father?" she asked, remembering the young girl dressed in pink and white, her hair a riot of blonde curls, sitting with the Earl and Countess of Aimsley.

"Oh, that's my cousin, Daphne," he replied, stunned she would describe Daphne exactly as his brother had earlier that morning. "Father has decided he wants a daughter, so he is borrowing her from Aunt Daisy until my mother..." He stopped and cleared his throat, not sure if he should mention the countess' condition.

"Has her baby?" Danielle finished for him.

"You know?" he asked in surprise.

Danielle shrugged. "She's in good company. Apparently, my mother is as well." Her gaze went inward for a moment. "Which is probably why she seems so determined to see us married," she murmured.

Anthony furrowed a brow at hearing this last bit, but he didn't reply. He reached for her gloved hand and kissed the back of it. "Wait a few minutes, and then come down to the gardens. We shouldn't be seen together." He was nearly out the door before he paused. "By the way, if my brother offers to take you home in our coach, do be sure to accept, won't you?"

Furrowing a brow, Danielle gave him a look of suspicion before she remembered she might be kidnapped. "All right," she agreed as he bowed and took his leave of the library. She remained seated on the sofa, finally settling back into the cushions until her head was tilted so she was staring at the ceiling. She had a thought to simply close her eyes and take a nap, and she might have, except the sensation of someone joining her in the room had her giving start.

"What are you doing here?"

CHAPTER 20
FLOWERS AND THE FUTURE

eanwhile, in the Morganfield gardens
"My, I don't recall ever seeing you wearing such a decorative waistcoat before," a familiar voice said from somewhere near where Andrew was admiring a newly-bloomed tulip. He was sure he had seen Danielle in this part of the gardens only moments ago, but now that he'd had a chance to extricate himself from the attentions of two matrons who wished to admire his waistcoat and make his way to the tulips, Danielle was no where to be found.

He straightened and glanced around. "Lady Dahlia?" he responded, watching as the young woman approached from where she'd been seated on a stone bench. Although the garden party was well attended, most of the guests had taken seats at the wrought iron tables immediately behind the house and were enjoying tea and cake. The men who weren't seated seemed intent on spying on the young ladies who were, peeking from behind hedgerows and discussing their options in a manner suggesting they intended to employ strategies befitting a military campaign in order to either gain notice or a promise of a dance at the next ball.

Dahlia paused in mid-step. "How did you know it was me?" she asked in surprise.

Andrew grinned. "I have known you since we were in leading strings," he reminded her. "How did you know it was me and not my brother?"

Grinning, she stepped up and threaded her arm through his. "Well, the waistcoat did have me confused at first, but I rather doubt Breckinridge would bother himself with a tulip," she replied. "Besides, you never appear quite as serious as he does."

"Impending duty does seem to age him somewhat," Andrew agreed, realizing his brother's plan of switching places wasn't going to work. He sobered. "He's very sorry about what happened yesterday." At seeing her arched brow, he added, "Something about a runaway horse that wasn't?"

Dahlia rolled her eyes. "I admit, I was quite vexed by what he did. At least, at the time. You see, I was having the ride of my life on a racehorse."

Andrew noted her expression of wistfulness. He thought it made her look far prettier than usual. "Ah. Was it the speed that had you enthralled?"

She grinned. "The speed, yes, but Vindication has such an even gait, and he's a most responsive mount. I've never had a ride like him," she claimed. "I think he shall be the only horse I ride in Rotten Row from now on."

"Lucky horse," Andrew commented, rather impressed by how passionate she could be about the former racehorse.

Turning her gaze on him, Dahlia furrowed a brow. "Oh, my. Should your brother be concerned?"

Andrew reddened. "At the threat of losing life and limb, I have assured Anthony I shall not pursue you for courtship, Lady Dahlia. My best hope is that I may one day call you sister."

Dahlia's eyes rounded. "Oh, my." She hadn't considered that she would gain another brother should she agree to wed Breckinridge. She certainly liked Andrew more than she did her own brothers.

They walked along in silence for a time before she said, "I'm not angry with him. Breckinridge, I mean."

Surprised by her comment, Andrew slowed his pace. "Does that mean you'll give him a chance to offer for your hand?" he asked, pausing to examine the early pink blooms on a rhododendron bush.

Pinching her lips together, Dahlia seemed reluctant to respond. "I wish there was a way I could be married to him without certain... certain responsibilities that come with it. At least, not at first."

Andrew straightened and stared at her. "And if that can be arranged? Would you accept his offer?"

Dahlia blinked. "What?"

"Explain what it is you want... and what you don't want," he encouraged her. "Tell him exactly what you've told me," he added. "I'm quite sure you two can come to some sort of agreement that you'll both find acceptable. At least, until it's absolutely necessary you start a nursery." He paused. "Besides, I rather imagine it will be a long time before Anthony inherits, given how old our grandfather was when he finally died, which means you'll be a viscountess in name only."

Dahlia stared at him a moment, her brows furrowing with suspicion. "You're saying I should bargain with Breckinridge?"

Andrew opened his mouth to respond but thought

better of it as he winced. "Just... talk with him is all," he finally encouraged.

"Mayhap when I see him next." She glanced around, apparently on the lookout for the viscount.

"Then perhaps you might be amenable to helping me," Andrew said.

Dahlia inhaled softly. "You mean with Danny?"

He nodded. "Please don't be alarmed if she doesn't return to Norwick House this evening. Mayhap make an excuse for why she won't be home for dinner? Say that she's dining with a friend and won't return until late this evening."

Her eyes widening in alarm, Dahlia glanced around again before she turned to stare at him. "What are you saying?" Her eyes widened even more. "Are you taking her to Gretna Green?"

Scoffing, Andrew leaned down and said in a low voice, "I'm only going to do what your father told me to do to secure her hand."

Dahlia's mouth dropped open as her eyes darted to the side. "Oh, dear," she murmured. "When... when might that have been?"

Andrew shrugged. "Yesterday. In the park. Directly after Lady Danielle took her leave of me. After I... right after I proposed marriage."

Looking as if she might swoon at any moment, Dahlia once again glanced around. "You say it was my *father*? You're quite sure it was not Uncle Daniel?"

One brow furrowing, Andrew said, "He *said* he was your father—"

"Oh," Dahlia whined. "Oh, dear. What did he tell you to do?"

Andrew was about to respond, but his brother strolled up and hooked his arm into Dahlia's free arm.

"Thank you, brother, for seeing to it Lady Dahlia had an escort, but I can take over now," Anthony said as he lifted Dahlia's hand to his lips before placing it back on his arm. "You might find the library more diverting," he whispered hoarsely. He didn't give Andrew a second glance but merely led Dahlia off toward the back of the garden.

Giving Andrew one last quizzical glance, Dahlia turned her attention on Anthony.

CHAPTER 21
KIDNAPPING IS AWKWARD

*M*eanwhile, up in the Carlington House library

"What are you doing here?" Andrew asked as he regarded Danielle. She was perched on one of the library sofas, the bell skirt of her peach gown spread wide on the cushions.

Pulled from the reverie she'd been experiencing since Lord Breckinridge had taken his leave—the effects of the hastily downed champagne had her feeling delightfully tipsy—Danielle gave a start and narrowed her eyes. "I might ask you the same thing."

Andrew reached for her hand and kissed the back of it. He didn't let go, though. "I was looking for you, of course. My brother..." He glanced behind him, as if he feared he'd been followed. "He implied I could find you here."

Danielle glanced towards the door, as if she feared being discovered alone with him. "I find I'm not yet ready for the Season's entertainments," she murmured, one brow arching when her gaze went to the hand he still held.

Lowering himself to one knee, Andrew continued to hold onto her hand. "Then allow me to escort you to someplace more private," he said before once again kissing the back of her hand.

Inhaling softly, Danielle regarded him with rounded eyes. With him kneeling before her, their heads were level, and she rather liked that she didn't have to look up at him. "More private than this?"

He nodded. "I think you'll like it. At least, I hope you do."

She regarded him with suspicion. "Is it far?"

He furrowed a brow. "Not far. We can be there in ten minutes," he claimed.

"Walking?"

"We'll go in the Aimsley coach," he said, hoping his brother wouldn't be too upset at discovering he had absconded with the equipage that had brought the two of them to Carlington House. He had warned him.

"My maid isn't with me today," Danielle said as an involuntary shiver passed through her. This had to be the kidnapping. "I came with Mother."

"We can speak with Lady Norwick on our way out," he suggested. "I'm sure she'll agree to be your chaperone."

Danielle scoffed. How would it be a kidnapping if he had permission? "We'll do no such thing," she said, rising from the sofa, surprised when her knees seemed perfectly steady. Apparently the effects of the champagne had worn off.

Andrew stood up. He didn't step back, though, which had him standing impossibly close to her. So close, his legs pushed against the front of her bell-shaped skirts. His hand still gripped her gloved hand, and for a moment she thought he had merely forgotten to let go. But she watched as he once again brought it to his lips and kissed her knuckles.

"If you're sure," he finally responded. He lowered the hand to his arm and led her out of the library, down the steps, and out the front door, trying hard not to hurry. Anxiousness had his heart racing. At any moment, he was sure she would change her mind and ask that he take her to her mother.

He relaxed upon seeing the gold-painted crest of the Aimsley earldom on the coach parked nearest to the front door. At least they wouldn't have to wait for the equipage to be brought 'round.

"Will you at least give me a hint as to where we're going?" Danielle asked as he waved to the coach driver. The servant immediately moved to open the door, giving Andrew a curious look as Danielle stepped up and into the ancient coach. Although it was old, its navy blue velvet interior was more elegant than most. She took the seat in the direction of travel and watched as Andrew bounded in and sat across from her. "Or at least tell me where you're taking me?"

Andrew waited until he felt the slight jerk that indicated they were in motion before he said, "To my townhouse."

Her brows lifted as did her lips. "You have a townhouse?" she asked in disbelief. She couldn't help the grin that accompanied the query.

Perhaps the champagne was still addling her brain.

He nodded. "I do. I cannot be married and continue to live in Aimsley House," he claimed. "It wouldn't be fair to my wife."

Danielle inhaled softly, suddenly sober. "What

wife?" His words implied he was already married.

Blinking, Andrew lost some of his resolve. "Well, whomever agrees to marry me," he hedged.

"Oh," she replied, relaxing into the velvet squabs before her brows furrowed. "What's wrong with Aimsley House?"

He shrugged. "Nothing, of course. But eventually it will be my brother's house, and his countess will be its mistress," he explained. "I should think my wife would want to run her own household. Decorate it as she sees fit. Host her own tea parties and such." He tugged at his cravat, wishing he hadn't allowed the valet to tie it so tight that morning.

"Have you moved in?"

He shook his head. "Not yet. I only just acquired it this morning," he explained, relieved his father had readily agreed with his reasoning. It had also helped that he hadn't even known the earldom was in possession of the property.

He had his mother to thank for that, apparently.

Before Danielle could respond, the coach jerked to a halt. Andrew glanced out the window, relieved to see they were in Bruton Street. Relieved to see the townhouse was fairly well maintained, even if the black window boxes beneath the ground floor windows didn't have any flowers in them. All the black shutters appeared in working order, as did the red front door, which featured a brass mermaid knocker.

"Where are we?" Danielle asked as the driver opened the coach door. Anticipation had flutterbies tumbling about in her stomach. Never before these past two days had she allowed a young man to escort her somewhere without the benefit of a footman or a lady's maid. She wouldn't have been allowed.

She rather doubted she was allowed now, except she was quite sure she had spotted her father watching the coach from the other side of the street.

"Number twenty-five, Bruton Street," Andrew replied. "The park is but a few streets that way," he said as he pointed west.

Danielle gingerly stepped down, allowing the driver to help as her gaze darted about. For the first time since they had left Carlington House, she worried who might see her in the company of a man.

Andrew offered his arm, and she quickly threaded hers through his elbow. "Have you met your neighbors?" she asked, her gaze going to where she was sure she had seen her father.

No one was there, though.

Andrew shook his head. "Not yet," he admitted. Given the townhouse's proximity to Grovesnor Square, he sorted that most in this neighborhood would be members of the peerage or wealthy merchants and bankers. "Shall we?"

Danielle once again glanced around. "Please," she whispered.

The front door opened even before they had a chance to employ the mermaid knocker.

"Parker?" Andrew guessed, recalling his mother's mention of the servant's name.

The butler bowed slightly. "I am, Mr. Comber. We've been expecting you."

Andrew's eyes rounded before he realized his mother had probably sent word that he'd be occupying the property. "Ah, very good. I expect we'll be staying at least the night and possibly another. It will depend on her ladyship," he said as he nodded toward Danielle. "If she finds the accommodations satisfactory or not."

"Very good, sir," Parker said as he stood aside to let them in.

About to put voice to a protest—she had no intention of spending the night—or two—Danielle realized she couldn't counter his words or the butler might jump to conclusions. Realize they weren't married. Or think she was Andrew's mistress.

"If we could have tea brought to the parlor in say... half an hour?" Andrew suggested.

"Of course, sir."

"And dinner at seven."

"Very good, sir. In the dining room? Or...?"

Andrew swallowed, realizing they weren't in possession of dinner clothes. He hadn't thought to bring any luggage. "The dining room will be fine," he replied, well aware Danielle was on the verge of protesting. "In the meantime, I'll take her ladyship on a tour of the house."

He watched Parker hurry off to the kitchens before turning his gaze onto Danielle. Her attention was on the hall, though, her eyes round with wonder. "Where would you like to start?" he asked, relieved she no longer seemed so nervous. Or about to protest.

Danielle scoffed. "What are you about?" she asked in a whisper.

He shrugged. "I merely wish to show you where we would live should you agree to marry me," he replied.

"Dinner?" she countered. "Touring a house won't take four *hours*."

He winced. "True," he hedged, wondering if he should tell her everything her father had told him he should do. At some point, he would have to tell her he had kidnapped her.

But not just yet.

CHAPTER 22
A PROPOSAL GOES SIDEWAYS

*M*eanwhile, back at Lady Morganfield's garden party

"What did my father tell you to do?" Dahlia asked as Anthony escorted her to the farthest reaches of the Carlington House gardens.

Anthony regarded her in surprise. "What makes you think he told me to *do* anything?"

Giving him a quelling glance, Dahlia huffed. "I just agreed to lie on behalf of my sister. Apparently your brother is taking her somewhere for an illicit *affaire*," she claimed.

Scoffing, Anthony said, "My brother is not capable of an illicit *affaire*," his smirk revealing a dimple that was rarely on display.

"You say that as if *you* are," Dahlia accused.

Anthony stopped and regarded her with an expression of concern. "I would be capable of such with you," he whispered. He glanced around, wincing when he realized there was little in the way of available hedgerows or trees behind which he could kiss her. The few that lined the area where the tables were located were already in use by other amorous couples. "I wish to apologize for what happened yesterday. I truly thought you were in danger," he said in a quiet voice. "That horse was running so fast. If something had happened to you... if you had been thrown from him, I would never forgive myself if I hadn't at least tried to save you," he claimed in a quiet voice.

Dahlia inhaled softly. "I wasn't in any danger, I assure you," she said. "But I appreciate your concern for me. I do, Breckinridge."

He lowered his head to hers, resting his chin on her forehead. "Call me Anthony. Please?" he countered. For a moment, he wished he could remove her hat. At least she had the peach rose-topped straw hat perched at a jaunty angle.

Her eyes widening slightly, Dahlia said, "All right." When he didn't offer anything else right away, she said, "I couldn't help but think you had more to say to me yesterday. When you were making your way out of the park? I apologize for my immediate reaction. That I didn't give you a chance to speak," she stammered. "To explain yourself. And then you raced off so suddenly."

Grimacing, Anthony pulled away slightly. Glancing about as if to discover if someone was watching them, he said, "I did intend to ask you something." When he was sure no one had directed their gazes onto them, he lowered his lips to hers and kissed her. Although their lips barely touched and the kiss was over almost as quickly as it had begun, he wondered if he could get away with another.

Dahlia stared up at him. "That's a rather curious means by which to ask a question," she whispered.

"You didn't mind, did you?" he countered.

Blinking, Dahlia shook her head. "No. Not at all," she admitted. All at once, she seemed discombobulated. Unsure of where she was. "If only all questions were so easy," she murmured.

Giving her a wan grin, Anthony took one of her hands in his. "Will you marry me, Dahlia?" Before she had a chance to answer, he added, "I know there is much to discuss. Negotiations that must occur. Agreements that need to be made," he said quickly. "We needn't live together right away if you'd rather not. I don't expect I'll inherit anytime soon, so duty won't be required forthwith, but..." He stopped when he saw her expression. "Oh, dear. What is it?"

Dahlia scoffed as her fists moved to her hips, including the one he was still holding onto. "Leave it to you to turn what should be a rather romantic moment into a... into a *business* proposition," she hissed.

"Davy," he whispered. "I know you don't wish to wed right away, but..." He grimaced at seeing her expression. Anger. Disbelief. "I must."

A combination of hurt and confusion had Dahlia near tears. "Oh, you know that, do you?" Her brows suddenly furrowed. "*Must?*" she repeated, just then comprehending his last word.

Wincing, he nodded. "By the end of the summer. No later," he stated, remembering he had enough funds in reserve to last him until then.

"Well, *that's* rather convenient," she countered. "You'll have the entire Season to find a willing young miss to marry," she huffed.

"Davy," he murmured, his brows furrowing in confusion. "I don't want a willing young miss. I want *you*," he said on a sigh.

Still smarting from his botched marriage proposal,

Dahlia shook off his hand. He'd been attempting to take possession of her right hand as he made his apology. She took a step back, fighting to take a breath between sobs that threatened to have tears streaming down her face. "Good day, Lord Breckinridge," she managed to say before she dipped a curtsy and then headed off toward the house at a rather fast pace.

Stunned by her sudden departure, Anthony balled his hands into fists and raised his face to the sky. He was tempted to let out a howl of frustration, but remembering where he was, he swallowed and struggled to breathe.

About to make his way toward the house—perhaps he could catch Dahlia before she took her leave of Carlington House—Anthony couldn't.

David Fitzwilliam stood in his way, his arms crossed over his chest, his expression suggesting he was not pleased.

CHAPTER 23

KIDNAPPING IS EVEN MORE AWKWARD

M eanwhile, at the Comber townhouse in Bruton Street

Danielle's gaze on Andrew didn't waver, although it held a hint of suspicion upon hearing his agreement as to how long it would be before dinner was served. "I cannot spend the night here," she said, although the hesitation in her voice suggested it wouldn't be hard to change her mind. She was obviously impressed by the townhouse. Her gaze had settled on the majestic marble staircase and the split landing halfway up to the first floor. From there, two sets of stairs led to two different corridors.

"Of course not," Andrew agreed, deciding it better he not share her father's plan. She might leave in a huff, and then he'd never talk her into marrying him. "Come. We'll take a tour of the house. Let's start in the very front," he suggested, leading her into a small room. Two windows looked out onto Bruton Street, their soft green velvet drapes pulled back in the center with tasseled tiebacks. White chiffon curtains hid the glass.

"A sitting room, do you suppose?" Danielle asked as her free hand skimmed over an escritoire. An Aubusson carpet covered the floor, looking as if it had never been walked upon. A couple of chintz upholstered chairs placed on either side of a small table were the room's only other furnishings.

"Your own salon," Andrew suggested as he led them out and into an adjacent room.

"Obviously the study," Danielle remarked, remaining near the door while Andrew made the rounds of the oak-furnished room. Dark green drapes framed the only window behind the modest desk, and shelves stuffed with leather-bound books covered half the wall while a fireplace took up the rest.

"Looks like someone liked to play cards," Andrew remarked as he studied a well-worn gaming table at the far end of the room.

Danielle's attention was on the books that filled the shelves. She gingerly stepped into the room to peruse the titles. One shelf featured foil-stamped titles such as "Modern Farming," "Horse Husbandry," and "The Fruit Tree Handbook." Another shelf contained a number of novels while another had her pulling a book out. She opened it on one arm and gasped when it fell open to the color plates located in the middle.

The same color plates Dahlia had shown her the week prior. She thumbed through the slick pages, her gaze darting to the illustrations of mostly naked bodies engaged in all manner of sexual relations.

"What is it?" Andrew asked as he joined her.

Danielle slammed the book shut. "Nothing," she said as her face bloomed with color. She quickly slid the book back onto the shelf.

Andrew jerked back in response. When she avoided his gaze, he said, "Danny?" in a soft voice.

She rolled her eyes and huffed. "The reason Davy and I don't wish to marry," she murmured.

He winced before his attention went to the book she had opened. Pulling it out, he read the title on the spine and said, "Oh." While Danielle pretended to admire an overstuffed wing chair, he flipped through the illustrations in the book. He couldn't help how his own face reddened at seeing some of the positions depicted. "I would never do this to you," he said, glancing up from one particularly embarrassing color plate to discover her leaning against the wall with her arms crossed over her bosom.

"Which one?" She couldn't help but wonder which illustration had him making such a claim.

He turned the book around so the color plate was aimed in her direction.

She rolled her eyes. "But you would do it with a mistress," she countered.

Andrew furrowed a brow. "I don't have a mistress, but even if I did, I... I would not do such a thing," he said before turning the page. "Nor this one." He continued to flip through the pages, his brows doing a dance between shock and careful consideration. After a moment, he moved toward Danielle.

Pressing herself more firmly against the wall, she gave him a suspicious glance. "What?"

"Come sit with me," he encouraged as he settled on a leather sofa, the book opened on his lap.

Reminded of the leather sofa in the Carlington House library, Danielle frowned, but she pushed away from the wall and joined him. She was careful to leave plenty of space betwixt them, though.

He showed her the first plate in the book. "I would very much like to do this with you," he said, indicating the missionary position, not bothering to add that it was the only one he knew. His limited experience had been with a tavern maid, and they'd had to be quick given she was the only server on staff that night.

Danielle glanced over at the drawing, her brows rising in apparent shock. "Like that? Completely... naked?" she asked in a whisper.

He hesitated before saying, "Not at first. But once we're more comfortable with one another..." He turned to the next page. "What would you say to riding St. George?" he asked, reading the caption below the illustration.

Moving closer to look at the drawing, Danielle inhaled sharply but then seemed to think on her response before saying, "Maybe."

Continuing to show her each color plate in turn, Andrew watched for her reaction before giving his own opinion. By the time they had finished perusing the color plates, their opinions varying between disgust, bewilderment, shock, and laughter, Danielle was sitting against him, and one of his arms had moved to rest behind her shoulder. He was about to kiss the side of her head when Parker appeared on the threshold.

As if he'd been caught in a compromising position, Andrew pulled his arm from behind Danielle and straightened. "Parker?"

"A tea tray has been delivered to the parlor, sir."

Attempting an air of nonchalance, Danielle quickly stood and said, "I'll see to serving, Parker."

"Very good, my lady," the servant said in his baritone voice. He nodded and disappeared.

Andrew saw to replacing the book on the shelf before

he offered Danielle his arm. "I believe the parlor is on the first floor," he said as he led them to the marble stairs.

"Is that a breakfast parlor?" Danielle asked as they were about to pass an open door.

Pausing in mid-step, Andrew glanced in the direction she indicated. "It is," he replied, wishing he'd had a chance to tour the house before bringing her. At least the floor plan seemed similar to most townhouses in Mayfair. "Would you like to see it?"

Danielle was about to say they could do so later, but he changed direction and took her into the room. A single window faced east, but afternoon light managed to illuminate most of the breakfast parlor.

"Rather nice sideboard," Andrew remarked, noting the carved doors and decorative shelf that ran the length of the piece.

Her attention on the table, Danielle sighed. "Four chairs," she remarked.

"You think we'll require more?" he asked, waggling his brows. He quickly sobered when he noted her quelling glance.

"We should discuss it," she countered. "How many children, I mean."

Heartened she seemed to be considering marriage, especially after their time in the study, Andrew offered his arm. "Over tea," he offered.

They made their way up the stairs and into the parlor. "It's a bit a small," Danielle remarked as she made her way to the chair in front of the tea tray. She went about preparing the cups as Andrew studied the fireplace and mantel.

"It is cozy," he said. "If you think it's too small, we might knock down that wall," he said, pointing to the wall opposite the fireplace. He disappeared from the room and returned a moment later. "It looks like a sitting room, and the fireplace is on the opposite wall, so we'd end up with a parlor with two fireplaces," he added, desperate to make her happy.

"Milk and sugar?" she asked, smirking at his attempts to bribe her into agreeing to marry him.

Andrew lowered himself into the chair opposite hers. "You remembered," he murmured.

Danielle gave a start. "Yes, I suppose I do," she said as she offered him his cup of tea on a saucer. "Biscuit? I'm not sure what these are." She held out a plate of biscuits. "There's no cake," she added.

"That's my fault. I'm afraid I didn't give the staff much notice that we would be here today."

"Have you even *met* the staff?" she countered, lifting a teacup to her lips.

Andrew inhaled to answer and then shook his head. "Truth be told, I only learned about this townhouse yesterday. My father didn't even know about it. Or didn't remember it was an Aimsley property."

Danielle furrowed a brow. "Then how did *you* discover it?"

Remembering his conversation with the late Earl of Norwick in the park the day before, Andrew scoffed. "Your father told me."

Blinking, Danielle nearly dropped her teacup. She glanced around the room, expecting to find her father casually leaning against one of the walls with his arms crossed over his chest. When she didn't see him, she turned her attention back to Andrew. "When?"

"Yesterday. Right after you left me in the park," Andrew replied.

"Oh, dear," she whispered. Her eyes rounded. "What else did he tell you?"

Despite not having taken a bite of his biscuit, Andrew swallowed. "Um... well, um...," he stammered.

Danielle set her teacup and saucer on the table. "*What* did he tell you?"

Andrew rolled his eyes. "Oh, must I say?" he whined. At her scoff, he sighed and said, "He told me to kidnap you."

Not expecting that particular response—even if she had been warned—Danielle stared at him before she glanced around. "Kidnap me?" she repeated. Her eyes rounded in pretend shock. "Is that what you've done?"

He shook his head. "Not exactly," he replied. "Not yet. You came of your own accord. Didn't you?"

Danielle couldn't argue his point. She had come willingly. He hadn't coerced her. Hadn't threatened her in any way. "And if I hadn't?" she asked.

He winced. "Well, I was to bodily remove you from the garden party, I suppose. Bring you here."

"And?" she prompted.

"Show you the house."

"Which you've done," she said.

"Well, not *all* of it," he argued. "You haven't seen the bedchambers. The mistress suite. The nursery."

She bit into a biscuit as if she were biting her tongue. "And once you had shown me all of the house? What then?"

Andrew sighed in resignation. "I was planning to propose marriage again. Give you the ring. Kiss you."

This last seemed to have her relaxing somewhat. "That's hardly kidnapping," she hedged. "I mean, what sort of ransom demand were you planning to make?"

"Your agreement to marry me," he finally admitted. "I wasn't to let you go until you had accepted my suit."

Danielle gasped, her eyes narrowing as she glanced toward the parlor door. "And if I didn't? Accept your suit?"

"Oh, Danny, please don't—"

"What were you to do if I didn't agree?" she pressed.

Andrew sighed. "You had to, Danny."

"So, do you intend to keep me here until I do?"

"Your father told me to keep you overnight, if necessary. *Thoroughly ruin you*, I believe is how he put it."

For a moment, Danielle looked as if she might be sick. "Oh," she mumbled, her gaze darting about as if she expected to find her father watching them.

For a moment, she couldn't decide if she should thank the ghost or hit him over the head with the fire poker.

CHAPTER 24
A TRYST IN THE LIBRARY

*M*eanwhile, back in the Carlington House
gardens

"Lord Norwick," Anthony acknowledged, giving the ghost of Lady Dahlia's father a slight bow.

"Breckinridge," David countered with a nod. "Still having trouble with my oldest, are you?"

Anthony was sure his face was bright red with embarrassment. "Just a slight set-back is all, my lord," he replied.

"Set-back?" David repeated. "At the rate you're going, you'll be in the last century before long."

Wincing, Anthony had a mind to plant a facer on the arrogant late earl. He didn't think his fist would make impact, though. "I thought to assure her we needn't be married immediately," he said.

"Turned it into a business dealing, did you?"

Remembering it had been the late earl's idea that he negotiate the terms of a marriage with Dahlia, Anthony frowned at David and crossed his arms, imitating the ghost's posture. "Aren't most marriages?" he countered.

David scoffed. "These days? Hardly," he replied. "It's not like in my day," he went on. "People are marrying for love. Or affection, at least. I had to learn that from my brother of all people."

Anthony furrowed a brow. "You botched your proposal?" he asked, not at all concerned he might be offending the ghost.

"Oh, I managed to avoid that issue entirely," David announced proudly. "I let my twin brother do the proposing. The courting. All those pink roses he bought for Clarinda? Saved me a small fortune. Then, when it was time for us to wed, I merely swooped in and claimed her as my own."

Anthony's mouth dropped open in shock as his arms fell to his sides. "Sir?"

"Daniel and I looked exactly alike. Clarinda couldn't tell us apart, so..." He shrugged.

"How hard did he hit you when he discovered what you had done?" Anthony asked, his expression growing fierce.

Furrowing his brows, David shook his head. "As I recall, there was no violence on his part," he replied. "He knew Clarinda and I had been betrothed since she was quite young..."

His words were cut off when Anthony's fist impacted his left cheek. Stunned, the ghost of David Fitzwilliam seemed to wobble a moment before his legs went out from beneath him and he crumpled to the ground.

Shaking his arm while he flexed his fingers, Anthony quickly glanced around to determine if anyone had seen him punch the earl. Although a few had aimed curious glances in his direction, no one seemed particularly alarmed.

Then it dawned on him that the ghost of Dahlia's father might not be visible to anyone else.

"What happened to your hand?" a male voice asked.

Anthony spun around to discover a fellow viscount, Sebastian Peele, heir to the Weatherstone earldom, regarding him from where he stood near a hedgerow. The rather tall man had been spying on the ladies seated at one of the wrought iron tables. "Ah, Lord Cougham. I heard you were back in town." He noticed Sebastian's look of concern and added, "Uh, I'm not quite sure. It suddenly just... hurt," he said as he once again gave it a shake. He glanced down at the ghost, and then side-eyed the other viscount to discover if he was even looking down at it.

He wasn't. Anthony relaxed some and shook out his hand again.

"Bee sting perhaps?" Sebastian suggested.

His eyes widening, Anthony nodded as he studied his hand. "Why, yes. Yes. I do believe you have the right of it. If you'll excuse me, I'll be off to wash it."

Sebastian merely nodded and continued his perusal of the young ladies beyond the hedgerow.

Glancing down at the still prone body of the late earl, Anthony decided it would be best if he wasn't around when the ghost awakened. The last thing he wanted was to be haunted for the rest of his life.

He turned to make his way to where all the matrons were having tea but had to stop short.

Dahlia stood staring first at him and then her father. "I saw what happened," she murmured. "Are you all right?" She stepped up close enough to take his gloved hand in hers.

Anthony blinked before he glanced first left and

then right. "Better than him," he replied. "Although I expect I'll be haunted for the rest of my life."

Dahlia afforded him a wan grin. "If it's any consolation, he scolded me before he did you," she said.

"Scolded you?" he repeated in alarm. "Whatever for?"

Dahlia rolled her eyes. "Might we go somewhere more... more private?" she asked. "Most of the matrons are going to Weatherstone Manor to admire the arrangements for Tuesday night's ball," she added, when she noticed that Anthony's attention was on the bevy of women who were departing the tables behind the mansion. "Including my mother."

Anthony watched as a number of countesses and viscountesses gave Lady Morganfield their regards. In only a matter of moments, it seemed half the garden party attendees had left the premises. He couldn't help but notice his father was still there, though, Daphne engaging him in what appeared to be a diverting conversation.

"Who's the cheeky chit flirting with your father?" Dahlia asked.

Anthony let out a guffaw. "That cheeky chit would be my cousin," he replied as he offered his arm. "Daphne. Father's current favorite," he added. "He desperately wants a daughter."

Tittering, Dahlia lifted a hand to her mouth. "He won't if she continues to talk his ear off," she murmured. "Poor man."

Stunned at seeing Dahlia so amused, Anthony took a moment to watch her. To note how the sun lit her face. To see the sparkle in her green eyes. The chestnut highlights in her hair. The way the peach of her gown complemented her complexion.

When she suddenly turned her attention on him, he pretended he had been staring at something behind her. "The library might be available now," he said by way of a suggestion of where they could go for privacy. When he saw her quelling glance, he quickly added, "I promise, I'll never tup you over a table."

Dahlia's eyes rounded. "Breckinridge!"

"You were imagining it. I could tell," he accused.

"How do you even...?" She clamped her mouth shut as a blush bloomed over her face. Combined with the peach of her gown, she now displayed more color than the nearby tulips. "Did Father speak of it with you?" she asked. From her manner, Anthony feared she was about to kick the prone earl.

"Never mind," he said as he once again offered his arm. When she didn't immediately take it, he took her gloved hand and forcibly placed it on his arm. "There are other far more important matters to discuss," he stated. "After I kiss you senseless," he added, remembering what Danielle had told him to do.

Although Dahlia's eyes once again rounded in surprise, a grin accompanied her expression of shock.

CHAPTER 25
REPERCUSSIONS OF A KIDNAPPING

*M*eanwhile, at the Comber townhouse
A grimace made Andrew appear far older than his one-and-twenty years. He was beginning to wish he hadn't followed the late earl's instructions to kidnap Lady Danielle. "I won't keep you here against your will, Danny," he whispered. "I promise. If you don't wish to wed me, then merely tell me now, and I'll return you to Carlington House. Or Norwick House, if you prefer," he said on a sigh. "I promise I won't ever call on you again. You can remain unmarried and go off to the Kingdom of the Two Sicilies and Greece by yourself. Mayhap I'll find someone else to marry, and our paths will cross in Rome. Or Athens." Just saying the words had him feeling sick.

Danielle straightened in her chair. "Oh, no, Andrew Comber," she replied, her hands going to her hips. "You're not getting off that easy," she announced.

"What? I'm not?"

She huffed and stood, which had Andrew quickly

coming to his feet. He watched as she moved to the window.

"Danny, what is it?" he asked, hurrying to join her. He looked out, wondering what she might be in search of.

"Do you see him?" she asked as she angled her head first right and then left.

"Him who?"

"My father," she said, exasperated. "I was sure I spotted him across the street. When we first arrived," she claimed before moving away from the window. She headed for the door.

"I haven't seen him since yesterday," Andrew replied as he followed her out of the parlor and up the stairs to the second floor. "Or last night, I suppose it was," he murmured when he recalled his nightmare. "What did you mean when you said I wasn't going to get off easy?" he asked as they reached the corridor.

"You're going to do *exactly* as my father command-ed," she said as she began opening doors and glancing in.

Andrew's eyes rounded. "I am?"

Danielle threw open another door, poked her head in, and moved onto the next. Upon opening this one, she stilled. "Oh," she breathed, annoyed she sounded like her mother.

"This is the mistress suite," he murmured. "I hope you like peach," he added, noting how her gown's color matched that of the counterpane and drapes, the uphol-stered chair in front of the dressing table, and the japanned screen in one corner.

She turned and gave him a wan grin. "Asks the man who is wearing a rather decorative peach waistcoat," she teased. "I almost didn't recognize you because of it," she added. "I suppose my father suggested you wear that color?" she asked as her hands gripped her skirts and held them out as if to display their matching shade of peach.

Andrew shook his head. "Anthony did, actually. It's his waistcoat. He thought we should switch places today, but it seems you and your sister can tell us apart regardless of what we wear."

She scoffed. "Of course we can. We've known you since you were in leading strings."

He inhaled and stepped forward, closing the space between them. "You're rather beautiful in peach. Surrounded by peach."

Danielle stared up at him. "As are you," she whispered, watching as his face lowered toward hers. Their foreheads touched before his lips settled on her lips. A moment later, and he had his arms around her back, pulling her against his front until her curves filled his voids.

When her arms finally wrapped around his neck, Andrew coaxed her mouth open with the tip of his tongue, sliding it over her teeth. He tasted the biscuit she'd eaten and the tea she had drunk before her tongue finally tangled with his.

Desperate for air, he pulled away and suckled her lower lip before finally allowing the kiss to end. "I could do that all day with you," he whispered.

She stared up at him. "I would let you," she replied.

"Does that mean you'll marry me?" he asked in a whisper.

Her eyes darted toward the bed. "Mayhap after you've thoroughly ruined me," she teased.

"Danny," he scolded, but he glanced down to discover she was already undoing his topcoat buttons.

"I think I should like to try what you showed me in the first color plate we looked at," she said, feeling rather emboldened.

Andrew blinked. "You would?" He noted how she was nearly finished undoing his waistcoat buttons.

"If that goes well, then you can be St. George," she went on, pushing the coats from his torso.

"I can?"

"By then, it will probably be time for dinner."

"It will?" He absently finished pulling off his coats and tossed them to a nearby chair.

She was in the middle of untying his cravat when she stopped and regarded him with a quelling glance. "Well, how long does it take? To make love, I mean?"

Andrew's mouth moved, but no sound came out.

"Not all night, surely?" she prompted.

He cleared his throat. "Seeing as how I've... I've not ever really done this before..." he stammered. "I mean, made love to a woman I... I love, I mean, I..." He stopped and swallowed, realizing Danielle was staring at him in awe. "What is it?"

"You love me?" she asked in a whisper.

He nodded. "Well, of course, I do," he replied defensively. "I have since I was... I was eight years old," he claimed. "That's why I want you to be my wife."

"And the money?"

Andrew frowned. "What money?"

Danielle sighed. "Your allowance?"

Careful not to react, Andrew said, "My allowance or lack thereof has no bearing on my wish to marry you," he stated, curious as to how she had learned about his father's edict.

She angled her head to one side. "What about your

wish to go to Greece?" Reaching up, she continued to undo his cravat.

He scoffed. "I want to take you to Greece, of course," he said. "And to the Kingdom of the Two Sicilies. But I want to do so with you as my *bride*. I want us to see those sights together."

Danielle sighed and stood on tiptoes to kiss him. "You might have mentioned it before," she teased, once she had finally pulled away, holding the length of white silk that had been wrapped around his neck as if it were a hard-won trophy.

"I thought I did," he countered.

"Well, thank you for making your intentions more clear," she said as she turned around, expecting him to undo her buttons. Instead, she gave a start when his lips touched the nape of her neck. He kissed her there and then directly behind her ear. "That tickles," she whispered, as one of his forefingers trailed along her hairline to the top fastening of her gown.

"I suppose I'll have to rebutton all these later," he murmured, struggling with the round mother-of-pearl discs.

"Not until it's time for dinner," she said, surprised at how different it felt to have his larger fingers undoing the buttons compared to those of her lady's maid.

When he had most of them undone, he spread the edges apart. She shivered as his fingers skimmed over the skin of her bare back above her chemise. A frisson shot through her when his lips brushed over the bumps of her spine, and she gasped. "Drew," she whispered, as yards of fabric were suddenly pulled up and over her head.

When she emerged from the gown, she inhaled softly. Despite the stays, chemise, petticoats and stockings she still wore, he was gazing at her as if she were naked. She took the opportunity to pull the hem of his shirt from his pantaloons, trying but failing not to notice how his arousal tented the form-fitting garment.

Andrew lifted the shirt from his body and tossed it toward the chair as he toed off his shoes. "May I remove that?" he asked, pointing to her stays.

Staring at his bare chest in wonder, Danielle didn't answer but merely presented her back to him again. "You don't have to undo the ties completely," she whispered. "Just loosen them." A moment later, and he was lifting her arms and pulling the stays over her head. She felt his tug on the ties that held up her petticoats, and they fell to the floor, one after the other.

"That's enough," she murmured, her lips trembling as she turned to face him. One of her hands went to his chest, skimming over the surface so that only one or two fingers made contact with his skin.

He inhaled sharply, and all at once, he seemed to become a different man. His eyes darkened upon seeing her rose-colored areolae through the translucent silk of her chemise. At seeing the dark triangle at the apex of her thighs.

Danielle pulled her hand away, but he captured it in one of his and placed it flat against his chest, directly over his heart, at the same moment his mouth descended toward one of her breasts. She inhaled sharply as his tongue laved over the mound. Even through the silk fabric, she felt the texture of it, felt the moisture and the heat. When her nipple pebbled, he worried it with his tongue and teeth. "Oh!" she cried out in surprise, now understanding why her mother made such a sound.

"Did I hurt you?" Andrew asked, lifting his head from her breast.

"No," she breathed as she shook her head. When her knees seemed to give way, and not from the champagne, Andrew lifted her into his arms. "What are you doing?" she whispered.

"Putting you on the bed," he replied, as he captured a handful of the counterpane and, with a flick of his wrist, had it stripped from most of the bed. He set her down and went to work on removing his stockings.

"Will you mind overmuch if I'm not wearing anything?" he asked, his breathing labored, and not just from having lifted her onto the mattress.

"I don't know," she whispered, holding herself up on her elbows. Every nerve ending in her body seemed to be firing all at once. She could feel her pulse in her ears. In her chest. And it positively throbbed in one particular spot near the top of her thighs.

Despite his nervousness, or maybe because of it, Andrew chuckled. He doffed his pantaloons close to the edge of the bed. Given how high the mattress was, his engorged manhood was hidden from her when he straightened.

He didn't have a moment to reconsider what he was about to do.

CHAPTER 26
A TRYST IN THE LIBRARY

*M*eanwhile, *inside Carlington House*
Despite the dwindling number of guests in the Carlington House gardens, Anthony decided it was best he and Dahlia find a more private place in which to discuss the matter of their future.

The library had certainly worked when he had met with Lady Danielle, and now he gingerly ducked his head around the threshold to be sure it wasn't still occupied by her and his brother.

When Anthony was assured it was empty, he pulled Dahlia into the room and through to the back. Once they were behind a row of shelves, he pulled her close, one of his arms across her back as if he feared she might attempt to escape his hold. Placing a hand along one of her cheeks, he sighed. "Please don't scream," he murmured.

Dahlia scoffed. "Why would I scream?" she countered. His lips were on hers only a second later, the kiss a combination of tentative moves and determined resolve. When she easily gave into his hold and began returning the kiss, he moaned and pulled away slightly.

"Because I've a mind to take your sister's advice," he whispered. His lips captured hers again, even as she seemed determined to put voice to a protest.

When he finally had to end the kiss so he might take a breath, she was quick to ask, "Whatever did Danny advise?"

Anthony chuckled, remembering how shocked he'd been at hearing Danielle's words.

Kiss her senseless. Get her into a bed and ruin her.

"Nothing I can do this very moment with you," he said sadly. "But I have every intention of eventually ruining you."

Dahlia's eyes widened. "Anthony," she whispered in a scold.

From the way she stiffened and her eyes darted in the direction of the door, Anthony feared she was about to bolt. "I know you didn't wish to hear a marriage proposal in the form of a business proposition, so I have decided to withdraw my proposal."

Blinking, Dahlia's mouth dropped open, but before she could say anything, Anthony took the opportunity to kiss her again. With her lips already parted, his tongue invaded her mouth. Swept over her teeth and across her tongue. Tangled with hers and then retreated as his lips once again claimed her mouth.

*T*he kiss might have gone on for a few seconds or a few minutes. Dahlia lost track of time and space, her senses only aware of the scents of lime and sandalwood and the feel of his lips on hers. Of his warm breath washing over her face and the steel of his arm across her back. Of how she was barely able to breathe.

How many times had she imagined doing this with him? How many times had she imagined him squiring her about town? Standing by her side as they shopped in New Bond Street or attended the theatre? Offering his arm as they entered a Mayfair ballroom or a *soirée*? Sitting next to her at a *musicale*?

What he did next she hadn't imagined. Or if she had, she hadn't known what it would feel like, for when his palm slid up her side and over to cup a breast, she gasped and pulled away from his kiss.

She immediately regretted her response.

Whatever he had done had something rather pleasant racing down her body. Something rather delicious.

Dahlia reached for his hand and placed it back onto her chest. "You merely startled me is all. Please, continue."

For a moment, Anthony's eyes seemed glazed over, as if he couldn't see her clearly. When they suddenly cleared, he glanced down at where she had placed his hand.

"Oh, dear. I suppose you were hoping they would be... rounder," she whispered, exhaling a sigh of disappointment.

"What?" Anthony countered, his gaze finally meeting hers.

"My..." She once again covered his gloved hand with her own and pressed it slightly. How was it she could feel his heat through the kid leather?

"It fits in my hand perfectly," he whispered. He lifted the hand to his mouth and pulled the glove off with his teeth, allowing the garment to fall to the carpeted floor below. Once again placing his hand over her breast, he gave it a slight squeeze.

Dahlia gasped, an "oh" escaping before she had a chance to swallow it. She had a quick thought that she might have sounded like her mother just then.

Anthony took the opportunity to undo the two frogs that held her pelisse closed and then slipped the hand beneath to fondle the breast. "See? Perfect," he murmured. "Has anyone else ever done this to you?"

Her eyes rounding with offense and her mouth following suit, Dahlia couldn't respond when he once again kissed her.

This time, the kiss was shorter. More punishing. Deeper and more intense. When he finally pulled his lips away, he used his thumb to circle the pebbled nipple behind her gown and stays. "Has anyone else ever done this to you?" he repeated.

Dahlia shook her head. "Of course not."

"Good," he replied as his hand moved to the other breast to cup it as his thumb brushed over the evidence of her arousal. Pulling his hand from behind the edges of her pelisse, he lowered the arm from across her back and then redid the frog closures on the garment.

"What are you doing?" she asked, breathless. The pleasurable sensations his simple ministrations had created were suddenly gone.

"Putting your clothes back to rights," he replied, his gaze darting to the window that looked out over the back gardens. "Seems the party is over, my lady."

Dahlia's attention went to the window, and she glanced out. Only a few servants were about in the gardens, retrieving champagne glasses and removing plates and cups from the tables. "So it is," she whispered sadly.

Anthony let out a huff. "Since you have made it clear you don't wish to discuss the details of a marriage with me, then I will take my leave of you."

"*What?*"

"Should you wish to marry me, Lady Dahlia, *you* shall have to be the one to do the proposing," he said before he bowed. "But I have a deadline I must meet, and as you said, the Season is about to start." He turned on his heel and took his leave of the library.

Dahlia blinked several times, her breaths shallow, as if she couldn't get enough air. "What?" she whispered in confusion.

If she hadn't been so shocked by Anthony's sudden departure—so surprised by his parting words and so offended by the anger that flowed from him in that last moment—she might have stomped her half-booted feet into the carpet and uttered an entirely inappropriate curse.

Instead, she leaned against the library shelf, crossed her arms over her chest, and allowed the tears to fall. She might have continued to cry for a half-hour or more but for what she heard only a moment later.

"There you are."

CHAPTER 27
RUINATION AND
RUMINATION

Meanwhile, back at the Comber townhouse in Bruton Street

"Am I supposed to be shivering like this?" Danielle asked as she watched Andrew divest the clothes from the lower half of his body. His top half was completely bare, the muscles rippling beneath his skin as he struggled to remove his pantaloons and who knew what else.

Andrew paused. "Are you cold?" he asked in alarm. His own body's temperature had increased to the point where he thought he might have a fever. It was made worse when his attention settled on Danielle. Positioned as she was on the bed and wearing only her chemise, nothing about the shape of her body—the mounds of her breasts, the tips of her nipples, the curve of her hips, the lines of her limbs—was left to his imagination.

"I'm quite warm. Feverish, even," she replied, lifting herself onto an elbow to attempt a glance at the rest of his body, still hidden beyond the edge of the bed.

When he noticed her gaze, Andrew lifted his

pantaloons to cover his arousal. "Anticipation, perhaps?" he suggested, realizing his own anticipation had every nerve ending on his body on high alert. One touch, and he feared he might explode.

Breathless, she nodded. She'd had a brief glimpse of his manhood before his hand hid it, relieved it didn't appear as large as those depicted in the illustrations in the book they had studied. Truth be told, the idea of being tupped over a library table didn't hold the same fear for her as the size of a man's manhood.

"Please, don't be frightened," Andrew murmured, giving up his attempt to cover himself in favor of climbing onto the bed. "I'll try ever so hard to be sure you're ready," he added before he kissed one of her breasts through the fabric of her chemise.

"I believe you," she whispered, inhaling softly at the renewed sensations he was causing. "Where... where do I put my hands? What do I do?" she stammered.

He briefly came up for air, his lips having moved down her body as his hands worked the chemise up enough to expose her belly. "Just... relax," he replied, grinning when she gasped as his lips took purchase on the pooch of her belly and suckled it. He moved his attentions lower, his tongue leaving a trail of moisture on her warm skin. When he gently blew on it, he watched in fascination as she quivered.

"That tickles," she said as she jerked beneath him.

"Should I stop?" he asked, sliding a hand beneath one of her knees to lift it. He didn't wait for an answer but kissed her inner thigh.

"Yes. No. Maybe." She lifted her upper torso and leaned on her elbows, her mouth dropping open when she realized where his head was located. "Andrew!"

His chuckle could be felt in how his entire body

vibrated on the bed. With his mouth pressed against her thigh, she felt the vibration through her leg and gasped at the combination of sensations she experienced.

Struggling to breathe, she was forced to lie back when one of his arms reached over the top of her body, his hand cupping a breast to push her down. She might have remained there but for what he did next.

"Andrew!" she scolded, once again coming up onto her elbows. "Whatever are you...?" She landed on her back when he lifted her other knee and his hands slipped beneath the globes of her bottom. "Oh!"

"Just... try to relax," he whispered. His tongue darted along the folds protecting her womanhood.

"Oh!" She clamped a hand over her mouth, remembering how only a few days ago, she had been chiding her mother over her repeated "ohs."

Now she understood.

The thought that her uncle might have been doing to her mother what Andrew was doing to her had her eliciting another "oh."

Determined to keep quiet, Danielle found she couldn't. Not when his tongue discovered her most private place. Not when its textured surface brushed over her engorged womanhood, not once, but over and over until she thought she might faint. Her hands clasped the bed linens, and she threw back her head as the sharp waves of pleasure coursed through her and over her and suddenly, Andrew was atop her, his mouth covering hers as his manhood sought her entry. He took each of her hands in his, pinning them to the bed as he lifted his hips and then drove himself into her.

Danielle's chest rose to touch his, her cry swallowed by his open-mouthed kiss. He stilled a moment, ended the kiss, and locked his gaze with hers. "Are you all right?"

She stared at him a moment. "I... I think so," she managed between gasps for air. Her gaze darted down to the space between their bodies. "It's not bad. But it does feel as if you're... you're far too large for me," she added on a wince.

Andrew nodded. "Being inside you is like being in heaven, Danny," he murmured. "But I don't wish to hurt you."

"It doesn't hurt. Not really. But... aren't we supposed to move?" she asked in a whisper.

He lowered his head to her shoulder. "I fear I'll come too soon," he replied, kissing her shoulder before he lifted himself by straightening his arms. "Hold onto my shoulders," he said as he gave up his hold on her hands. "And lift up your knees if you can."

Following his instructions, Danielle felt his manhood press into her more deeply. "Oh, that's better," she murmured.

"Oh, I love you, Danny," Andrew whispered before he kissed her on the lips.

Her eyes rounding in wonder, Danielle returned the kiss and then lifted her hips.

Half groaning, half chuckling, Andrew said, "I'll move now."

He pulled himself most of the way out despite how she clenched in response. "You have to let go," he whispered hoarsely. "Although it is..." He struggled to breathe. "Rather good like this."

Danielle finally understood his meaning, attempting to relax her inner muscles. She hadn't even realized how she'd been clenching on his manhood. When he thrust into her, she inhaled sharply. "Oh!

That's much better," she whispered, her hands moving from his shoulders to slide down his sides, her fingers barely skimming over his skin.

Andrew shivered. "That tickles." He couldn't help the burble of laughter that erupted as he shifted his back beneath her hold.

Danielle giggled, once again lifting her hips in anticipation. "Am I doing this right?"

Sobering, he took a breath and then retreated part way and pushed into her again. This time her hips met his, and he nodded. "Perfect," he managed to get out as he repeated his retreat and thrust, glad when her hands tightened their hold on his back.

Watching how the cords of his neck appeared as he lifted his head and hearing his labored breathing, Danielle did her best to match his moves in the dance as old as time. She might have continued, but ceased her movements when Andrew suddenly stilled. His chest rising well above hers, he looked as if he'd been stabbed in the back, an expression of pain crossing his features before warmth spread inside her lower body.

"Oh!" Danielle said as he pushed once more into her. One of his hands cupped a breast. He lowered himself onto one elbow, his face ending up on the other breast. "Oh!" she cried out when his mouth covered a nipple and his tongue laved over it.

Andrew couldn't help the chuckle that erupted from him. He nearly cursed but managed to swallow it before he moved to once again kiss her on the lips. "Thank you," he whispered, right before he passed out.

Stunned, Danielle moved a hand to the side of his face, relieved when she could feel his warm breath wash over it. She wondered how he could sleep at a time like this, when every single nerve ending of her entire being was abuzz with excitement.

Bit by bit, she took inventory of her body, carefully lowering her feet to the bed. She was aware of how the fullness of his manhood seemed to slowly subside. Of how his body, only a moment ago taut with strain, was completely relaxed. Of how his hair felt like silk where it fell onto her upper arm.

Once her breathing returned to normal, she felt a kiss on the side of her breast. "Oh!" she said with a start, immediately chiding herself for sounding like her mother.

Andrew's chuckle rumbled through her. "Your breasts are so plump and soft," he murmured. "So perfect."

She inhaled softly. "You don't think they're too large?"

The bed shook with his chuckle. "They're perfect, my sweet. Everything about you is perfect." He placed another kiss on the soft flesh.

Swallowing, Danielle stared at the painted ceiling above, contemplating what they had just done. Contemplating his words. "Are you saying that because you wish to make love to me again?" she asked. Not that she would mind. There was something positively wonderful about how her body felt at that moment. Alive. All buzzy and warm and aware.

"I'm saying it because it's true," he countered. "Although, now that we have made love, of course I wish to do it again. Again and again, for the rest of our lives," he whispered. "I love you."

Danielle gave a start, angling her head in an attempt to better see him from her vantage. "You really do?"

"*Now* will you marry me?" he asked as he lifted his head onto her chest again. "I do love you, Danny. I always have, and you know it."

Danielle speared her fingers through his dark hair and sighed. "If I say yes, does that mean you have to take me home?"

Blinking, Andrew regarded her with suspicion. "Well, I was hoping we could have dinner together first," he replied. "If you'd like to spend the night in your new home, we could send a note to Norwick House. Explain you're spending the night with a friend—"

"Friend?" She giggled. "Oh, no, Andrew Comber. I'm going to send a note claiming I've been kidnapped, and that I don't wish to be rescued."

He chuckled a moment but quickly sobered. "As much as I like that idea—and I do think it's a brilliant idea—I fear I might end up dead at the hands of the Earl of Norwick for having ruined you before I was given permission to do so."

Danielle rolled her eyes. "Father gave you permission," she reminded him.

Fearing her words had summoned the ghost of David Fitzsimmons, Andrew glanced around the bedchamber. Relieved the late earl wasn't hovering about, he said, "Nevertheless, I think it's best I take you home after the dessert course. Until then..." He left the bed to find his waistcoat and the pocket watch within. Opening the watch case, he aimed it so the dim light from around the drapes illuminated the crystal. "We have an hour until dinner."

"And the rest of the house to tour," she reminded him as she climbed off the tall bed. "I could use some more tea."

"I'm starving," Andrew agreed, his eyes darkening as he watched her gather up her petticoats and stays.

"There are some biscuits in the parlor," Danielle said as she shook out her stays. She giggled when she realized he had entirely different biscuits in mind as he pulled her into an embrace.

"Marry me?" he whispered.

She nodded as she tossed aside the stays and petticoats. "Oh, all right," she replied with a grin. "I'll marry you. But first, I think I'd like to learn more about how to ride St. George."

Andrew blinked. "Now?" He glanced over at the bed and then back at her. He stepped back and bowed. "My lady, I am honored to meet you. I am St. George."

She gave him a teasing grin. "It's very good to meet you, St. George," she replied as she waggled her brows.

It was nearly an hour later before they dressed for dinner.

CHAPTER 28
A FATHER'S ADVICE

*M*eanwhile, in the Carlington House library
"There you are."

Dahlia gave a start, straightening and turning to regard the rather tall man who had spoken the three simple words. "Oh, Father," she replied. "You startled me."

David Fitzwilliam furrowed a brow and approached her with a look of concern. "What happened?"

She glanced up at him and gasped. "I might ask the same of you," she countered, one of her hands reaching up to his bruised cheek. Although she hadn't felt a bit of sympathy for the ghost when Anthony had punched him, she did now.

"Oh, that's nothing," he replied with a wave of his hand. "I, uh, earned it," he added as his brows rose. "I may have prodded a certain viscount harder than I intended." He glanced around. "By the way, where is Lord Breckinridge?"

Dahlia's face bloomed with color at the same moment she wondered what he'd said to have Anthony practicing his pugilist moves on the ghost. "He's gone. He... he withdrew his offer of marriage."

David sobered, his expression turning quite serious. "Oh, did he now?"

"I didn't wish to engage in a business negotiation," she went on. "If I want him as a husband, I must be the one to ask for his hand."

The ghost of her father seemed to consider this bit of news with a good deal of confusion. "That's unexpected," he murmured.

"I cannot blame him," Dahlia replied sadly. "I haven't exactly given him any reason to think I want to be married to him. Other than returning his rather passionate kisses," she explained, apparently unaware of what she was admitting.

"Passionate kisses?" the late earl repeated, his arms crossing his chest in a most imposing manner.

"Well, they were. At least by my standards," she said. "Which are not to be taken with much consideration, I suppose."

He frowned. "First kisses?" he guessed.

She nodded. "Were yours like that?" she asked.

David's eyes darted sideways. "They might have been. I might need a bit more detail before I can agree or disagree," he hinted.

"Was Mother the first woman you kissed?"

Blinking, he moved to stare out the window. It was several moments before he spoke. "No," he finally replied. "Her late aunt was my first. Arabella," he murmured. When Dahlia gasped, he turned to regard her. "I loved Arabella. Met her whilst I was in university," he went on, his gaze still on the gardens. "It's unfortunate you never had a chance to meet her. She died in an awful accident. A long time ago."

Unsure of what to say to his admission, she moved to join him at the window. "Did you love Mother?"

He glanced down at her and nodded. "Oh, yes. Daniel did, too. Maybe more than I did at first, damn him. But I am living proof..." He paused and winced. "I *was* living proof that a man could love more than one woman in his lifetime," he stated.

They stood in silence for a time before Dahlia said, "What should I do, Father?"

He shrugged. "That all depends. Do you... do you love him?"

She winced. "I did for part of today," she replied. "I have in the past."

"So... most of the time?" he prompted.

"Yes," she finally admitted after a moment of consideration.

"Can you see yourself with him in the future? Imagine yourself with him in your house? Sharing your secrets and kissing one another for no reason at all? Can you see yourself with him at the theatre? Attending a ball or *soirée* together? Sitting side-by-side at a *musicale*?"

She inhaled softly, wondering how he knew her thoughts from earlier. "I have, yes."

"In bed together?"

Her eyes rounding, Dahlia regarded him with shock. "Father," she scolded.

"As I recall, you were considering spinsterhood, not about to allow a man into your bed, which is an admirable trait for a virtuous young lady."

Dahlia's face colored as she swallowed. "I think it was more about not wanting to be bent over a library table," she said. "I'm not about to suffer the indignity."

David settled against the wall, his arms crossing as

he gave her comment some thought. "You could begin with that as a negotiation tactic," he murmured, ignoring her wince at the word 'negotiation.' "Are there other situations you think you would not like?"

Her eyes darting sideways, Dahlia seemed reluctant to answer. "This is rather difficult to discuss with one's father," she complained.

He pulled his chin into his neck, which had it disappearing behind the folds of his cravat. "Pretend I'm not."

She scoffed. "It's rather difficult to discuss it with a man."

"Pretend I'm your mother."

A quelling glance followed, which had David allowing a long sigh. "Your sister then. Surely the two of you have discussed the issue."

Dahlia crossed her own arms. "We have. After I discovered the book—"

"This book?" he interrupted, referring to an open tome that seemed to appear from nowhere and rested over one of his arms. The color plates in the middle were on full display. He flipped through the pages even though his attention was on Dahlia.

"How...?"

"I am a ghost," he said with a shrug. "Now, I can understand how some of these positions might seem rather improbable," he added as he held onto one end of the book and studied one of the color plates sideways. He turned the book upside down and then angled it in another direction. His brows arched up nearly into his hairline. "Or impossible."

"That's what *I* thought," she said, her eyes widening as she stepped over to stand next to him. Her gaze settled on the page he'd been studying. She shivered in disgust.

He turned the page. "What about this one? It's your mother's favorite. At least, it was until she did this to me," he said as he turned the page. His brows waggled. He showed her a page depicting a woman straddled over her lover.

Dahlia winced. "Did she emit a lot of 'ohs' whilst doing that to you?" she asked.

David chuckled. "As a matter of fact, she did," he claimed. "I adored the sounds she made," he whispered, his words barely audible. "After bedding a number of courtesans, your mother was a refreshing change. I didn't even mind that I pledged never to bed another but her."

Studying his face for signs of artifice, Dahlia asked, "Did you live up to your pledge?"

He gave her a wan grin. "I did. I showed her what I liked, and she accommodated me. I returned the favor to ensure she wouldn't end up in some young buck's bed—or your uncle's," he confided, as if he was speaking with his best friend at his club.

Intrigued by his words, Dahlia indicated the color plates. "What do you suppose you were doing to her when Danny and I were conceived?"

His face lit up with a huge grin. "Now that's easy," he said as he flipped to the first page. "The most basic way of making love," he claimed, referring to the missionary position. "Hard on my knees given my age at the time, but..." He shrugged. "I didn't really feel anything past my..." He suddenly glanced down at her and cleared his throat, as if he realized their discussion was entirely inappropriate. "Well, never mind about that."

"Father!" she complained. "How am I supposed to learn about making love to a man if I don't know anything?"

"Your husband will tell you," he countered. "Or he should." He paused a moment. "Or he'll show you."

Danielle gave him a curious glance. "What if I don't like it? Any of it?"

David looked as if he'd been slapped across the face, which, given his purpling cheek from Anthony's punch, was to be expected. "You will," he replied. "At least, you should. Any man worth his salt will know exactly what to do. He has to if he wishes to father an heir," he explained.

"You didn't," she said quietly.

David regarded her with a furrowed brow. "I would have, given another chance," he claimed. "I wanted girls first, though."

Her eyes rounding in surprise, Dahlia said, "You did?"

He nodded. "Of course. Older sisters are necessary for their brothers, I think."

"*You* didn't have any sisters," she reminded him.

"Exactly my point. Which is why I was the proprietor of *The Elegant Courtesan*," he replied. "Where else was I going to learn about what women truly want?"

"You mean you bedded those women?" she asked in shock.

He once again pulled his chin into his neck. "Heavens, no," he replied. "I never engaged in that way with those girls," he added. "They were my employees."

"Then how did you learn what women truly want?"

The ghost of her father once again leaned against the wall, the book disappearing from his arm. "I listened. When they talked in the parlor. When they gossiped in the corridors. When they conferred with the madame. Women can be most enlightening when they don't think anyone is listening," he said wistfully.

"How will I know what I want?" she asked in a whisper.

David furrowed a brow. "Oh, you'll know what you want. From the moment you murmur that first 'oh,' you'll know," he assured her.

Dahlia stared at her father for several seconds before she allowed a nod. "Since Anthony withdrew his offer of marriage, I don't know that I want to marry him," she whispered.

"Yes, you do," he replied. "For if you don't, you'll regret it for the rest of your life. He'll marry some insipid miss, father an heir and a spare, and then take a mistress so he doesn't have to listen to his wife complain about the cook and housekeeper while she tups the footman."

"Father!"

"Trust me, Breckinridge's future is not a good one unless you are in it."

Dahlia inhaled softly, her gaze going to the garden beyond the window. "Oh, my," she murmured.

When she turned to say that she would give the viscount another chance, she discovered she was alone in the library.

CHAPTER 29

SECOND THOUGHTS LEAD TO A DECISION

M̃eanwhile... Anthony Comber, Viscount Breckinridge, marched out of Carlington House feeling a combination of anger and regret, disappointment and exhilaration.

"That will teach her to toy with a man," he said to no one in particular.

He stopped short, his gaze going up and down Park Lane. The ancient coach bearing the crest of the Aimsley earldom was no where to be found, as were most of the carriages that had delivered the attendees of Lady Morganfield's garden party earlier that afternoon.

His brother's words came back to him in a flash. Andrew had warned him that he would be taking the coach—and Lady Danielle—for some sort of tryst.

About to walk to Aimsley House, he was stopped short when someone called out to him.

"Lord Breckinridge?"

Anthony turned to discover a driver waving at him

from next to a glossy black equipage bearing the crest of the Norwick earldom.

"Yes?" he replied, turning to make his way toward the driver.

"I was told you might require a ride, my lord."

Furrowing his brows, Anthony couldn't imagine his brother making the arrangements on his behalf. Before he could ask, though, the driver said, "Lord Norwick, sir. He didn't wish for you to have to find a hansom cab this time of the day."

"Norwick?" Anthony repeated, his brows furrowing. He glanced back toward the house. He had a brief thought to ask which one and then remembered that there really was only one current earl. The other was a ghost and apparently invisible to all but him.

But had the current Earl of Norwick attended the garden party? He didn't remember seeing Daniel Fitzwilliam amongst those strolling the gardens. Anthony indicated the house. "Is he still...?"

"I think so, sir. I can't imagine where else he'd be. I didn't see him come out."

Anthony was about to step into the coach when he paused. "What about Lady Dahlia?"

The driver's eyes darted to one side. "I'm to wait for her, too, sir."

For a moment, Anthony thought to decline the offer. Use the opportunity to be alone for the half-hour or so it would take for him to make his way to Aimsley House.

What's the worst that could happen if he accepted the offer of a ride, though? Dahlia and her father—or uncle—would find him in the coach. She would either insist he get out, or she would apologize profusely and perhaps propose marriage.

Or she would simply ignore him.

Surely Lord Norwick was arguing on his behalf with her right this very moment.

Wasn't he?

Launching himself into the coach, Anthony took the seat facing away from the direction of travel and settled into the navy blue velvet squabs. The cushions were far more comfortable than those of the Aimsley coach, and he was soon dozing as images from earlier in the day flitted across his mind's eye.

Dahlia, as she sniffed the petals of a tulip, looking every bit like the spring blooms that surrounded her. Dahlia, in the library, seated on a dark green sofa and speaking with him as comfortably as if they'd been married for their entire lives. Dahlia, in his arms as he kissed her senseless. As his hands roamed over her soft body and took liberties to which he wasn't yet entitled.

He could certainly imagine what else he might have done. Stripped her bare. Removed his own clothing. Carried her to one of the green sofas before throwing the bolt on the door. Made mad, passionate love to her as the scents of vellum and vanilla surrounded them. Kissed her senseless and fallen asleep with her atop him, their legs entwined and her head nestled into the space between his neck and shoulder.

Given their heights, they would have required a longer sofa for true comfort, though. He imagined them instead sneaking into a guest bedchamber further down the corridor. Making mad, passionate love in a bed and then holding one another as their breaths evened and they fell asleep in one another's arms.

Yes, that's what he wished they could have done. That's what they could be doing this very night if matters hadn't taken such an awkward turn.

Anthony might have fallen asleep completely, but the Earl of Norwick appeared as if from nowhere.

"I do hope you appreciate what I've had to do on your behalf," David Fitzwilliam complained as he crossed his arms and regarded Anthony with a stern expression.

Anthony hadn't felt the coach jerk when the earl stepped in, and now he wondered if he had fallen asleep. Perhaps this was merely a bad dream. "My lord?" he responded, blinking his eyes several times. He hoped the earl hadn't noticed his arousal.

Apparently, he had.

"Like your cock, I think I have my daughter thinking straight now," the late earl claimed. "Quite an accomplishment, if you ask me." He scoffed. "Always thought the Scots had the right idea, what with their hand-fasting custom and all. Would have saved many an English marriage from certain failure."

"Sir?"

The ghost gave him a quelling glance. "Young ladies are proving far more vexing than they did back in my day," the late earl stated, oblivious to Anthony's look of astonishment. "Back then, they didn't even *know* about the marriage bed until the night of their betrothal. Or their wedding," he quickly amended. "Which I suppose is how I'm going to have to explain your brother's reason for bedding my youngest daughter on this day. When her mother finds out—"

"She'll be thrilled," Anthony said in a quiet voice, remembering how joyous the Countess of Norwick had appeared as she engaged in conversation with the other matrons of the *ton*, when the topic of her daughters had been raised and she spoke of Danielle and Andrew.

How had the countess known Andrew was about to

whisk her youngest off? Kidnap her, his only demand an agreement to wed him?

Had the ghost told the countess what was about to happen?

Or had Andrew told her?

He probably asked permission, Anthony thought in dismay. *And she gladly gave it.*

"Lady Norwick *is* thrilled," Anthony said in a whisper, amending his original comment.

David gave a start as he considered the words. "I suppose you're right." His eyes rounded. "Which bodes well for me," he added quickly. "I really hate leaving her angry with me."

Furrowing his brows, Anthony asked, "Why would she be angry with *you*?"

Inhaling as if to respond, David finally gave his head a shake and sighed. "Because I died too early. Left her. All alone and pregnant with twins girls." He visibly shivered. "*I* would be angry with me."

Anthony's eyes darted sideways. He didn't think the late earl had much of a say in the manner of his death. "If it's any consolation, sir, I do believe your brother was good about stepping in on your behalf. At least, that's my understanding."

David held up a finger as he brightened. "That's right. Now she's angry because the girls announced they wanted to be spinsters." His expression once again grew serious. "*That's* why I'm here. That's why *you're* here," he said as he pointed the finger at Anthony.

"Sir?"

"Dahlia's on her way to the coach this very moment. I've given her the what-for and made it clear what she needs to do. Don't bungle this again, Breckinridge."

"*Bungle* it, sir?" Anthony repeated. He straightened on the bench, his brows raised in indignation. "Sir, might I say, *I* am not the one who turned down a perfectly reasonable marriage proposal?"

"She said you withdrew your offer of marriage," David accused.

Scoffing, Anthony stared at the earl in disbelief. "Wouldn't *you* have?" he countered. "Sir, I may not have the means by which to continue life as a gentleman past this autumn. By then, I *must* be married," he stated. "I cannot change the circumstances of how I came to be in this predicament, but I can ensure that I am not forced to endure it much longer," he added on a huff, his gaze directed out of the coach window. "If your daughter doesn't wish to marry me, then I shall find someone who does. Tuesday night at the Weatherstone's ball, if need be."

Rather proud of his speech—of his willingness to take on the ghost of an arrogant earl—Anthony inhaled as his attention went back to David Fitzwilliam.

Or rather an empty bench. For the ghost was no longer there.

"Damnation," Anthony muttered, at the same moment the coach door opened and Lady Dahlia appeared.

CHAPTER 30
A CONFRONTATION IN THE COACH

C arlington House, Grand Hall
Feeling as if she was a thief as she quietly made her way out of the Carlington House library and down the main stairs, Dahlia breathed a sigh of relief when she made it to the Grand Hall without being seen.

Or at least, she hadn't thought she'd been spotted.

"Allow me to get the door for you, my lady," the butler said as he passed her on the way to the vestibule.

"Oh, thank you, Alfred," Dahlia replied brightly, despite the sob that nearly robbed her of breath. When she noticed his look of concern, she allowed a shrug. "I didn't wish to put a damper on the good cheer out in the gardens, so I had a cry up in the library."

"Ah," he replied, his brows furrowed. "I do hope her ladyship wasn't the cause?" he ventured.

She shook her head. "Oh, never. Lady Morganfield is always the most gracious hostess," she replied. "I fear it was over a marriage pro..." She stopped, just then realizing she was commiserating with a servant. "Well, never mind. It's over."

"Not for him, certainly?" Alfred countered, his head angling to one side.

Dahlia blinked. Had the butler overheard her and Anthony in the library?

Or the ghost of her father?

"Why do you say that?"

Alfred glanced towards the door. "Lord Breckinridge, my lady. He left here looking ever so... glum."

Dahlia's eyes rounded. "He did?"

The servant nodded as he opened the door. "I'm quite sure if you hurry, you might be able to set him to rights."

Her gaze going to the pavers leading from the house to the street, Dahlia wondered if the butler's comment was meant to be taken as a challenge. "Oh, I'll set him to rights," she replied with a prim grin.

Determined to marry the viscount, she marched out the front door and followed the pavers directly into the Norwick coach. She nearly screamed when she discovered who was already seated within. "Breckinridge?" she whispered. About to step back out of the equipage—for a moment she thought she might have entered the wrong coach—Dahlia finally took the seat opposite the one Anthony was in.

"Forgive me, my lady. Your driver insisted." He moved to stand, but Dahlia shifted her legs to prevent him from departing the coach.

"Don't go," she said.

He stared down at her. "You're sure?"

"Your life depends on it," she replied, indicating he should be seated.

Anthony's eyes rounded at the same moment the

He felt her inhalation of breath as her chest pressed into his.

"Oh, Anthony," she whispered. This time, she initiated the kiss, her lips opening to coax his to do the same. One of her hands reached up to grip his shoulder as she deepened the kiss, and she gave a start when his tongue touched hers. When she finally pulled away, she regarded him with a wistful expression. "Should I ask your father's permission to marry you?" she queried.

"Yes. No. Maybe," Anthony responded, finally chuckling. "Probably my mother," he said gently. He pulled her into an embrace. "If it's all right, I'll go into Norwick House with you. Ask to speak with the earl."

Dahlia nodded. "I don't have a ring for you," she murmured. Then her eyes rounded before she suddenly straightened and then pulled a glove from her right hand. "Oh, but I do." She wrenched a gold band with a green gemstone from a forefinger and held it out to him.

Chuckling again, Anthony removed a glove and allowed her to slide it onto his pinky, the only finger upon which it would fit. "I have one for you," he said as he reached into his waistcoat pocket.

"You do?"

"Well, of course. I did propose marriage yesterday and then again today," he reminded her.

Dahlia inhaled softly as he opened a small ring box to display a sapphire gem mounted on a gold band. "It's beautiful," she whispered. She watched as he slid it onto her finger, grinning in delight when it fit. "Oh, it's perfect."

The coach stuttered to a halt and the familiar jerking motion of the driver stepping down from his bench had them straightening in their seat.

---

respond
yet. "We
accused.

"Good
matters wo

"Carefu
the rest of y

"You say
she countere
appeared on

"Never h
announced.

"I punche
in a whisper.

"Oh, he d
before she turi
ghost. "Father,'
this... this *medd*

"Not until y
his chin thrust
know, your sister
the mistress suite
marital—"

"Sir!" Anthony
When he noted
surprise, he added,
honor, if I'm to ui
say," he added in wai

"At least your bi
tions," the ghost cour

Dahlia inhaled.
asked in a whisper.

Anthony winced.
share what he knew,

realizing she was commiserating with a servant. "Well, never mind. It's over."

"Not for him, certainly?" Alfred countered, his head angling to one side.

Dahlia blinked. Had the butler overheard her and Anthony in the library?

Or the ghost of her father?

"Why do you say that?"

Alfred glanced towards the door. "Lord Breckin-ridge, my lady. He left here looking ever so... glum."

Dahlia's eyes rounded. "He did?"

The servant nodded as he opened the door. "I'm quite sure if you hurry, you might be able to set him to rights."

Her gaze going to the pavers leading from the house to the street, Dahlia wondered if the butler's comment was meant to be taken as a challenge. "Oh, I'll set him to rights," she replied with a prim grin.

Determined to marry the viscount, she marched out the front door and followed the pavers directly into the Norwick coach. She nearly screamed when she discovered who was already seated within. "Breckin-ridge?" she whispered. About to step back out of the equipage—for a moment she thought she might have entered the wrong coach—Dahlia finally took the seat opposite the one Anthony was in.

"Forgive me, my lady. Your driver insisted." He moved to stand, but Dahlia shifted her legs to prevent him from departing the coach.

"Don't go," she said.

He stared down at her. "You're sure?"

"Your life depends on it," she replied, indicating he should be seated.

Anthony's eyes rounded at the same moment the

coach lurched into motion. "How so?" he asked as he carefully lowered himself onto the bench seat.

Dahlia remembered her father's words. "It seems if you don't marry me, you'll end up with an insipid young miss, father an heir and a spare, and then take a mistress so you don't have to listen to your wife complain about the cook and the housekeeper while she tups the footman."

The words tumbled out before she could censor them, and at the last moment, a gloved hand went up to hide her mouth. When the ghost had said them, he had done so with all the seriousness of a man at a funeral. Now they sounded almost funny.

Apparently, they did to Anthony as well, for a grin lightened his face and he chuckled. "Let me guess. My mother told you that?"

Her eyes rounded. "No. Father did."

Settling back into the velvet squabs, Anthony regarded Dahlia for a moment, now worried the ghost might have had a conversation or two with his mother. He sighed. "He had a long talk with me, too, although he didn't mention the insipid miss."

"When was this?" she asked in alarm.

"He left only a moment ago. Just... disappeared."

She sighed. "He does that."

"Well, he is a ghost," Anthony remarked.

Her eyes once again rounded. "You *know* that?"

Wincing, Anthony nodded. "I probably should be petrified with fear, but I find the old coot rather interesting."

"Old coot?" she repeated in disbelief. "Aren't you worried that he'll... he'll—?"

"Haunt me?" Anthony finished for her. "What do you think he's been *doing* these past few days?"

It was Dahlia's turn to wince. "I'm so sorry." When she noted his furrowed brows, she added, "This is all my fault." She couldn't help the sob that accompanied her words. She'd been attempting to swallow it since stepping into the coach.

"May I join you?" he asked as he nodded to the bench upon which she sat.

She nodded and scooted over to give him room to sit next to her.

"Why do you think that?" he asked, his arm resting on the squabs behind her shoulders so he could sit closer to her.

"I should never have looked at that *damned* book," she whispered.

He leaned over and kissed her on her temple. "Now I know you're upset," he whispered. "You so rarely curse," he added when she gave him a quelling glance. "I take it you are referring to the book about sexual congress?"

Dahlia gasped. "Did my father tell you about *that*, too?" she whined as her face bloomed with color.

Chuckling, Anthony said, "Actually, your sister did." When he saw anger in her eyes, he added, "Don't be cross with her. I'm glad she did. Otherwise, how would I know about your fear of the marriage bed? *You* certainly weren't going to inform me."

"I'm not supposed to know about such things," Dahlia countered.

"But now that you do know a thing or two, is that the *real* reason you don't wish to marry me?"

"*I* never said I don't wish to marry you," Dahlia countered. When she saw his look of confusion, she added, "I just didn't wish for us to have to *negotiate*."

Anthony straightened, deciding it best he not

227

respond to the comment about negotiating, at least not yet. "Well, you've certainly vexed your father," he accused.

"Good, because he's done nothing but make matters worse," she complained on a huff.

"Careful what you say, or he might haunt *you* for the rest of your life," Anthony warned.

"You say that as if you do expect he'll haunt you," she countered. She gave a start when David Fitzwilliam appeared on the seat opposite.

"Never have truer words been spoken," the ghost announced.

"I punched him in the jaw," Anthony reminded her in a whisper.

"Oh, he doesn't hold it against you," Dahlia replied before she turned an expression of frustration on the ghost. "Father," she scolded. "You really must stop this... this *meddling*."

"Not until you two agree to wed," David replied, his chin thrust out in determination. "I'll have you know, your sister is at this very moment ensconced in the mistress suite of her new home, happily engaged in marital—"

"Sir!" Anthony scolded. "Have a care," he added. When he noted how Dahlia stared up at him in surprise, he added, "You're besmirching my brother's honor, if I'm to understand what you were about to say," he added in warning.

"At least your brother knows how to follow directions," the ghost countered. "*You* certainly don't."

Dahlia inhaled. "What's he talking about?" she asked in a whisper.

Anthony winced. Struggling to decide if he should share what he knew, he finally relented when she pressed him to speak. "Andrew kidnapped your sister and took her to his townhouse. He wasn't to let her go until she agreed to wed him, and if she didn't, he was to ruin her."

Blinking, Dahlia gasped. After giving her father a look of disgust, she turned her gaze back on Anthony as her eyes rounded. "Andrew has a *townhouse?*" she asked, her manner suggesting she was impressed.

It was Anthony's turn to blink. "*That's* your response to learning your sister is being thoroughly ruined?"

Dahlia shrugged. "Danielle was always going to be Andrew's wife, so I hardly think it matters," she replied dismissively. "Now they'll finally be wed. They'll go on his Grand Tour together," she added with a grin. "Why, I'm almost jealous."

"You are?" Anthony asked, displaying his confusion.

Turning her body on the bench so she faced him, Dahlia was about to respond when the coach came to a halt. "Oh, dear," she murmured.

"Allow me," David said as he knocked on the trap door. When the driver's face appeared, he said, "Nor-wick House."

Stunned by the sight of the earl in the coach, the driver blinked several times before nodding. "Right away, guv'nor."

"Thank you, Father," Dahlia said as the coach merged into the late afternoon Park Lane traffic. She regarded Anthony a moment and sighed. "I admit I was hurt when you withdrew your proposal," she stated. "I was angered by the thought that your proposal was made with terms and conditions to be attached at a later date—"

"You needn't make them sound so odious,"

Anthony interrupted. Before she could respond, he added, "We could be married in name only. Live at Aimsley House—we wouldn't have to share a bed, at least for a few years—and then, when you allowed it, or when it was necessary, then we could live as husband and wife," he reasoned.

Dahlia stared at him a moment before she dipped her head. "Oh," she whispered. "Is that all?"

Anthony angled his head to one side in an attempt to see her eyes. "What did you think I meant?"

Straightening so she could look up at him, Dahlia said, "I thought you were going to inform me of your intentions to take a mistress, and tell me what nights you intended to be at your club, what nights you expected to join me in my bed, and what entertainments you required me to attend and..."

Her words were cut off when Anthony's lips captured hers. He kissed her for several seconds, watching as her lashes lowered over her eyes and a tear spilled out of one corner. When he pulled away, he wiped the tear away with his thumb and kissed both her eye lids. "No mistress, mayhap Tuesdays and Fridays—although I could easily be talked out of it— whatever nights you'll welcome me in your bed, and which ever ones you wish to attend," he whispered.

Dahlia swallowed. "Oh." She rolled her eyes at hearing her breathy response. "Then... will you marry me?"

He lowered his forehead to hers. "Oh, I suppose," he replied on a huff before his face brightened with a huge grin. He kissed her forehead and turned to remind her father he already had the man's permission, but the ghost of David Fitzwilliam had disappeared.

"Could you be just a little more enthusiastic about it?" Dahlia asked on a huff.

Pulling away, Anthony grinned at her. "I will when I get to do to you what my brother has no doubt been doing to your sister on this day," he teased.

The oddest shiver had Dahlia's eyes widening. A pleasant frisson that seemed to have her entire body awakening to possibilities. Perhaps sharing a bed with Anthony would not be so bad. "Mother warned me I might be expected to give up my virtue before the vows were spoken," she murmured. Straightening on the bench, she glanced around. "Not here, though," she said, as if she was already plotting where she might give him her virtue. "I don't want us to be discovered half-naked in here," she added, indicating the opposite bench.

Anthony chuckled. "Of course not. When I make love to you, it shall be in a comfortable bed. We shall have privacy. However...," He glanced at the empty bench. "We probably wouldn't be the first to make love in this coach, given what I've learned about your father," he murmured, quite sure the Earl of Norwick and his countess had engaged in a tumble or two on the opposite bench.

"Have you?" she quickly countered. "Been caught in a coach tupping someone?" she clarified.

He gave a start. "No, I assure you, I have not," he claimed, his manner suggesting he was offended she thought him capable of such a scandal. "I have thought about it, though," he admitted. Before she could react, he added, "I imagined it would be with you. Whilst on a long trip. I cannot think of a better way to alleviate the boredom of travel than have you sitting atop me."

He felt her inhalation of breath as her chest pressed into his.

"Oh, Anthony," she whispered. This time, she initiated the kiss, her lips opening to coax his to do the same. One of her hands reached up to grip his shoulder as she deepened the kiss, and she gave a start when his tongue touched hers. When she finally pulled away, she regarded him with a wistful expression. "Should I ask your father's permission to marry you?" she queried.

"Yes. No. Maybe," Anthony responded, finally chuckling. "Probably my mother," he said gently. He pulled her into an embrace. "If it's all right, I'll go into Norwick House with you. Ask to speak with the earl."

Dahlia nodded. "I don't have a ring for you," she murmured. Then her eyes rounded before she suddenly straightened and then pulled a glove from her right hand. "Oh, but I do." She wrenched a gold band with a green gemstone from a forefinger and held it out to him.

Chuckling again, Anthony removed a glove and allowed her to slide it onto his pinky, the only finger upon which it would fit. "I have one for you," he said as he reached into his waistcoat pocket.

"You do?"

"Well, of course. I did propose marriage yesterday and then again today," he reminded her.

Dahlia inhaled softly as he opened a small ring box to display a sapphire gem mounted on a gold band. "It's beautiful," she whispered. She watched as he slid it onto her finger, grinning in delight when it fit. "Oh, it's perfect."

The coach stuttered to a halt and the familiar jerking motion of the driver stepping down from his bench had them straightening in their seat.

"Time to do battle with the earl," Anthony murmured as the coach door opened.

"Hardly," Dahlia countered with a watery grin. She allowed the driver to help her step down to the pavement. "Lord Breckinridge will require a ride home," she said before turning her attention back to Anthony. "He'll be so glad to hear of your intentions, he'll probably double my dowry."

"I'll wait," the driver acknowledged.

Thinking his future wife was merely teasing, Anthony joined her outside the coach and offered his arm.

CHAPTER 31
AN EARL IS ALMOST TOO ENTHUSIASTIC

In front of Norwick House
"I don't know why I'm so nervous," Anthony murmured as he stopped before the front door of Norwick House.

One of her arms on his, Dahlia regarded him with a sympathetic grin. "There's no need to be nervous. My uncle will be quite reasonable."

The front door opened, revealing the butler. The older servant's gray brows rose in surprise as he stepped aside.

"How do, Belvedere?" Dahlia asked as she entered. "Can you let the earl know Viscount Breckinridge wishes a word with him?"

"Is the earl even in residence?" Anthony asked, thinking Daniel Fitzwilliam might be at his club or about to go into dinner. He removed his hat, expecting to wait.

Belvedere gave a slight bow. "I'll let him know you're here, sir."

Anthony and Dahlia watched as the servant made

his way to the study, and when he disappeared from view, Anthony reached for Dahlia's gloved hand. He lifted it to his lips. "Should I tell him you were the one to propose?" he asked in a teasing whisper.

"You could, but he wouldn't believe you," she replied without humor. "He'll think you know something scandalous about me, and that's how you convinced me to marry," she added as she rolled her eyes. She nearly scoffed when she realized what she had done—picked up a most unladylike trait from the ghost of her father.

"Do I?"

Dahlia blinked. "Do you what?"

"Know something I shouldn't?" Anthony asked in a whisper.

Scoffing, Dahlia couldn't help the blush that colored her cheeks. "We've shared a coach without the benefit of a chaperone—"

"Your father was with us—"

"—and you've kissed me quite thoroughly—"

"Because your sister told me to."

"—and I've kissed you quite thoroughly—"

"Not *that* thoroughly," he said with a smirk.

"—and we've spoken of," her voice lowered to a whisper, "sexual congress."

He grinned, glad for the quiet moment with her. He didn't know quite why, but he loved seeing the color in her cheeks. Loved seeing how she could appear so vulnerable despite how she usually behaved—confident, bossy, and far too serious. Almost cold.

Perhaps that's why he had always thought she would make a suitable countess. Why he hadn't expected to ever have feelings for her beyond those of friendship and respect.

Seeing her like this—remembering how her lips had felt pressed against his—he had a thought that there was much more to Dahlia Davida Fitzwilliam than he knew. Why else would his cock be hardening at this very moment? Why else would he be experiencing an overwhelming desire to kiss her? To strip her bare? Take her to a bedchamber and prove to her she would enjoy the marriage bed?

"Why are you looking at me like that?" Dahlia asked in a whisper.

"Like what?"

Her eyes rounded. "Like you wish to eat me alive?"

Aware Belvedere was on his way back to where they stood, Anthony held up a gloved finger. "Hold that thought," he said with a quirked brow.

"Wh...?"

"Lord Norwick will see you now, my lord," Belvedere announced. He took Anthony's hat and placed it on a shelf before turning around to lead Anthony through the hall and to the earl's study.

Anthony gave Dahlia's hand another quick peck before he disappeared, well aware she would probably remain just outside the door and attempt to eavesdrop on the proceedings. There was a strategically placed chair directly adjacent to the study's entrance.

"Breckinridge," Daniel Fitzwilliam, Earl of Norwick, said as he held out his right hand. "To what do I owe the honor of your call this time of the evening?"

"I apologize for the hour, sir. You're probably about to go into dinner," Anthony said as he shook the earl's hand. He found the man's resemblance to the ghost of Dahlia's father rather uncanny and then remembered the two had been twins.

"In a few minutes," Daniel agreed. "Have a seat."

"I wanted you to know that I have accepted Lady Dahlia's proposal of marriage," Anthony stated as he took the chair in front of the desk.

About to be seated at the mahogany desk that seemed to take up most of the space in the masculine study, Daniel paused and stared at the viscount. He held up a finger. "I think you might have mixed up what it was you meant to say," he commented with a grin as he settled into his leather chair. "You're no doubt nervous, but for no reason at all."

Shifting uncomfortably in his seat, Anthony said, "I admit, I did propose to her ladyship again today—at the garden party—but I withdrew the offer when I sensed Lady Dahlia was not interested in pursuing a marriage with me."

Daniel angled his head to one side, his gaze displaying his suspicion. "She has made comments that would suggest she wasn't interested in marrying *anyone*," he agreed. "So... what happened?"

About to mention the earl's dead twin brother and his role in the matter, Anthony realized he couldn't. Not without sounding like he was a candidate for Bedlam. "Uh..." He cleared his throat. "Um... second thoughts?" he offered lamely.

His brows furrowing, Daniel stood up and moved to the study door, about to call for Belvedere and ask that Dahlia be summoned. When he opened it, Dahlia nearly collided with him. She'd been leaning against the door, listening intently to their conversation.

"Uncle!" she said brightly. "I was just about to knock," she claimed. Her gaze went to Anthony. "Lord Breckinridge," she added with a curtsy.

Even as Anthony rose to his feet, Daniel was eyeing

his niece with a good deal of suspicion. "Is it true you proposed marriage to Lord Breckinridge?" he asked, almost as if he intended to admonish her.

Dahlia swallowed. "I did," she replied with a nod. "Please don't hold it against him, Uncle," she pleaded. "Father has been vexing us both all day—"

"David?" Daniel interrupted in alarm.

She bobbed her head and watched as her uncle turned his attention on Anthony. "*Both* of you?" he asked in a quiet voice.

Anthony nodded. "I met him yesterday, sir. In the park. He told me what to do to gain Lady Dahlia's hand, and when it didn't work, I withdrew my proposal."

Daniel's gaze darted between his niece and her betrothed. "Does he *know*?" he asked Dahlia in a whisper. He surreptitiously nodded in Anthony's direction.

She sighed. "If you're referring to the fact that my father is a ghost, then yes, he knows," she replied. Her eyes widened. "He even planted a facer on him during the garden party," she added proudly.

"*Davy*," Anthony scolded in a hoarse whisper.

"Oh, if only I could have been there," Daniel said wistfully. "I might have managed to get a shot in myself," he added as he pantomimed a punch into the air.

"Actually, you were there, sir. But I believe your back was to the area in which it occurred at the garden party," Anthony explained. "I tried to be sure no one paid witness."

"I didn't realize a ghost could be punched," Daniel murmured, his attention on his mind's eye.

"Neither did I, sir. But I was rather incensed at the

time, and I didn't take a moment to consider whether it would work or not."

"Oh, no doubt. He's an insufferable, narcissistic, stubborn,—"

"*Please* don't say anything else, Uncle," Dahlia interrupted, "or you'll have him making an appearance here," she added in a hushed voice.

"Oh, quite right," Daniel replied. He regarded Dahlia a moment and then straightened. "I have some details I need to discuss with Lord Breckinridge. I'll see you at dinner—"

"Actually, sir. I was wondering if Lady Dahlia might be allowed to join me for dinner at Aimsely House this evening," Anthony said. "I was hoping we could announce the news to my family."

Daniel shrugged. "Fine with me," he replied. He turned back to Dahlia. "Go on up and change clothes. Be quick about it. You don't want to keep your future husband waiting," he ordered.

Dahlia dipped a curtsy. "Yes, sir," she replied with a grin. "Should I have my lady's maid join us?"

Frowning, Daniel said, "I hardly think a chaperone is necessary. You're betrothed now."

"Yes, sir," she said before she hurried off.

Returning to his chair, Daniel said, "Now, where were we?"

Nervous, Anthony regarded the earl a moment before he said, "Despite her having proposed to me, I thought it best I ask your permission for her hand. I already have the late earl's permission—he gave it yesterday in the park."

"We're well beyond that now, Breckinridge," Daniel stated. "We're onto the matter of her dowry. Thirty-thousand pounds if you take her to wife before the end of April."

Anthony's eyes rounded. "Sir?" Thirty-thousand pounds was well beyond the usual twenty-five-thousand pounds for an earl's daughter.

"My countess has informed me there will be another spare heir or daughter in the house before summer comes to an end," Daniel announced proudly. "When the boys are back in residence, it would be best if Dahlia had a new situation."

Blinking, Anthony thought about what his mother had said the day before. "Lady Norwick will be in good company, sir, given my mother is also with child."

Surprised by this revelation, Daniel lifted a brow. "They'll both be in good company. Why, Everly informed me only last night that his countess is expecting," he remarked, referring to Harold Tennison, Earl of Everly. "With any luck, Stella will finally give him a spare heir."

Anthony had already learned the news of Alexander Tennison's betrothal—as had every young miss in Mayfair and every young buck who'd had to compete for their attentions when Alexander was in the same room. "The Everly earldom will be in good stead," Anthony said. "Alexander has proposed to a jeweler's daughter, which means the most handsome heir in all of Mayfair will no longer be a bachelor," he added.

"Tuesday night's ball will be quite a spectacle," Daniel murmured. "I rather imagine Weatherstone will delight in having all these betrothals announced. Pray tell, shall we have him include yours?"

Anthony dipped his head. "Of course, sir."

"Very well. Now, back to business. I've a country

house in Sussex. Norwick Park. It's entailed but available should you wish to use it on occasion."

"Very good, sir," Anthony responded. He hadn't considered other perks that might come with marrying Dahlia Fitzwilliam.

"I rather imagine my countess will wish to arrange a large wedding on behalf of her eldest—"

"I would expect nothing less, sir."

"—Especially since she won't have the benefit of doing it for her youngest," Daniel added wistfully.

Anthony blinked. "Sir?"

Daniel furrowed a brow. "Oh, in my discussions with your brother, we agreed to a quick wedding for him and Danielle."

"You did?" Anthony straightened on his chair, wondering when Andrew had met with the earl. He had assumed his younger twin was still off wooing Danielle.

"They'll be off to Greece soon," Daniel said proudly. "This is an auspicious day. Both girls betrothed?" He shook his head. "I would never have guessed it. In fact, I'm thinking I may wait until later this evening to tell my countess of the betrothals. Otherwise the entire dinner conversation will be about wedding preparations." He turned his attention back to his desk. "I'll have the dowry details drawn up and delivered to Aimsley House by day after tomorrow."

Anthony inhaled softly, hoping Dahlia wasn't sharing the news with her mother this very instant. "Thank you, sir." He paused a moment. "What time should I return Lady Dahlia here this evening? So I can let my mother know she can't keep her in the parlor all night?" he added in a teasing voice.

Daniel regarded the viscount with an assessing glance. "Is midnight too soon?"

Shaking his head—he had expected something closer to ten o'clock—Anthony said, "Not at all, sir." He stood. "We should be off. I don't wish to be late for dinner at Aimsley House."

"Of course." Daniel held out his right hand. "Best wishes and good luck," he added as he shook Anthony's hand.

"Thank you, sir."

Anthony gingerly opened the study door, half expecting Dahlia to fall into his arms. When she didn't, he stepped out, his attention immediately going to the marble staircase.

Dahlia was halfway down the stairs, her head held high and her gaze directed straight in front of her.

Dressed in a dinner gown of peach satin with matching gloves, her hair done up in an elegant chignon held in place with a jeweled comb, she looked the part of a future countess.

His current viscountess.

He swallowed and took a steadying breath.

Moving to collect her at the bottom the stairs, Anthony offered his arm. "My mother is going to be thrilled. My father is going to faint, and my brother is..." He paused, furrowing a brow.

"Is going to be *my* brother even before you are Danielle's," she whispered.

"Your uncle mentioned theirs was to be a quick wedding, but then, so must ours be."

Dahlia paused before the door to allow Belvedere to help her with a mantle. "And why is that?"

"He says we must marry by the end of April," Anthony replied as he helped himself to his top hat.

Grinning, Dahlia took his arm. "Well, that gives us... four weeks," she replied, her eyes rounding slightly. Her gaze settled on Anthony's, and the strangest sensation of excitement and anticipation passed through her.

She wondered why he was staring at her as if he was seeing her for the very first time. For a moment, she thought he was going to kiss her again, but with Belvedere standing next to the open door, she knew he wouldn't dare. This was Anthony Comber, Viscount Breckinridge. He wasn't a rake or a rogue, a scoundrel or a libertine. He wouldn't do anything improper.

Not yet, at least.

Inhaling slightly, she added, "Or less. I wouldn't mind."

Curious as to her apparent change of heart, Anthony merely nodded, and the two took their leave of Norwick House.

He waited until they were in the coach before he stole a kiss or two.

CHAPTER 32
A DINNER REVEALS MUCH

*M*eanwhile, at the Comber townhouse in Bruton Street

Seated at opposite ends of the dining room table, Danielle watched as a footman delivered their first course. Andrew's attention had been on her since he had held her chair and then took the carver at the other end. She waved, her cheeks flushed from what they had been doing.

He waved back. "I have an idea," he said as he pushed back on his chair. The footman paused in his duties.

"Sir?"

"We're going to change places. I don't wish to sit so far from my lady," he explained, as he moved his place setting halfway down one side of the table.

"Understood, sir." The servant quickly moved Danielle's serviette to the seat across from Andrew's and then held the chair for her.

"Much better," Andrew said as he settled into his chair.

"You're going to play footsie with me, aren't you?" Danielle accused with a grin.

He scoffed. "Were my intentions that apparent?" he teased, after he was sure the footman was out of earshot.

Danielle sipped her soup, her brows rising in appreciation. "This is very good," she remarked. "Who's your cook?"

Andrew blinked. "You mean *your* cook?" he countered with a grin. "I've absolutely no idea," he said. "Remember, I haven't yet met the staff."

"We'll have to do that, perhaps on the morrow," she replied.

"I'll see about a license as well. When would you like to hold the ceremony?"

Danielle's eyes rounded. Despite his repeated marriage proposals, her thoughts on this day hadn't been on an actual marriage ceremony. Not with what he'd been doing to her up in the mistress suite. "I suppose that will be up to Mother," she murmured. "Have you a date in mind?"

"If we marry soon, we can be off to Greece before it grows too hot there."

Grinning, Danielle leaned forward. "And the Kingdom of the Two Sicilies?"

"We can go there first, if you prefer. Visit Sicily. Go up to Rome. Over to Greece. Whatever you'd like, Danny." He finished his soup and regarded her a moment.

"What is it? Do I have something on my face?" she asked, lifting a hand to her cheek.

He chuckled. "Only the most beautiful blush I've ever seen you display," he replied. "I do hope I help put it there."

"Rake," she accused.

Sobering, he said, "Until a couple of hours ago, I would have argued with you—"

"A couple of hours ago, and I wouldn't have thought you capable." The words were delivered without humor, although she managed a teasing grin and an arched brow after a moment.

Straightening in his chair, Andrew frowned. "I suppose I do come off rather like milquetoast."

Danielle gave a start. "I would not say that," she countered, just as the footman appeared with the next course. "You've always just been... you."

Andrew waited until the footman had placed the fish course in front of them before he said, "Predictable?"

Blinking, Danielle regarded him with confusion. "Not all the time."

"Boring?"

She shook her head, glad they were once again alone in the dining room. "Never boring. You've always been the fun one," she said. "Not a care in the world, unless you were having trouble in school."

"I was always having trouble in school."

"I missed you terribly when you were at Eton."

Andrew's eyes widened. "You did?"

She scoffed. "But of course. You were practically my best friend."

Despite not having taken a single bite of his fish, Andrew swallowed. "And now?"

Danielle inhaled softly before a brilliant smile brightened her face. The light dimmed, though, before she asked, "May I be both your best friend and your wife?"

Andrew's mouth opened as he seemed to have

trouble breathing. "God, I hope so," he whispered. He quickly glanced around the dining room, as if he meant to make sure they were still alone. Then he pushed away from the table and stood from his chair.

Watching in wonder as he rounded the table and made his way toward her, Danielle let out a squeak when he pulled her out of her chair and into an embrace.

He kissed her. Deeply. Thoroughly. And kept on kissing her until he finally had to come up for air.

"Oh!" Danielle gasped, her eyes wide with surprise.

"Now... I fear I *am* guilty of the label of rake."

Her eyes darted sideways. "As long as you're not doing it to anyone else," she hedged.

"Only you, Danny," he said before he kissed her once more.

His arms laden with the next course, the footman reappeared in the dining room and froze in place. He seemed unsure of what to do, first turning around as if he intended to go back into the butler's pantry. Then he paused and sighed. Making his way around the kissing couple, he placed the dishes on the table, refilled the wine glasses, and made his way out of the dining room.

Danielle ended the kiss this time, her eye lashes fluttering as if her eyes had to adjust to the candlelight. She glanced at the table. "I do believe the next course has been served," she murmured.

"Oh, good," Andrew said as he stepped away. He helped her back into her chair. "I'm starving."

Giving him a grin, Danielle tucked into the meal. "We really must ensure we don't lose this cook," she remarked.

"I'll see to it Parker has a word with him," Andrew replied.

"When will you move in?"

Andrew paused a moment. "I hadn't given it any thought. I shouldn't wish to be here without you—"

"You should move in," she interrupted. "I'll have my maid pack my things so I can join you once we're married."

"Oh, must we wait that long?"

Danielle blinked. "Drew!" she scolded. "I cannot live here before the vows."

"We'll hardly be moved in before we depart on our wedding trip," he countered. "You must let me know what the house lacks so that I can see to it it's taken care of whilst we're on our trip."

Grinning, she said, "Then I shall come with my mother and Davy. I'm sure they'll have opinions."

Andrew chewed his meat and frowned. "I don't suppose you could... you could come of your own accord? By yourself? Some afternoon when I'm in residence? I'm quite sure I'll be in the study desperately learning everything I must for our wedding trip."

"Wouldn't I be interrupting?" she teased.

He nodded vigorously. "That was my thought, of course!"

They both chuckled and then sobered as they regarded one another.

"You never did tell me how many children you want," Danielle said quietly.

Inhaling softly, Andrew allowed a shrug. "As many as you wish to give me, I suppose. More than one, I hope."

Danielle waved a hand. "Let's start with three and see how it goes."

"Triplets?" Andrew asked in alarm.

Tittering, Danielle said, "Of course not. One at a

time," she added. "If only you could have seen your face just then. I don't think I've ever seen you look so frightened."

"I was, if only for your sake," he explained. "Mother has complained many a time about how difficult it was for her when she was expecting Anthony and me."

"My mother, too," Danielle said.

"I do not wish for you to suffer. And I cannot bear the thought of losing you."

Danielle inhaled as Andrew made his claim, touched by the sadness in his voice. "I do believe I love you, Andrew Comber," she stated.

Andrew stilled, his meal forgotten. "I really wish I didn't have to take you home this evening."

Danielle's eyes darkened. "Who says you do?"

The sound of a clearing throat had the two of them turning their attention to the man who stood in the dining room doorway. "I do," David Fitzwilliam, the late Earl of Norwick, announced.

"Father!" Danielle said in surprise. "You told him he could keep me here overnight," she added in a whine.

"If you didn't agree to marry him," the ghost countered. "There will be plenty of time for bed after you're wed."

Her brows furrowing, Danielle asked, "Whatever happened to your cheek?"

He paused, a hand going to the side of his face. "Never mind about my shiner. Your future brother-in-law packs quite a punch when he's incensed."

Danielle gasped.

"I'll see to taking her home as soon as we've completed the dessert course, sir," Andrew said, his eyes round with fear. He had stood as soon as he saw that it was the late earl who had interrupted their dinner, and now he wondered what had his brother so angry he would punch the ghost.

"Well, do stay long enough so you can have a glass of port," David said, waving a hand.

Andrew exchanged glances with Danielle before he said, "I shouldn't wish to leave my bride-to-be all by herself in the parlor, sir."

David rolled his eyes. "You can have the port while she has a glass of claret," he argued.

"Yes, sir. Very well, sir."

"Have her home by eleven."

"Yes, sir."

Andrew once again glanced over at Danielle. When he returned his attention to the door, the ghost was gone.

Very slowly, Andrew settled back into his chair. "He's gone."

"He does that," Danielle murmured, returning her attention to her meal.

"Do you suppose he'll continue to pay calls like that even after we're wed?" Andrew asked on a wince.

Danielle furrowed a dark brow. "I rather doubt it. Mother implied he hadn't paid a call since shortly after his death—before she wed Uncle Daniel," she explained.

"So... once your mother was remarried, he stopped appearing?"

She nodded. "Exactly."

His eyes darted sideways. "I'll see if Father will lend me the blunt for a special license," he said, thinking if they wed quickly, the ghost would leave them alone. "Perhaps we can be wed in a couple of days."

Danielle gave him a brilliant smile. "Then Mother can concentrate on Dahlia's wedding," she said happily.

"You're sure she won't mind? Not doing a big wedding for you, I mean?"

His bride-to-be grinned. "If it means my father's ghost won't be haunting us any longer? I'll be sure of it."

It was five minutes of eleven when Andrew delivered Danielle to the front door of Norwick House.

"I may not see you before the ball Tuesday night," Andrew whispered. "Will you save both waltzes for me?"

Danielle gave him a brilliant smile. "I will." Her eyes rounded. "Oh, Lord Weatherstone will want to be the first to announce our betrothal," she breathed, remembering how the ancient earl insisted that his first ball of the Season feature the betrothals that had occurred over the winter months.

"I'll escort you down the stairs," Andrew promised, at the same moment Belvedere opened the door. Unable to kiss her in the presence of the butler, Andrew merely kissed the back of her hand. "Wish me luck."

A quarter-of-an-hour later, he completed a discussion with Daniel, Earl of Norwick, and took his leave as he displayed a huge grin of relief.

CHAPTER 33
A DINNER WITH A FUTURE FAMILY

eanwhile, at Aimsley House

As soon as Hummel had opened the front door to allow Anthony and Dahlia to enter Aimsley House, Anthony knew something was different. Although the hall was quiet, muted conversations were occurring elsewhere in the house.

"Good evening, sir, my lady. Dinner is about to be served," Hummel said as he took Dahlia's mantle.

"Lady Dahlia will be joining us this evening. Can you see to it another place is set at the table?"

"Already done, sir," Hummel replied. "Lady Aimsley is expecting you both for dinner."

Anthony gave a start and then remembered his mother had insisted he invite Dahlia for dinner.

"Lady Dahlia will take Mr. Comber's place since he is having dinner at his townhouse this evening."

Dahlia exchanged a quick glance with Anthony, well aware her sister was with Andrew. She had looked for her at Norwick House, and her lady's maid had confirmed Danielle hadn't returned from the garden party. *Oh, she's having dinner with a friend,* Dahlia had said, remembering to cover for her sister's absence.

"I'm so glad my presence won't be an inconvenience for your mother," Dahlia whispered.

Anthony chuckled. "Even if it was, she would take delight in it," he replied quietly. "Besides, she's the one who insisted that I invite you."

He took Dahlia's hand, and when the butler was making his way toward the dining room, he kissed her. He grinned at seeing her eyes widen in surprise. "You have the softest green eyes," he murmured. He held up his left hand. "Like the emerald in the ring you gave me." He wiggled his pinky.

Dahlia blinked. "Yours are so blue," she countered. "They match the sapphire in the ring you gave me."

She was about to stand on tiptoe to kiss him again when the sound of a clearing throat had the two turning to discover Adam, Earl of Aimsley, standing outside the dining room. "Well, what have we here?" the earl asked as he made his way in their direction.

"I've brought a guest for dinner, Father," Anthony said.

Dahlia dipped a curtsy. "How do, my lord?"

"Father, Lady Dahlia has agreed to be my wife," Anthony said with a slight nod. "We're to be married sometime in April."

Grinning, Adam took Dahlia's gloved hand and lifted it to his lips. "Ah, then my wish to have a daughter will come true," he said jovially. "Best wishes are in order. Come. Join us in here," he said as he waved them into the dining room.

The eyes of Diana, Countess of Aimsley, and

Daphne Streater widened upon seeing Dahlia enter on the arm of Anthony. "Mother, may I have the honor of presenting my betrothed, Lady Dahlia?"

Diana stood, her look of astonishment turning to a huge grin. "Oh, you most certainly can," she replied as she hurried over to greet Dahlia. "Even though I knew this news would be coming soon, I cannot tell you how glad I am that it's today," she gushed.

"Oh?" Dahlia replied, her nervousness dissipating. She knew this family. Had known them her entire life. Well, all except for the blonde girl who stood regarding her with a curious expression. "How do?" she said as she dipped a curtsy. "I believe I saw you at the garden party earlier." Although she might have looked like Little Bo Peep when she was sitting with the earl, the girl certainly didn't now. She wore a dinner gown that was nearly a replica to that of the countess'.

"This is my niece, Daphne," Diana said as she held out a hand in the girl's direction. "We're borrowing her from my sister for a while."

Daphne dipped a perfect curtsy. "How do, my lady?"

Dahlia didn't have a moment to consider Diana's odd comment before she said, "It's very good to meet you." She curtsied to the young girl.

Turning her attention to Anthony, Daphne said, "You might have introduced me to Lady Dahlia at the party earlier."

Anthony chuckled as he pulled out a chair for Dahlia. "You appeared far too preoccupied," he replied. "I seem to remember you flirting with a number of boys."

Daphne's eyes rounded as did her mouth. "I did no such thing," she replied, her fists going to her hips.

"Anthony," Dahlia scolded. "You shouldn't tease your cousin like that."

Grinning as he took the chair opposite of Dahlia's, Anthony looked suitably sorry and apologized to his cousin. "Perhaps it was the boys who were flirting with you," he suggested.

Straightening in her chair, Daphne turned her gaze on him and said, "They were, as a matter of fact," she replied. "Why, if I hadn't warned him off, Xercioius Roderick would have kissed me by the daffodils," she added in disgust.

Rather amused at hearing this bit of news about one of the grandsons of the Marquess of Reading, Adam chuckled. "Sounds as if he'll be the new Rake of Reading," he commented at the same time several footmen appeared with the first course.

Dahlia glanced at Anthony and realized he'd been staring at her when he quickly turned to regard his cousin with a grin. "He's your age, is he not?"

Her eyes rounding in horror, Daphne stared at Anthony. "He is," she acknowledged. "Oh, dear. Do you suppose he intends to propose marriage soon?" she asked in a whisper. She turned her attention on Dahlia. "Cousin Andrew proposed to Lady Danielle when he was only eight years old," she said.

Anthony sobered. "Little pitchers have big ears," he whispered.

"I'm well aware," Dahlia replied, suppressing a giggle at the young girl's comment. "She's my sister."

Emboldened to continue—the adults were including her in their conversation—Daphne said, "Well, if she does marry Cousin Andrew, I do hope the ghost doesn't haunt her, too."

Dahlia swallowed, her gaze immediately going to

Anthony. "A ghost?" she repeated in as light a voice as she could manage.

"He and the ghost were talking last night and woke me up. Twice. And Andrew looked quite frightful this morning, what with his hair going off in all directions, so I know he was quite vexed by the haunting." Daphne's hands waved about around her head as if to illustrate what she meant.

"Daphne," Diana said in a quiet rebuke. "They will be no more talk of ghosts this evening." To the rest of those at the table she added, "I've assigned Daphne to another bedchamber since Andrew apparently talks in his sleep."

"Hmph," Anthony said after he'd swallowed a spoonful of soup. "I don't think I've ever heard Andrew talking in his sleep," he murmured.

Realizing he made the comment to further torment his cousin, Dahlia tried to hide a smirk even when she said, "Anthony!" in a hoarse whisper. When she turned her attention back to Daphne, she found the girl beaming in delight at her, as if Daphne had decided Dahlia was her new best friend. "You'll have to tell me what you know about your cousin Anthony," she said in a conspiratorial voice.

Daphne's shoulders lifted as her head dipped before she glanced over at her much older cousin.

"Oh, no you don't," Anthony said to Daphne, his grin belying his words. When his gaze turned on Dahlia, he found her staring at him in awe. For a moment, he was sure he saw adoration in her eyes. When she didn't immediately look away but instead gave him a grin followed by a daring wink, he was sure she was reassessing her opinion of him. "My betrothed might come to realize I'm not the overly serious man she's known over the years."

Daphne grinned. "He's not a stick in the mud," she said to Dahlia.

Diana and Dahlia both tittered. "I can't say I ever thought *that* about him," Dahlia agreed. "But I do appreciate his sense of responsibility."

"As do I," Adam stated. "In fact, I'm going to put him in charge of seeing to it all the tenant cottages of the earldom are completely replaced with new ones," he stated.

Everyone at the table turned to stare at the earl. "You are?" Anthony asked. He dared a quick glance first at Dahlia and then at his mother.

"It was Andrew's idea to replace them. He has a good point. The maintenance issues would be ongoing, especially given the poor condition of the roofs. Makes more sense to build new, modern versions. No more thatched roofs," Adam explained.

"When would this rebuilding campaign start?" Anthony asked.

Adam shrugged. "I've already sent a note to the foreman. I'm thinking they should all be done before next winter, if that's possible."

Anthony's expression took on a look of concern. "So soon?"

Dahlia immediately understood his dilemma. "We can wait and take our wedding trip in the winter. The weather in Greece will be far more hospitable then," she reasoned.

His expression changed to one of awe. "Are you quite sure? I shouldn't want you to be disappointed."

Giving him a shrug, Dahlia said, "I won't be.

Besides, it sounds as if we'll have to do some traveling if you're to oversee the construction," she reasoned.

"You can stay at the country house in Wiltshire," Diana said brightly. "I would dearly love it if you could run the Aimsley Park household while you're there," she added, turning her attention to Dahlia. "Seeing as how I'll be in confinement."

Well aware of Anthony's gaze on her, Dahlia inhaled softly. "Of course, my lady. I would be delighted to do it," she replied.

"Then it's all set," Adam announced happily. The footmen reappeared with the next course.

"Will you still tutor James and me?" Daphne asked of her aunt.

"I expect so, darling," Diana replied with a grin. "How else are you going to learn equations?"

Beaming, Daphne tucked into her meal and kept quiet while the adults carried on their conversations.

When it was time for her and Diana to retreat to the parlor for tea, Daphne waited to ask as to why Dahlia didn't join them until after her aunt was settled onto the settee in front of the fireplace.

"Your cousin is giving her a tour of the apartments they'll be living in after they're married," Diana replied. "And then he has to see her home." She sighed contentedly. "I expect Lady Dahlia will be moving into Aimsley House this next month."

After Diana had dropped a lump of sugar into it, Daphne accepted her cup of tea and sipped it. "Is he going to make love to her?" she asked in a whisper.

Diana nearly choked on her tea, her eyes wide at hearing the query from the nine-year-old. "Daphne," she scolded. She stared into her teacup and allowed a wan grin. "I hope so," she whispered. "I dearly hope so."

CHAPTER 34
A TOUR LEADS TO TORMENT

eanwhile, in the late earl's apartments
"Truth be told, I've never stepped foot in these rooms," Anthony said as he led Dahlia to the apartments in which they would live once they were married.

"Not even when you were a child?" Dahlia asked in disbelief.

He shook his head. "I was never allowed, so of course I was even more curious," Anthony replied with a grin. "I used to stand outside this door and try to peek through the keyhole," he added as they stopped. He turned the handle and gave the door a shove.

Pausing as if he expected someone to jump out from behind the door, Anthony gave Dahlia a quick glance. "After you," he said.

"Coward," she teased. A moment later, she stood breathless. "Oh!"

Anthony gave her a worried glance, but then saw the look of awe on her face. "Was your 'oh' because you... like it, or because you're—"

"It's gorgeous," Dahlia murmured. She spun around in place, attempting to take in the decor and furnishings all at once. "I don't know what I was expecting, but certainly not this," she added as she hurried over to admire the painting above the fireplace. "A Fitzsimmons," she breathed as she studied the landscape featuring a folly next to a pond. A pair of swans swam on the water's surface, and clusters of flowering bushes were scattered about behind the Greek temple-like folly.

Relieved at Dahlia's first reaction to the apartment, Anthony began his own perusal, daring a glance into one of the bedchambers. From the hunter green fabrics and dark wood finishes, he was fairly sure it was the master suite. "I think I shall be very comfortable in here," he commented. He made his way to the other bedchamber door and opened it at the same time Dahlia's tour of the sitting room brought her to the same spot.

"Oh!" she gasped. "I love it," she said as she gazed into the mistress suite. "I'm not sure why I was expecting pink." She giggled upon realizing the bedchamber was decorated entirely in sea foam green and peach.

Grinning at her enthusiasm, Anthony watched Dahlia as she made her tour of the bedchamber, one hand skimming over surfaces and occasionally resting on an object she had stopped to admire. Seeing her like this, he remembered why it was he had thought of no one but her to be his wife.

Even during dinner, he'd been struck by her loveliness, by her patient and kind manner with Daphne, by how she so easily accepted the change in plans for their wedding trip and how she had seemed honored by his mother's request that she run the Aimsley Park house-hold during their residence.

"I really wish I could make love to you right now," he blurted.

Dahlia paused in her study of the dressing table, turning to regard him with a curious expression. "Is there a reason you cannot?" she countered.

He swallowed. "I told your uncle I'd have you home by midnight."

Her gaze went to the mantel clock above the fire-place. "Does it take a long time?" she asked. "To make love?"

Anthony glanced at the clock and shut the door. He leaned against it as he visibly swallowed. "I suppose that depends," he said in a quiet voice. "I really wanted to take my time. Undress you slowly, and kiss every inch of you," he whispered.

Dahlia was in his arms in an instant, her hands wrapped around his neck as she stood on tiptoe and kissed him. "Or you could just get on with it," she whispered after she'd pulled away slightly. "I probably won't like it much. This first time," she reasoned. "It's best we get it over with, don't you think?"

"Davy," he responded softly, his brows furrowing. "I want to make it so you *will* like it," he added before he kissed her. When he pulled away, his eyes darkened. "And I think I know how."

A shiver of anticipation shot down Dahlia's spine. Another rather pleasant shiver shot through her abdomen. "Oh!" she breathed, really wishing she didn't sound so much like her mother. "What should I do?"

"*Undo* is more like it," he replied. "All of my buttons," he added as his hands, still on her back, began undoing the fastenings of her gown.

Her fingers made quick work of both his top coat and his waistcoat, but when they moved down further, she froze and inhaled sharply.

Anthony shrugged. "That's me. That's what you do to me, Davy," he whispered.

Her eyes rounded. "Does it hurt?"

He swallowed. "That depends on whether or not we do this."

"Oh, we're doing this," she insisted, apparently unaware the bodice of her gown had fallen forward to reveal her corset.

"I wish for you to ride me," he stated.

Dahlia blinked. "Ride you? Do you mean—?"

"Like a horse, yes," he replied. "But astride," he quickly added, noting her look of confusion. "Like you would Vindication, but without the riding habit. And boots."

"Oh!" She nearly rolled her eyes at hearing herself. "All right." She stepped back and pushed her gown down her body, stepping out of the satin puddle and tossing it onto a nearby chair. She undid the ties of her three petticoats and allowed them to drop to the floor before she gave him a look of uncertainty. "If I need to remove my corset, you're going to have to help," she murmured.

Having frozen in place, mesmerized by how she simply disrobed before his very eyes without so much as a single request that he turn around, Anthony stared at her. "Of course," he finally said, after she had stepped out of the halo of white muslin petticoats and turned her back to him.

He pulled on the tie that held the corset closed, his fingers gently tugging on the crossed laces to loosen them.

"You'll have to go faster than that," she complained. "Or we'll only have time for a quick ride."

"Of course, my lady," he said, nearly cursing when his fingers refused to work properly.

"Although you already seem to be warmed up," she said with a titter.

"You have the right of that," he replied. He couldn't help the humor that sounded in his voice. This was not at all how he expected his first time with Dahlia to go.

"Are your coats still on?"

Anthony doffed both coats in two swift moves, determined that they be off in case she turned around before he was quite finished with the corset. "They're off." In a moment, he was afraid he would be, too, given how his cock throbbed.

"And your shirt?" Her head turned so her chin rested on her shoulder.

"Not yet. There's the matter of my cravat," he replied.

Dahlia turned around completely. "Tug it down whilst I undo this," she said as she worked to untie the knot in the length of silk.

Gingerly, Anthony pinched the bottom edges of the corset and pushed it down over her hips at the same moment she began unwrapping the cravat from around his neck.

"You're too tall," she stated.

Anthony immediately dropped to his knees, his gaze going to the underside of her breasts, visible due to the sheerness of her chemise. His first thought was to push his face into her belly as a means to block out the erotic sight, but her corset was still in the way. He managed to get it completely off of her when he felt her hands pulling on his shirt. He raised his arms, and the white linen passed in front of his face on its way over his head.

Still on his knees, he glanced up to find her staring down at his bare shoulders and back. He placed a hand on the side of her knee and slid it up one thigh beneath the chemise.

"I think I should like to leave my stockings on," she whispered.

"Very well," he replied, his hand moving to cover her mons. He heard her inhale sharply. "But I shall take mine off."

"Am I to ride you here?" she asked, obviously not pleased with the idea.

"On the bed," he said quietly. He managed to stand, disappointed he had to give up his vantage. He toed off his shoes, slipped one arm behind her knees and one behind her shoulders, and lifted her onto the bed. Her hands immediately went to wrap around his neck, the look on her face one of surprise. "Is something wrong?"

She shook her head. "You did that so easily," she murmured.

"Well, you're light as a feather," he teased before he kissed her forehead.

He had his stockings stripped off a moment later, and his pantaloons and smalls followed, although he struggled to push the smalls over his engorged manhood.

How ever would he last long enough to provide her a ride?

"Might I be allowed a moment to pleasure you first?" he asked in a whisper.

Dahlia's eyes rounded. "What are you going to do?"

One brow arched in reply, and Dahlia let out an

Her breathing having settled into a more normal rhythm, Dahlia nodded in the pillows. "I think so."

"Are you ready to go for a ride?"

She nodded again. "How do I do it?"

"Up on your knees. Face me. You won't need a mounting block," he added as she gingerly followed his instructions.

She straddled him, although she was careful to avoid touching his manhood—at first. "Is this the pommel?" she asked as she gripped it.

Anthony nearly sat up as he let out an "oomph." "Careful, my sweet. You'll have me coming before you've even left the stables," he warned.

But Dahlia's attention was on his manhood, one hand holding it while a finger caressed the silken skin. "It's so soft," she whispered.

Clearing his throat, Anthony said, "Hardly."

She glanced up and saw his look of offense. "Soft and hard," she amended. "So smooth. It feels like my velvet riding habit."

When he didn't respond with anything other than a guttural agreement, she slid her thumb over the top of it and watched as a clear bead of moisture formed. "Oh," she murmured, once again passing her thumb over the top.

"I really need you to mount me," Anthony whispered, as if he were in pain.

"I'm supposed to sit... on *this*?"

He nodded, hoping she wasn't going to change her mind.

"Oh, all right." She lifted her hips and centered herself over his manhood as he held it in place.

"You can go as slowly as you... *oomph*," he managed before she slid down partway on him. "You may wish to lean forward and... maybe place your hands on my shoulders," he suggested.

She inhaled. "I don't think it's going to fit," she whispered. Although Anthony expected her to claim it was uncomfortable, she seemed determined to make it work.

Anthony lifted her hips slightly and then pulled her down, his eyes closing as his manhood slid inside her as far as it would go. "Your horse is ready whenever you are, my lady," he said on a happy sigh.

Dahlia's gaze raked down his torso, from his face to where their bodies were joined. She bent her arms until her breasts were pressed onto his chest, and she studied how he reacted. When she used her tongue to lick one of his nipples, he jerked beneath her and his eyes rounded.

"You know how to make your horse happy," he said on a chuckle. When she bit his nipple, he bucked. "You minx!"

She moved then, lifting her hips and lowering them as she gripped his shoulders. "Are you ready to go faster?"

He nodded. "I am."

Once she established a tentative rhythm, Anthony gripped her hips to help guide her. "Ride me," he begged. "Harder."

He watched as Dahlia's expression displayed her determination, watched as she increased her rhythm as he began thrusting up with his hips. When he was sure he could no longer hold back his ecstasy, he rubbed a thumb along the space where their bodies met.

Dahlia's eyes rounded and her breath caught, and from the way she clenched on him, he knew her ecstasy had begun.

When his body seized and he held his breath, she straightened and leaned back slightly. Both lost to the after effects of their race, there was a moment when time seemed to stop, when Dahlia seemed to stay suspended above him. Then all at once, she flattened her torso onto his and moved her hands to grip the sides of his body.

"Oh," she said between gasps for air.

"Don't you mean 'whoa, pony'?" he countered, attempting to catch his own breath.

She grinned into the side of his neck as he wrapped his arms around her back. "It's not exactly like riding Vindication," she murmured. "But I do believe I enjoyed it more."

Anthony allowed a sigh of relief. "I'll be your pony whenever you'd like," he whispered.

She lifted her head to regard him with a wistful expression. "As long as you're my husband the rest of the time," she replied.

"Always, my sweet," he assured her. "I can be both at the same time." He held her face between his hands and kissed her until the mantel clock chimed eleven times. "Speaking of time, I need to take you home."

Dahlia moaned her disappointment.

"I'll help you dress," he offered.

"How do I dismount?"

Anthony chuckled as he moved his hands to her hips and lifted her until his softened manhood was free of her. He twisted and lowered her until she was on her back. "Stay there while I see to finding a cloth for you in the bathing chamber."

About to protest, Dahlia instead settled onto the bed and closed her eyes. She wondered what he had done to her. What he had touched to set off such intense sensations. Such sharp darts and rolling waves of pleasure. Although the pleasure had subsided, in its place, her body seemed wide awake. Sensitive. Tingly.

She was reveling in the aftermath when she felt a bath linen drape over her thighs and a kiss on her forehead.

"Come, my beautiful betrothed. Time to get dressed."

Although she didn't like it, Dahlia allowed him to lift her to her feet. He helped with her corset and tied the petticoats once she'd had them pulled up. Buttoned up her gown and saw to his own clothes, although he skipped pulling on the cravat.

At a quarter of twelve, he escorted her to the front door of Norwick House. He kissed her on the lips and the back of the hand and reminded her to grant him both waltzes at the Weatherstone's ball. The moment before he departed, he said, "Whatever you do, Davy, please don't change your mind about marrying me."

As Belvedere opened the door, Dahlia gave Anthony a wink. She disappeared into the house without a word.

CHAPTER 35
A DAUGHTER RETURNS

A quarter past eleven o'clock in the evening at Norwick House

After poking her head into several rooms in search of her mother, Danielle practically tip-toed into the parlor upon discovering the countess ensconced in her favorite settee. The light from a roaring fire cast the room in a comfortable glow, its warmth welcome after spending time out in the chilly night air.

"Did you miss me?" Danielle asked brightly as she joined Clarinda Brotherton Fitzwilliam in front of the fire.

Clarinda glanced up, her expression suggesting she'd been deep in thought. "Why, not at all."

"What do you mean you didn't miss me?" Danielle asked as she regarded her mother with a curious expression. She had expected being kidnapped might result in some consternation at Norwick House.

Enjoying a cup of tea and her second biscuit after an especially quiet dinner, Clarinda glanced around the parlor as if she thought there might be someone else there. The interruption of her reverie by the youngest of her twin daughters had her shrugging. "Dahlia said you were having dinner with a friend. I do hope it went well," she replied.

Danielle blinked. "It did, actually. The meal was exceptional, as was the company," she replied. "That is, until Father showed up. Otherwise, I might still be there."

The countess regarded her with alarm for a moment. "He was there? The ghost?"

Rolling her eyes, Danielle joined her mother on the settee. "I have seen him far too many times on this day," she complained. "But no more. Once I'm married, I'm quite sure he'll leave me alone."

"Probably," her mother agreed, helping herself to another biscuit as if she hadn't comprehended all of what her daughter had just said. "Speaking of marriage, I paid witness to a most romantic proposal today."

Danielle's eyes widened. "Oh? Who?"

Clarinda allowed a brilliant smile. "Sebastian Peele proposed to Lady Vivian today. At Weatherstone Manor. She had a faint in the front salon, and he swooped in and caught her and then announced that they would be wed. Weatherstone will formally announce it Tuesday night during the ball."

"Finally," Danielle said under her breath, half-wishing a proposal had been witnessed for her sister and Anthony. Vivian Wentworth, the only daughter of the late Earl of Roth, was at least three years older than Danielle, and the exceedingly prim and proper miss had always held a candle for the very tall and very improper viscount and heir to the Weatherstone earldom, despite his reputation for acts of derring-do and racing coach-and-fours in the middle of the night.

"Tuesday night's ball will be filled with announcements of marriages and betrothals," Clarinda went on. "It would be so wonderful if Dahlia and Anthony could be included, don't you think?"

Boggling, Danielle shook her head. "Didn't she say anything about it at dinner?"

Clarinda gave a start. "Why, she wasn't here for dinner," she replied. Her brows furrowed. "Wasn't she with you?"

For a moment, Danielle wasn't sure how to respond.

Had Dahlia spent the evening with Anthony? Had Dahlia dined with him under the pretense that she was with her? "Oh, of course," Danielle replied with a wave. "How could I forget?"

"Your hat certainly didn't provide you with any protection from the sun today," Clarinda remarked. "Why, you're cheeks are especially flushed."

Danielle blinked, realizing that neither her hat—or rather the way in which it had been pinned to her hair —nor the sun, had anything to do with the color her face displayed. "I suppose they are," she replied. "Seeing as how I accepted Andrew Comber's marriage proposal."

Clarinda's eyes widened. "*What?* When was this?"

"After the garden party," Danielle replied. "He proposed at least three times today," she added with a shrug. "Father gave him permission. And Uncle spoke with him as well, apparently sometime before the party," she explained. "We're going to Greece and to the Kingdom of the Two Sicilies for our wedding trip. Maybe as soon as next week, if Andrew can secure a special license."

Her mother stared at her in awe. "Well, that's...

that's wonderful," she whispered. "Whatever had you changing your mind? Only a few days ago, you announced you were going to be a spinster," she accused.

Danielle considered telling her mother all about the kidnapping but thought better of it. "Andrew was very insistent," she replied. "And Father was on his side."

Clarinda beamed in delight. "I'm so happy for you," she said as she pulled her daughter into a hug. "Andrew has loved you his entire life—at least, that's what his mother has said—and I rather think you adore him, too, do you not?"

Dipping her head, Danielle remembered that afternoon and the revelations she had experienced with Andrew. "I love him, Mother," she admitted.

"Of course you do. And you'll love running your own household," Clarinda said, pulling away slightly. One of her brows furrowed. "Where will you live?"

Grinning, Danielle said, "A townhouse in Bruton Street. It belongs to the Aimsley earldom, and Lord Aimsley has given it to Andrew. For us to live in."

"Why, that's an exceptional address," her mother remarked. "You'll be close to Berkeley Square." She suddenly sobered. "Now what's this about leaving for Greece next week?" Her joy seemed to disappear with her query.

Danielle was about to respond, but her uncle appeared on the parlor's threshold. "I understand best wishes are in order," he said with a grin as he approached the two women.

"Who told *you*?" Clarinda asked as he kissed her on the forehead.

"Why, the lucky groom-to-be, of course. Mr. Comber paid a call on me this morning. We've already discussed the particulars," he explained. "Finished up a moment ago." He turned his gaze onto Danielle. "So... it sounds as if you'll be on your way to Greece next week?"

Danielle beamed in delight. "Oh, Uncle, I can hardly wait," she replied. "We'll start there and then go to the Kingdom of the Two Sicilies. We're saving Rome for last. Did he tell you about the townhouse?"

Grinning at her enthusiasm, her uncle took the chair adjacent to the settee. "Indeed. Apparently it has an exceptional cook and is ready for you to move in."

"I've taken a tour," Danielle admitted. "Earlier today. I'm to have my lady's maid pack whatever I'm not taking on the trip and have it moved to the house so it will be ready for when we return." She squealed in delight.

"Mr. Comber seems as if he has all well in hand," Daniel remarked. "In fact, it seems Andrew is even more in love with you than his brother is with Dahlia," he added. "Of course, Anthony has always been the more serious of those twins."

Danielle's blush deepened. "As I am in love with him," she replied on a sigh. "Oh, Uncle, I can hardly wait to run my own household and..." Her eyes rounded. "What's this about Anthony and Dahlia?"

His gaze darting to Clarinda, Daniel realized he would have to tell her about the other betrothal. "Our eldest had her own good news today," he hedged.

"Did she?" Clarinda asked in alarm. "Why didn't you mention it during dinner?"

Daniel swallowed. "Uh... um... I thought perhaps she should be the one to tell you," he stammered.

As if on cue, Dahlia swept into the parlor, her face flushed and displaying a happy expression. "Oh,

Mother! Uncle! Danny! I've the most *wonderful* news," she said, nearly breathless as she hurried to the settee. Despite the width of her bell skirt and those of her sister and mother, she wedged herself onto the settee and beamed in delight. When her sister didn't say anything, Dahlia sobered, "How was the kidnapping?"

Her mouth dropping open in disbelief, Danielle gave her sister a quelling glance. "I agreed to wed Andrew after he proposed again. Twice," she replied, deciding it best she not acknowledge the mention of a kidnapping. "I rather adored how determined he was to secure my hand," she added sweetly.

"Anthony agreed to marry your sister after *she* proposed," Daniel said, his quirked brow suggesting he was still rather amused by the situation.

"Uncle!" Dahlia groused. "You didn't have to mention that."

"*You* proposed?" Clarinda asked in alarm, her manner suggesting she was a bit miffed her husband hadn't told her about Dahlia's betrothal. Her look of horror abated somewhat. "Well, you certainly aren't the first aristocrat's daughter to do so, I suppose."

"Anthony did propose first," Dahlia countered on a huff. "Twice, actually. But when I hesitated because he spoke of negotiating the terms of our marriage, he withdrew his proposal. And Father was most unhelpful. I think because he was probably still embarrassed by how Anthony punched him in the face during the garden party."

Her eyes once again widening in alarm, Clarinda exchanged a quick glance with Daniel before their gazes swept the parlor, as if they expected the ghost of the late earl to make an unwelcome appearance.

"If you're looking for Father, he won't be bothering

us again," Dahlia announced. "Unless we don't wed, in which case it seems he'll be back to haunting us," she added as she turned to face her sister. "Andrew said you were going to wed next week, but Lady Aimsley is of the opinion we should wed together."

"Oh, that really would be preferable," Clarinda commented.

"Except I made a deal with Anthony that he would wed Dahlia by the end of April," Daniel countered. "He agreed."

Clarinda inhaled as if to complain but instead allowed a shrug. "Well, then I suppose we shall have to arrange a quick wedding for the both of you," she suggested, feigning disappointment.

"Although we're both planning to go to Greece on our wedding trips, we won't be going when you do", Dahlia explained. "Lord Aimsley has asked Anthony to oversee the construction of new tenant cottages at Aimsley Park, and Lady Aimsley has asked me to run the household there."

"Oh, you'll love Aimsley Park," Clarinda replied. "And Wiltshire isn't that far away I suppose. When will you go on your wedding trip?"

"As soon as the cottages are finished. Hopefully this winter," Dahlia replied. "The weather won't be so hot in Greece."

"We may not see you there," Danielle commented. "I think our plan is to end our trip in Rome. So romantic," she added on a sigh. She straightened and announced, "Mother already has plans for my bedchamber."

"Hers as well," Clarinda said, referring to Dahlia's bedchamber.

"*What?*" Dahlia scoffed. She quickly brightened.

"Oh, but I don't mind. I've already seen my new bedchamber, and I like it very much," she claimed, her cheeks reddening at the thought of what Anthony had done to her there only the hour before. She furrowed a brow. "What plans do you have for my bedchamber?"

Clarinda patted her midsection. "I might be having twins again."

Both daughters rolled their eyes in unison, which had Daniel chuckling. "Oh, dear God. You looked just like your father when you did that."

Holding their forefingers to their lips, Dahlia and Danielle *shushed* him, but their efforts were too late.

As if summoned by his brother's words, David Fitzwilliam, the late Earl of Norwick, appeared in the middle of the parlor.

CHAPTER 36
PARENTS OF GROOMS MAKE
A PLAN

Eleven o'clock that evening, Aimsley House
Stepping down from the ancient coach, Andrew Comber regarded the front of Aimsley House and grinned.

He felt a stirring in his loins when he remembered what he'd been doing earlier that afternoon. A sense of relief that the young lady he had loved for most of his life had agreed to be his wife. A slight ache in his heart that he'd had to say good night to her only a few moments ago.

Their parting kiss—a stolen kiss as he was about to leave her at Norwick House—had been far too brief and left him wanting to do it again and again.

But mostly he felt a sense of calm now that he knew he'd be spending the rest of his life with her.

Had the ghost of David Fitzwilliam not appeared when he had—if he hadn't told Andrew what to do to gain his daughter's hand—Andrew wasn't sure he would have been successful. That the current Earl of Norwick had been so accommodating when he had paid a call on the gentleman earlier that morning merely reinforced his knowledge that he was doing the right thing by marrying Danielle Fitzwilliam.

Rather proud of what he had accomplished on this day, he entered Aimsley House and greeted Hummel as if he were a long lost friend.

The butler regarded him as if he'd drunk too much at his club, but Andrew ignored the older man's scowl as he made his way to his father's study.

He found Adam Comber lounging on one of the sofas, a glass of brandy in one hand and a book in the other. "Father?" he said as he knocked on the door.

Adam lifted his head and gave a start at seeing his younger son. "There you are," he replied. "We missed you at dinner. A rather lively affair given your brother's guest," he added as he straightened on the sofa.

"Didn't Anthony tell you where I was?" Andrew asked as he gingerly stepped into the study.

"The townhouse. Yes, he mentioned you were giving it a go. Tell me, what did you think of your dinner there?"

Andrew nodded. "The cook is excellent, sir. The company, even more so."

Giving his son a look of confusion, Adam said, "Oh?"

"Lady Danielle joined me for dinner, Father. I proposed again to her, you see, and this time she accepted," he replied, his chest puffing out.

"You're in good company," Adam replied, his manner rather serious as he stood and joined Andrew in front of the desk.

His eyes darting sideways, Andrew asked, "Does that mean Anthony was successful? With his proposal?"

Chuckling, his father nodded. "*Her* proposal, as it

happens. Indeed. He brought Lady Dahlia to dinner this evening. I don't think I've ever seen those two look so besotted with one another," he commented.

Andrew blinked. "Anthony? *Besotted?*" he repeated.

His father chuckled again. "Lady Dahlia even more so," he said. "She'll make a right proper countess some day."

"No doubt," Andrew agreed.

"So," Adam said before he inhaled deeply. "We'll not only be gaining a new babe in this family, but *two* daughters as well. Your mother will be thrilled when she hears your news."

"Thank you, Father. But one of the terms Lord Norwick set forth is that Lady Danielle and I must marry by the end of April. I plan to secure a license and see if we can't be married by next week."

The earl shrugged. "Fine with us," he replied. "We're going to need your bedchamber, after all."

Giving a start, Andrew said, "Oh?" His brows furrowed. "Are you expecting guests?" He almost asked if Daphne's brother was going to be moving in, too, but thought better of it.

"Just expecting," Adam said with a grin. "Can't leave the new addition in the nursery too long," he added.

Wondering if his father might be teasing him, Andrew dipped his head. "I shall be moved out of my bedchamber before I depart for Greece."

"Ah, capital," Adam replied, setting his book on his desk. He drained the rest of the brandy in a single gulp. "I'll see to it your allowance is restored within the week."

Andrew blinked. He had almost forgotten about his allowance. "I appreciate that, Father." He paused a moment. "Do you think I should tell Mother my news now? Or should I wait until breakfast?" he asked, thinking he was about to be dismissed.

"I'm on my way up to her bedchamber now. I can tell her if you'd like," Adam offered.

"Thank you, sir, but..." Andrew glanced around before adding, "I think I should be the one to tell her." He was anxious to see her reaction. Curious as to what she would say when hearing his good news. "See you in the morning."

He left the study and climbed the stairs, curious as to his father's reaction to his news. Although he hadn't expected outright elation from the man, he had expected more than the tepid response the earl had exhibited.

Rather than going directly to his bedchamber, he instead stopped at his brother's.

A few minutes later
Adam Comber climbed the stairs in a hurry, attempting two at a time. He finally had to slow his pace or risk sounding like a huffing bear at the Tower of London.

When he burst into his wife's bedchamber, Diana gasped and gripped the edges of her dressing gown together. She blinked before her eyes widened. "Is something wrong? You look as if you've seen a ghost!"

Her husband struggled to catch his breath. "Not at all. My plan worked. Completely."

She gave him a quelling glance. "You mean the one where our sons are forced to marry for blunt?" she asked on a huff.

Adam froze in place, realizing at once his countess

was miffed with him. "Andrew has always wanted to marry Lady Danielle, and now that she has accepted his proposal, he will. Probably next week," he replied defensively. "Now, you have to act surprised when he tells you at breakfast in the morning." When she didn't seem any less annoyed at hearing his news, he asked, "What's wrong?"

Tears pricked the corners of Diana's eyes. Before she could answer, Adam rushed to pull her into his arms. He had learned long ago it was far better to keep her close than to keep his distance when she was on the verge of tears. "What is it, my sweet?"

Her head fell against his shoulder, and he was quick to place a hand at the back of it and kiss her temple.

"Will we ever see Andrew again?" she asked, her query broken up by a sob.

His eyes darting to the side, Adam said, "Well, of course. He'll be at breakfast in the morning. Probably here throughout the day. Tomorrow is Easter. At the ball Tuesday night—" He let out an "oof" when Diana punched him in the gut.

"I meant *after* he marries," she countered. Tears streamed down her face.

"Oh," Adam replied, understanding her concern. "It's true he plans to take his bride to Greece and the Kingdom of the Two Sicilies for their wedding trip," he said quietly. "But they will return to Mayfair after that."

"And live in their own house," she murmured, sniffling.

"They will," he agreed. "Not even a mile from here, though," he reminded her. "I expect we'll see our son almost every day." He pulled a handkerchief from his waistcoat pocket and dabbed her cheeks with it.

"My boys weren't supposed to marry so young," she whispered.

"Your boys weren't supposed to break the rules when it came to their behavior at university, either," he said, a bit more forcibly than he intended. From the way she jerked in his arms, Adam knew he had said the wrong thing. "*My* boys weren't supposed to break the rules," he quickly amended.

"How many rules did *you* break by the time you were their age?" she countered.

About to respond, Adam inhaled softly. "Uh... are you expecting a numerical answer? Or... just in general? Because I may have lost track by the time I was sixteen or so."

Diana gave him a quelling glance. "Adam. You expect our sons won't occasionally break the rules, and yet you did constantly—"

"Not *constantly*."

"All the time—"

"Not *all* the time."

"Most of the time."

At this point, Adam clamped his mouth shut. When her eyebrows arched, as if she expected a rejoinder, he said, "I agree. It was most of the time."

She scoffed.

"I expect better of them, though," Adam whispered. "Just because I was able to get away with behaving badly doesn't mean I'm going to allow them to." He sighed. "Besides, they both seem to be looking forward to married life. Andrew is practically chomping at the bit to say his vows. Next week, in fact."

Diana plucked the handkerchief from his hand and wiped it over her face. "I admit Anthony didn't seem as bothered by the prospect as I expected," she murmured.

"A couple of days ago, he looked like he'd been scheduled for an execution. What do you suppose happened?"

Despite his hold on her, Adam shrugged. "Who knows? Mayhap the ladies feared becoming old maids—"

"They were *willing* to be spinsters," Diana argued, remembering what Clarinda had told her over tea.

"So they had a change of heart," Adam reasoned. "We are talking about our sons here. Our handsome, well-behaved, well-liked and intelligent boys who will once again have their allowances."

Diana sighed as she seemed to relax in his arms. "I'll speak with Clarinda on the morrow," she murmured. "She'll know the reason."

"There's my sweet," Adam said, before he kissed her on the forehead. "Of course Norwick's countess will know. It's not as if the threat of a ghost or a demon changed their minds."

Furrowing her brows, Diana regarded her husband with a rather odd expression. "I should hope not. Now take me to bed."

Adam blinked. "Yes, my lady," he replied, a grin splitting his face. "If I haven't told you already, I adore you when you're with child."

"Well, good, because I'm going to be like this for several more months," she warned with an arched brow.

His own brows waggling, Adam grinned. "You say that as if it's a bad thing, my sweet, and nothing could be further from the truth."

He had the dressing gown stripped from her body and his own clothes off in a matter of moments. Ignoring the ache in his knees, he lifted her onto the bed and made mad, passionate love to her. Before he passed out, he managed to bestow a kiss on her temple and another on her lips.

Watching her husband while he slumbered, Diana sighed softly. There were benefits to marrying a former rake, even if his knees weren't as young as they used to be.

*M*eanwhile, at the opposite end of the second floor

Using the back of a knuckle, Andrew tapped on his brother's bedchamber door, hoping Anthony wasn't already abed.

"Come," he heard from within.

He gingerly opened the door wide enough for his head to poke in, fearing he might be the victim of a thrown shoe or boot. When nothing came sailing through the air at him, he stepped into the room and closed the door. "Anthony?"

"Here," his twin replied as he emerged from the dressing room wearing only a shirt and his pantaloons. It was apparent Andrew had interrupted his brother's preparations for bed.

"I came to give you good wishes. Father said you and Lady Dahlia are to be wed," Andrew commented as he leaned against the back of the door.

Anthony grinned. "We are," he said on a sigh. "It's been a challenging but rewarding day. And you? Are best wishes due for you?"

Andrew nodded. "It took some doing, but Danny agreed to marry me. Norwick has given his permission as well, so we'll wed next week and be on our way to the Mediterranean," he said with a huge grin.

"I don't suppose I could talk you into holding off

for a week or two?" Anthony asked as he settled a hip on the edge of his bed.

Blinking, Andrew moved to lean against one of the carved posters. "Are you planning to marry before the end of April?" He crossed his arms and then bent a knee so the toe of his shoe was pointing into the carpet, much like he remembered the ghost doing. When he seemed to teeter on the verge of falling over, he wondered how the ghost remained upright. Andrew quickly put both feet flat on the floor.

"Seems we must if we're to make Lord Norwick's deadline," his brother replied. "Here I thought our father's edict was ridiculous."

"Lord Norwick's deadline?" Andrew frowned, not expecting *both* girls to have to marry by the end of April.

"I must marry Lady Dahlia by the end of April," Anthony stated. "Which is fine with me." He removed his stockings as he watched for his brother's reaction.

"Same for me with regards to Danny. But I don't mind," Andrew remarked. "The sooner the better, now that I know what to expect."

Anthony's brows furrowed. "Whatever do you mean?"

Andrew dipped his head. "Danny and I... we made love this afternoon."

Leaning forward, Anthony regarded him with rounded eyes. "You had to *ruin* her to get her to agree to marry you?" he asked in alarm.

Quickly shaking his head, Andrew said, "Not really. I mean, she didn't give me an answer until afterwards, but I truly think she would have said yes if I'd merely pressed my suit," he explained.

"Drew," Anthony said quietly, a hint of rebuke in

the simple word. He scoffed. "I cannot believe *you* would do such a thing."

"Why ever not? We spoke of it earlier. Before the garden party. Her father insisted I ruin her."

"I know, but that doesn't mean I believed you were going to *do* it," Anthony argued.

"Did you ruin Davy?"

Anthony gave a one-shouldered shrug. "I might have kissed her quite thoroughly. Spent some time alone with her without benefit of a chaperone," he admitted.

"But you had Lord Norwick's permission," Andrew hinted.

"I had a *ghost's* permission," Anthony countered. "Hardly the authority in this matter."

"He certainly thought so, though," Andrew murmured. "I know I cursed him—"

"I punched him in the face," Anthony interrupted.

"—but I truly think he knows what's best for his daughters. That *we* are best for his daughters," Andrew went on.

"I suppose you're right," Anthony finally replied.

"Did *you* have to agree to conditions with Davy?"

Anthony's expression conveyed confusion for a moment. Despite thinking they would have to agree to a number of conditions before she would give her answer, she had proposed. Negotiations hadn't really been necessary. "I did not. In fact, she's..." He paused and shook his head. "She's acting as if she feels *affection* for me."

Andrew chuckled. "Well, of course she is. Because she does," he stated. "Any fool could see that." He gave a start when he saw how his brother stared at him. "What?"

Shaking his head, Anthony said, "I suppose I am a fool then, for I did not realize it until dinner this evening."

Furrowing a brow, Andrew asked, "What happened?"

Anthony rubbed his face with his palms. "She was dressed in peach, and she was positively *perfect*," he whispered. "Behaved as if she was already a countess. Endeared herself to Mother and Father—,"

"They've always held her in high regard."

"—and was so good to engage Daphne in conversation."

"Oh, dear. That must have been interesting," Andrew remarked, not sure if *he* could hold his own in a conversation with his female cousin.

"For a moment, I was afraid Daphne was going to be welcome to come along on our wedding trip to Greece," Anthony continued, his eyes rolling.

Andrew's chuckle burbled forth before he sobered. "Is that why you wish for me to wait to marry Danny? Because you're going to Greece, too?"

"Something like that," Anthony agreed. "Actually, I wanted you to stand with me at my wedding, and you can't do that if you're fifteen-hundred miles away and already atop the Acropolis."

Andrew regarded his brother with new-found respect. After what had happened at university, he had thought they might end up estranged—merely acknowledging one another's existence when social engagements required it and otherwise avoiding one another's company. "Will you stand with me?" he countered.

"Well, of course."

"I'll speak with Danny about it at the ball Tuesday

night," Andrew said. "Perhaps she's having a similar conversation with her sister on this night."

Anthony's eyes rounded in alarm. "Oh, dear. I suppose they're going to tell each other every detail of what happened today."

His face paling at the thought of Danielle telling her sister what she'd done in the mistress suite at the townhouse, Andrew let out a groan. Upon further reflection, he thought Danielle would keep the details to herself. Know that if she shared too much, word might get to her mother or the earl.

"Good thing you had Norwick's advice to kidnap Lady Danielle," Anthony commented.

"I'm not sure how good it is if the advice came from a ghost, though, brother," Andrew replied.

It was Anthony's turn to chuckle. "Point taken."

CHAPTER 37
A GHOST GIVES HIS LAST REGARDS

eanwhile, back at Norwick House

The ghost of David Fitzwilliam crossed his arms and regarded the four people who stared at him with looks of confusion and horror. "What?" he asked, all innocence.

"Your face," Clarinda said as she stood and rushed over to him. "I don't think I've ever seen you like this," she said as she was about to cup his bruised cheek with a hand. She quickly pulled it away as if she'd been burned. "As I recall you never took part in a bare-knuckle mill when you were alive."

David raised a hand to his cheek and winced. "Oh, that." He rolled his eyes. "One of my future son-in-laws," he remarked. "Don't know which one. Can't tell them apart," he added with a shrug.

"It was Anthony," Danielle stated.

"Danny!" Dahlia said in protest.

"Well, I don't want him haunting Andrew for the rest of his life," Danielle said in a hoarse whisper.

"Oh, so now Anthony has to be haunted for the rest of his life?" Dahlia countered on a huff.

"You *do* know that I can hear everything you say?" the ghost asked rhetorically.

"No," everyone responded in unison.

"What brings you here so late in the evening?" Daniel asked as he stood from his chair. He placed his fists on his hips as he regarded his ghost of a brother with an expression of impatience.

David shrugged. "I thought to give my best wishes to my daughters is all," he replied.

"Thank you, Father," the twins said as they dipped curtsies.

"Make sure their dowries have been arranged."

"I've already seen to everything," Daniel responded.

"Everyone set for Tuesday?"

Several pairs of eyes blinked before Clarinda asked, "Are you referring to Lord Weatherstone's ball?"

It was David's turn to blink. "That's *Tuesday* night?" he asked, displaying a look of confusion. "Oh. Well, I was thinking of the weddings, but I suppose it's too soon for those," he murmured. He held up a finger. "Weatherstone will insist on having his butler announce the betrothals, so be sure to enter on the arms of your young men," he said, his attention on the twins.

Dahlia and Danielle exchanged glances. "Andrew and I already talked about it," Danielle said.

"Oh, dear. I expect Anthony will wish to know what color gown I'm wearing. I learned over dinner with his parents and his cousin Daphne that he always likes his waistcoats to match whatever it is I'm wearing."

Danielle suppressed the urge to giggle. "They might

look alike, but Andrew is nothing like his brother otherwise," she remarked.

"So, now that you've given the girls your regards, was there anything else?" Daniel asked, apparently anxious to be rid of his late brother's ghost.

"I wish to give my congratulations to Clarinda for being with child," David replied.

Clarinda blinked, about to ask how he knew. Then she remembered he had known about the twins—both sets of them—back when he had first appeared as a ghost shortly after his death. "Thank you, darling."

"You'll just give birth to one babe this time," David added with a quirked brow.

A profound look of relief passed over Clarinda's face. "Oh, David, that's so good to know."

"That means you'll only need one of our bedchambers," Dahlia commented.

"It would be good to have another guest bedchamber," Clarinda countered.

Both twins displayed grimaces. "I do believe they're anxious to get us out of the house," Danielle whispered.

"Of course they are," their father stated. "Can't have you girls underfoot when they'll be wanting to tup in every room of the house. Including your bedchambers."

"Eww!" The sound of protest came from Dahlia, whose eyes immediately rounded. "Are you implying a library table might be involved?"

David pulled his chin into his neck while he deliberately ignored Clarinda's look of shock. "I didn't say anything about a library table," he replied. "So... if that's it, then I suppose I'll see you again sometime in the future. Mayhap when the babes are born?"

Dahlia and Danielle exchanged quick glances. "Babes?" they repeated in unison.

"Don't. Ask," their uncle Daniel warned in a low voice.

"Yes, the babes," David replied, ignoring his twin. "The six cousins will be the best of friends and vex you both to no end," the ghost went on in delight. "Just you wait until you have to marry *them* off," he added with glee. When his comment was met with horrified stares, he said, "Well, I'm off."

And with that, the ghost of David Fitzwilliam disappeared.

One after the other, those left in the parlor fell into their chairs and exchanged uncertain glances.

"Well, if there really are to be *six* cousins and I intend to have only three children, that means you'll have the other three," Dahlia said to Danielle.

Danielle grinned, remembering that she and Andrew had already discussed the matter of children over dinner. "Three sounds perfect," she said on a sigh.

CHAPTER 38
PREPARING FOR A BALL

Tuesday, April 2, 1839, Aimsley House
          "You're wearing that waistcoat?" Anthony asked in disbelief as he regarded Andrew from the threshold of his brother's bedchamber. He was dressed in his very best evening clothes and an embroidered waistcoat of bright blue silk.

Andrew opened his black superfine top coat and glanced down at his silver metallic waistcoat. "Too flamboyant, do you think?"

Sighing dramatically, Anthony disappeared for a moment. He returned with a gold waistcoat embroidered with vines and leaves done in silver metallic threads. "Wear this one. It will go much better with Lady Danielle's gown," he instructed.

His eyes rounding, Andrew asked, "How is it *you* know what Danny will be wearing to the ball?"

"I asked Mother to find out," Anthony replied as he helped Andrew into the gold waistcoat.

"Is it your intention to always match your bride's gowns when dressing for entertainments?" Andrew asked as he buttoned up the waistcoat. He turned to regard his image in a cheval mirror and his brows shot up. "I rather like it," he remarked. "A bit more sedate."

"I should like us to look as if we've taken care in our choices, especially when we're dancing a waltz together," Anthony replied. "Dahlia is wearing a blue gown, by the way," he said as he indicated his own waistcoat.

"I suppose you know what color Danny is wearing?" Andrew asked, not expecting him to know.

"Sapphire blue satin with a gold sarcenet overskirt and gold soutache braiding along the neckline."

Andrew blinked. "I have no idea what that is."

"Of course you don't, which is why I need to see to your choice of waistcoat," Anthony countered. "Are you ready? We don't want to be late."

"I am," Andrew replied, slipping his feet into his dance shoes.

"Father says Weatherstone will insist we be announced this evening," Anthony went on as they headed for the stairs. "We'll descend the stairs into the ballroom with our ladies on our arms. That should stave off any young bucks who think they might have a chance at the twins."

Andrew frowned. "You make it sound as if we own them," he replied. "They are allowed to dance with others, you must know."

His brother scoffed. "Just because she's allowed doesn't mean I want Dahlia to be dancing with every man who approaches her."

Stopping at the bottom of the stairs, Andrew stared at his brother. "A week ago, and you wouldn't have given it a second thought to see Davy dancing with someone else," he accused.

"A week ago, I wasn't..." Anthony clamped his mouth shut.

"What? A week ago you weren't *what*?"

Anthony dipped his head. "In love with her," he whispered. He rolled his eyes. "I cannot believe I just said that."

Andrew gave a start as he stared at his twin. "Humbling, isn't it?" he asked in a quiet voice.

Still reeling from having put voice to his feelings for Dahlia, Anthony frowned. "What do you mean?"

His attention going to their parents as they descended the stairs, Andrew jerked his head. "To allow another to own your heart? I've been living it my whole life, as have they," he explained.

Anthony's gaze followed suit, and the twins stepped aside to allow the couple to complete their descent to the marble floor of the hall.

"You two look rather dashing," Diana said happily. The dark green satin ballgown topped with a gold sarcenet overskirt set off the emerald-jeweled comb she wore in her hair. "As do you, darling," she quickly added, her gaze turning to her husband.

"I think I may have chosen the wrong waistcoat," he replied, referring to his jewel-toned tapestry garment.

"Nonsense. There's no reason for your waistcoat to match my gown," she replied.

"That is a gold sarcenet overskirt," Anthony said to Andrew, indicating his mother's gown.

Andrew rolled his eyes. He surreptitiously reached out and fingered the gold, though, his expression suggesting he was impressed.

"Yes, it is, and it cost your father a fortune, so do be

careful in the coach, won't you?" Diana said with a teasing grin.

"Where is Cousin Daphne?" Anthony asked, half-expecting the youngster would be included in the night's entertainments.

"I sent her home with her brother after they finished their classes this afternoon," Diana replied. She glanced up at Adam. "Apparently your father didn't realize how talkative nine-year-olds can be when they've been given permission to be so."

His head dipping down as if he was attempting to avoid a sword swipe, Adam said, "I've learned my lesson."

"Does that mean you no longer want a daughter?" Anthony asked in concern. Although he hadn't welcomed the idea of having a younger brother or sister when he learned his mother was with child, the idea had grown on him, especially when he considered Dahlia might have a babe in the next year. The two babies would occupy the Aimsley House nursery at the same time.

"Oh, I still want a daughter," Adam assured him as he led them to the front door. "But only at breakfast and dinner. Mayhap at tea."

Diana cast a quick glance in his direction as Hummel helped her with her mantle. "And if it's a boy?"

Adam chuckled as he escorted her to the Aimsley town coach. "A boy?" He scoffed. "This babe will be a girl," he insisted.

Anthony and Andrew exchanged amused glances before they stepped into the coach.

· · ·

*M*eanwhile, at Norwick House

"I can't find my gold slippers," Dahlia complained as she entered Danielle's bedchamber. "Do you have them?"

Sitting perfectly still at her dressing table whilst Peterman used the curling iron on her hair, Danielle regarded her sister's reflection in the mirror. "They're in the dressing room," she replied. "Do you have the silver slippers?"

"Right here," Dahlia replied, as she dropped the shoes onto the floor next to Danielle.

"This is a very bad idea," Danielle remarked, mentally counting how many seconds Peterman held the hair in the iron.

"Why do you say that?" Dahlia asked as she stepped in front of the cheval mirror. She smoothed the gold sarcenet overskirt of her blue satin gown before slipping a foot into a gold slipper.

"Mother told Lady Aimsley which gowns we were wearing, and I'm fairly sure she did so because Anthony always wants to know so he can wear a matching waistcoat," she replied. "If I'm wearing your gown, it means his waistcoat won't match."

"Both gowns are blue," Dahlia replied. "Besides, you look gorgeous in silk de Naples, and I do not."

Danielle scoffed. "You're being ridiculous. We look the same."

Dahlia was about to argue but realized she couldn't win. Except for their hair, they did look alike. "Are you nervous?"

"Only that my hair is about to burn," Danielle replied. "Peterman," she scolded.

The lady's maid let the lock of hair out of the iron

and stepped back. "That's the last one, my lady. I'll just pin up these last curls, and you'll be ready to go."

"Why should I be nervous?" Danielle asked as she turned to regard her sister with a furrowed brow.

"We're to be announced. Go down the stairs on the arms of our betrothed. Dance the first dance with them. Everyone will be watching," Dahlia replied, obviously anxious at the prospect.

"If we leave now, we'll be one of the first ones there, and we'll be the ones watching everyone else descend the stairs," Danielle argued.

"Only if Anthony and Andrew arrive when we do," her sister reminded her.

Danielle grinned. "I'm not nervous," she stated. She sobered. "Davy? What is it? What's this about?" She waved for Peterman to leave them alone, and the lady's maid dipped a curtsy and scurried from the bedchamber.

"Anthony made love to me," Dahlia blurted.

Danielle blinked and then giggled. "You say that as if you never thought it would happen," she whispered. "I did wonder at your high color the other night. And you were babbling." When her sister continued to stare at her as if the world might be ending, Danielle added, "You are in good company. Andrew and I made love Saturday."

Dahlia's eyes rounded. "How come you didn't tell me?"

"I'm telling you now. I wasn't about to say anything the other night with Mother and Uncle and Father in the parlor." She winced. "Besides, Father probably knows what we did."

"Oh, do you think he was watching?" Dahlia whined.

"I was *not* watching. Either one of you," the voice of David Fitzwilliam stated. "I do have better things to do."

The girls gasped and turned to stare at the ghost of their father. "Father! You frightened us," Dahlia scolded.

"I frighten myself sometimes," their father replied. "Now, what are you still doing here? Aren't you supposed to be on a ship to the Continent? For your ten-year anniversary trip to Greece?"

Exchanging confused glances, the twins said in unison, "We're not yet married."

David covered his face with a hand. "Oh." He paused. "Forget what I just said. You're supposed to be at Weatherstone's ball."

"We were just about to leave," Dahlia said.

"Well, get on with it then," he urged. "I would have thought by now you would have realized I won't frighten you if you don't invoke my name."

The twins blinked when he disappeared from the bedchamber.

Danielle scoffed. "He might have mentioned that a few days ago," she whispered. She glanced over at Dahlia, who was displaying an expression of amazement. "What is it?"

Turning to regard her sister with a brilliant smile, Dahlia whispered, "We're going to Greece for our ten-year anniversary!"

Giggling, Danielle led her sister to the door. "We won't be going anywhere if we don't leave now," she replied. When they were halfway down the corridor, she asked, "Did you like it?"

"Like what?"

Danielle gave her sister a quelling glance.

"Oh! Oh, I—"

"You sound exactly like Mother."

"—did. Very much. And I've given up trying not to say 'oh,'" she added as her chin went up. When she noticed Danielle's smirk, she said, "What else can I possibly say when I'm in the throes of passion?"

Danielle giggled. "Ooh. Yes. Please," she replied, mimicking what she remembered from her experience.

"In a bed?"

Slowing her steps as they descended the stairs, Danielle said, "Yes. In the townhouse. Where else would we make love?"

Dahlia shrugged. "Over a library table?"

"You didn't."

Rolling her eyes, Dahlia sighed dramatically. "Not yet, but it might be in my future."

Scoffing, Danielle accepted Belvedere's help with her mantel and the two followed their mother and uncle into the Norwick town coach.

CHAPTER 39
A BALL REVEALS ALL

Nine o'clock in the evening, Weatherstone Manor Breathless, the Comber twins entered the vestibule of Weatherstone Manor at a near run. "They're probably already here," Anthony murmured, worry in his voice. "Cursing our tardiness."

"Danielle doesn't curse," Andrew remarked, even though he had heard her use a choice term or two in their two decades of knowing one another. "And the Norwick coach hasn't yet arrived."

"How can you be sure?" Anthony asked as he handed his greatcoat to a footman.

"I looked," Andrew replied. Despite the chill in the air, he had left Aimsley House without a coat. "Come. There's a receiving line," he said as he led the way through the hall to where Lord and Lady Weatherstone were standing together, greeting their early guests. Beyond them were the wide stairs leading down to the ballroom, potted palms posted on either side. Fresh pineapples had been mounted atop the stair railings.

"Mother raved about the decor over breakfast this

morning," Andrew commented as he joined the receiving line.

"How did she already know of it?"

"Apparently most of the ladies of the *ton* were invited here for tea whilst they were at the garden party Saturday," Andrew explained. "Daphne had our father all to herself for quite awhile," he added with a smirk.

One of Anthony's brows quirked. "Oh, is that why he wasn't at breakfast this morning?"

"I think she talked his ear off, asking so many questions and such. Mother said he was quite vexed," Andrew commented.

"Hmm." Anthony took Lady Weatherstone's hand in his and kissed the back of it. "You look especially lovely this evening, my lady. You will save a dance for me?"

Agnes Peele, Countess of Weatherstone, scoffed. "Oh, Breckinridge, save your dances for the younger ladies, and do let me be the first to wish you well."

Anthony gave a start. "You already know Lady Dahlia has accepted my marriage proposal?"

"Young man, it's my business to know these things. But if you really must know my source, you need look no further than your mother. Lady Aimsley sent word this morning. Something about hoping you wouldn't change your mind."

"Change my mind?" Anthony whispered. "I wouldn't. I haven't," he insisted. His brows lifted. "Has Lady Dahlia?"

Lady Weatherstone's attention flitted to her husband. "Not that I'm aware," she replied.

"That's a relief," he whispered. "Thank you, my lady." Anthony went on to Lord Weatherstone and inhaled to tell him his news.

"Well, if it isn't one of the lucky young men who are about to be caught in the parson's mousetrap," William, Earl of Weatherstone, said jovially. "Where is your lady?"

"Here, my lord," Dahlia said as she hurried up to join Anthony. She curtsied to the countess and gave the earl her gloved hand.

"Best wishes to you both." Weatherstone's gaze fell on the two people next in line—Andrew and Danielle. "To all of you," he amended. "Do be sure to tell my butler so he can announce you." He waved toward the stairs, where Gilbert was posted as if on guard. "I do feel great pride in my ball being the harbinger of good news."

"Yes, sir," Anthony replied before he bowed, and the four continued to the top of the stairs.

Andrew turned his gaze on Danielle, his brow furrowing when he noticed her gown wasn't quite as Anthony had described.

"What is it?" Danielle asked, noting his curious expression.

"You look lovely in that gown," he whispered.

"It's my sister's. She insisted I wear it, and she's wearing mine," Danielle explained.

"Oh, so that's what a gold sarcenet overskirt looks like," he murmured, glancing over to where Dahlia stood facing Anthony. The two were staring at one another, Anthony holding onto one of Dahlia's gloved hands. "Sort of like a golden bird cage."

Danielle grinned. "And you wore a waistcoat to match it," she said, pretending sadness. "I really wish I had put up more of a fuss when she asked me to exchange gowns with her," she added.

"I could switch my waistcoat with Anthony before

we go down," he offered, about to head toward the other couple.

"Don't," Danielle whispered. "There's really no need for your waistcoat to match my gown," she added as she watched her sister interact with the viscount, her expression showing concern.

"I rather think my brother will be the one to insist," Andrew replied, smirking. He sobered. "Are you all right?"

Danielle's eyes widened. "Of course."

"I mean because, well..." He sighed as the color in his face heightened. "Because of what we did Saturday. I feared you might be having second thoughts or—"

He couldn't finish his thought when Danielle's lips suddenly took his. He was so stunned she would kiss him while they stood at the top of the stairs, he barely had a chance to return the kiss, and once he did, she ended it as quickly as she had begun it.

He blinked as she gave him a brilliant grin. "No second thoughts," she said with a shake of her head. "And I rather doubt Dahlia is having any, either. I think she's heels over head in love with Breckinridge."

Andrew blinked, his gaze darting to where his brother and Dahlia were still standing, engaged in quiet conversation. Deciding he wouldn't switch waistcoats after all, he turned to Gilbert and said, "Mister Andrew Comber and his betrothed, Lady Diana Dorothea Fitzwilliam."

"Drew!" she scolded. "Hardly anyone knows my real name," she added when he gave her a questioning glance.

"Now they will," he replied with a grin. "Or at least those in attendance. There's hardly anyone here yet." He led them to the middle of the top step and waited for the butler to announce them.

A quick glance in Danielle's direction found her gazing down onto the ballroom. He'd nearly forgotten how overwhelming the Weatherstone ball could be. Those already in the ballroom wore colorful gowns and satin evening clothes. The gas-lit chandeliers bathed the ballroom in a golden glow. Faint strains of music drifted from the quintet of musicians playing on a raised dais. The tables of champagne and other refreshments were already surrounded by gentlemen engaged in raucous conversations. A few wallflowers had taken up residence with the potted palms that lined the wall adjacent to the French doors.

Despite what would eventually become a crush below, Danielle displayed a pleasant expression, and then she allowed a brilliant smile when Gilbert announced, "Mister Andrew Comber and his betrothed, Lady Diana Dorothea Fitzwilliam."

Aware of the heads that turned to regard their arrival, Andrew straightened and placed a hand over Danielle's as they descended.

Before they had made it to the bottom of the stairs, the announcer called out, "The Lady Helen Tennison, Mister Alexander Tennison, and his betrothed, Miss Margaret Ewen."

"Alex!" Danielle whispered in excitement. When they reached the bottom of the stairs, she forced Andrew to turn around so they could greet the newly betrothed couple and Alexander's sister, Helen.

"Best wishes to you both," Danielle gushed.

"And to you," Alexander replied, before introducing Margaret. "I wasn't aware you two had finally decided to make it official," he said as his gaze went to the top of the stairs.

"Only last Saturday," Andrew said, frowning when his brother and Dahlia weren't the next ones in line to come down the steps. "You will afford me a dance, Miss Ewen?" he added.

Margaret's eyes rounded. "Yes, of course," she replied, when Alexander gave her a nod of approval.

"And I expect a dance with you," Alexander said to Danielle.

"Anything but a waltz," she replied. "I've promised both of them to Drew."

"A Scottish reel, then," Alexander remarked with a smirk.

"Alex!" she scolded, knowing Lady Weatherstone never had a Scottish reel included at her balls. "I'll save you a cotillion," she insisted.

New to the *ton* ball experience, Margaret appeared confused by their banter, but Alexander soon took her off to a cluster of well-wishers.

Danielle glanced back up the stairs. "Where's your brother?" she asked.

Andrew pulled her aside upon seeing the next couple set to descend the stairs. "The library?" he guessed, his brows waggling.

"The Right Honorable the Earl of Trenton, the Right Honorable the Countess of Trenton, and Mr. and Mrs. Gabriel Wellingham," the baritone voice of the butler called out. Before they were halfway down the stairs, he added, "The Right Honorable the Earl of Haddon and The Right Honorable the Countess of Haddon."

Andrew displayed a huge grin as his cousin, Juliet Comber Carlington, Countess of Haddon and future

Marchioness of Morganfield, descended the stairs on the arm of her much older husband, Christopher Carlington.

"She looks happy," Andrew remarked.

"He looks as if he's hit his head," Danielle said with worry, sure the earl had a bruise on his forehead.

"Probably hit it on a headboard," Andrew whispered. When Danielle realized what he meant, she raised a glove hand to hide her giggle.

Upon hearing her scolding, *"Andrew,"* he added, "Juliet says it keeps him humble. She already has him wrapped rather tightly around her little pinky."

Danielle tittered. "Are you wrapped around mine?"

Andrew arched a brow but didn't reply as he watched his cousin and her new husband make their way to the French doors at the back of the ballroom. "They're already off to the gardens," he remarked, his brows continuing to waggle.

"Mr. Thomas Grandby and the Lady Victoria Grandby," the announcer called out.

"What a gorgeous gown," Danielle said as she watched the Duke of Staffordshire's daughter walk down the stairs. Victoria was wearing an orchid gown with a full skirt. White tulle surrounded the neckline and trailed down to a huge bow at the back of her waist. "It's perfect with her dark hair," she added in awe.

"They're off to the gardens as well," Andrew commented as he watched the second set of newlyweds follow their friends out the French doors. "I would think it would be too chilly to go out to the gardens."

Danielle gave him a quelling glance. "I suppose it all depends on what they're *doing* out there," she said, arching a brow.

Andrew's eyes widened. "Oh!" he responded, which had her tittering.

"The Right Honorable Viscount Hexham and the Right Honorable Viscountess Hexham," the butler called out.

Danielle inhaled softly as her gaze darted back to the stairs. George Grandby, Viscount Hexham, and Anne Wellingham, daughter of the Earl of Trenton, had only been married a few months and had recently returned from their wedding trip.

The Fitzwilliam and Comber twins had been in attendance when the pair had become betrothed at a dinner party at Torrington House only the December prior.

"Anne looks as if she's positively glowing," Danielle said on a happy sigh.

"And George looks as if he's spent a good deal of time in the sun," Andrew chimed in.

"That's because they've just returned from Italy," Danielle said. "With any luck, we'll look like that in a few months," she added with a wink in his direction.

"What do you suppose has become of my brother and your sister?" Andrew asked as he led her toward the refreshment table.

"I can't imagine they're having second thoughts," Danielle said as she accepted a glass of champagne.

Andrew furrowed a brow, hoping his brother wasn't reconsidering the arrangements he had made with Dahlia. All had seemed perfectly fine earlier that afternoon.

. . .

*M*eanwhile, in an alcove near the top of the stairs

"What is this about?" Dahlia whispered as Anthony pulled her into an alcove, away from the Weatherstone Manor butler and other prying eyes.

"I want you to be sure," Anthony replied, lowering his forehead to hers.

"Of course, I'm sure," Dahlia replied, leaning back to regard him with alarm. "Why ever would you think I'm not?"

Anthony winced. "You've had over two entire days to think about it. All day. I... I feared you might have changed your mind."

Dahlia shook her head, her brows furrowing in worry. "You've changed your mind," she accused, one of her hands coming up to cover her mouth.

"I have not," Anthony replied. "Especially after what happened the other night. I'm in love with you, Davy," he claimed. "I merely wanted to make sure you were still of a mind to marry me before Gilbert announces it to the entire *ton*," he whispered. "I ruined you thoroughly, but if for some reason you had a change of heart—"

"I haven't changed my mind," Dahlia stated. "Now have you changed yours?"

He shook his head. "I have not."

Dahlia angled her head as she regarded him with suspicion. "Breckinridge," she said with a hint of warning.

"Anthony," he corrected her. "Or you can call me Tony, like you did the other night," he said, his eyes darting to the side. "I rather liked how you said it. All breathy and bossy and needy all at the same—"

Dahlia stood on tiptoe and took his lips with hers, essentially cutting off his comment. When she released him, she regarded him with an arched brow. "Mother always said it is a woman's prerogative to change her mind. However, I have not," she stated. She took a deep breath and let it out before adding, "Now, can you honestly say you still wish to marry me?"

Despite the number of aristocrats who waded through the receiving line and despite those who hovered nearby waiting their turn to descend the stairs, Anthony wrapped his arms around her shoulders and pulled her hard against the front of his body. His lips nearly crushed hers in a punishing kiss, which had several nearby ladies gasping in shock and one earl saying, "The library is down the hall, Breckinridge," whilst a marchioness sighed and said, "Oh, how I miss young love."

When Anthony finally released Dahlia, he said, "Yes. God, yes. And if we don't make our way down those stairs this very minute, I shall take you to the library and have my way with you," he warned, pretending to ignore those who stood nearby. Surreptitious glances were occasionally aimed in their direction.

Dahlia's eyes widened. "Oh, will you?" she asked, with far too much enthusiasm.

Anthony blinked, his eyes widening. "You *minx*," he accused. His expression soon displayed a brilliant smile.

Giggling, Dahlia placed an arm on his. "If only you could have seen your face just now," she murmured happily. "Why, I think you were more shocked than you were Saturday night."

"That's because I was," he replied, finally offering his arm. "Now, before you change your mind..." He hurried them over to the top of the stairs. "Viscount Breckinridge and his betrothed, Lady Dahlia Davida Fitzwilliam," he said to the butler.

Gilbert called out the announcement, a smirk appearing as he watched the couple descend the stairs. He was quite sure that by the time of next year's ball, there would be a number of new members to the *ton*.

EPILOGUE

*S*ix months later, at the Aimsley townhouse in Bruton Street

Weary from their voyage across the Channel, Mr. and Lady Andrew Comber made their way into the Aimsley townhouse in Bruton Street and accepted Parker's greeting with tired nods.

"Your correspondence is on your desk in the study, and there have been some deliveries for you, sir. Wedding presents, I believe," Parker said. "I've left them on the table here in the hall."

"I'll see to writing thank you letters in the morning," Danielle said, her hand going to her rounding middle. "I want nothing more than to take a nap right now."

"Anything of note?" Andrew asked, helping Danielle with her mantle. Footmen were already seeing to bringing traveling trunks in from the equipage that had delivered the couple from the docks in Wapping.

"Ah, yes. The delivery from Chippendale's," Parker remarked.

Danielle and Andrew exchanged glances. "Furniture?" she asked in awe. "Orders from Chippendale's take months to fill," she whispered.

"Indeed," Parker replied. "The card indicated it was from one David Fitzwilliam. A relative, no doubt? I had it taken upstairs to the library."

Danielle inhaled softly.

"Come, we can stop on the way up to your bedchamber," Andrew said as he offered his arm. "And then I can tuck you into bed."

Danielle tittered as they made their way up the stairs. "I adored Greece," she murmured. "We must go again."

"I liked Greece, but I do think Rome was my favorite of all the places we went," Andrew said as they entered the library.

"Because it was romantic?" Danielle asked, her head landing on his shoulder.

"That and the light," he replied. "You looked positively gorgeous under that Italian sun," he added, one of his hands smoothing over her middle. "And you still do here in London."

"Bounder," she replied as she turned her attention on the newest piece of furniture in the library.

A library table.

While Andrew chuckled, Danielle gave him a quelling glance. "It's not funny," she said as she lifted the card from atop the library table. She read it before she handed it to her husband. "Not funny at all."

Andrew took the note and read the missive, all the while grinning.

To the newlyweds,
*   I could think of no better wedding gift than a*

*library table from Chippendale's. I'm quite sure you
will put it to good use.*

Yours in service,

David Fitzwilliam

*P.S. If my brother should ask, then you may tell
him I charged it to the Norwick earldom.*

"You have to give him credit," Andrew said as he
returned the note to the top of the table. "He's a most
enterprising ghost."

Danielle rolled her eyes before they rounded. "Oh,
dear. I wonder if he had one delivered to my sister?
Dahlia will be furious."

"Over a table?" Andrew asked, his brows furrowing.

"A *library* table," she clarified. "Father knows how
she reacted to the..." Danielle paused, remembering
how she, too, had reacted to the book on sexual
congress. How she had reacted at seeing the color plate
featuring a woman being tupped over the edge of a
library table.

"Oh, I remember that color plate," Andrew
murmured, his grin still apparent. "And I am quite sure
my brother has seen it, too." He pulled her close. "It's
merely a table, my sweet. And that's all we shall use it
for," he added with a grin before escorting her to the
mistress suite.

eanwhile, at Aimsley House
"The tenant cottages are complete,
and the workers have all moved in," Anthony said to his
father as he and Dahlia greeted the Earl of Aimsley in
his study. "And all is well at Aimsley Park."

"Glad to hear it," Adam said as he rose from his

desk and made his way to where they stood. "Will you be off to the Continent now?"

"Next week," Anthony replied. "We're going to have dinner with Andrew and Danny before we leave. Discover the best places to go and such," he added.

Diana joined them, pulling Dahlia into an embrace and giving her son a peck on the cheek despite her rounded belly. "You two look as if you've enjoyed the country."

"Oh, very much," Dahlia replied. "The weather was perfect when it wasn't chilly, and we made so many friends in Wiltshire."

"Then you're no doubt looking forward to a warmer climate, Adam remarked.

"Oh, we are," Anthony assured him. "Is there any correspondence I need to see to here?"

"A few notes, a couple of invitations," Adam replied. "Several wedding gifts arrived while you were at Aimsley Park. Hummel had a footman take them up to your apartments."

"Including one from Chippendale's," Diana added, her eyes indicating how impressed she was by the gift. "There's a card on it, but I didn't peek," she claimed.

"A piece of furniture?" Anthony guessed.

"Indeed. It's beautiful, and I think there was a perfect place for it in your salon," his mother added.

"Well now I'm curious," Dahlia said, anxious to head up to the apartments."

"As am I," Anthony remarked. "We'll get settled, and I'll come down later to see to the correspondence," he added as he offered Dahlia his arm.

Dahlia hurried up the stairs with him, commenting on how glad she was to be back in London. "I did love running the household in Wiltshire and the country air was divine, but I did miss the entertainments," she said as they moved on to the next flight of stairs.

"I never thought I would, but you're right. I think we shall have to split our time betwixt the two houses, at least until I inherit," Anthony replied. He paused as he pushed down the handle of the door to their apartments. "Will you allow me to carry you over the threshold?"he asked as he gave the door a gentle shove.

Dahlia grinned. "Again?" She let out a shriek and a giggle when he lifted her into his arms and used a booted toe to kick the door open as wide as it would go.

He chuckled as he set her down in the middle of their sitting room. The two glanced about before he shrugged. "Looks like it did when we left it," he commented. He noted how his wife stared at something in the connecting salon, and his gaze followed hers to the new piece of furniture. He let out a guffaw. "Is this some sort of joke?" he asked, hurrying to the note that sat in the middle of the inlaid wood top of an elegant maple and ebony library table.

He unfolded the note as Dahlia stood still in the middle of the sitting room, her hands on her hips.

"Who's it from?" she asked, almost sure she knew the answer before Anthony scoffed.

"Your father," he replied.

Huffing, Dahlia marched over to the table and plucked the note from Anthony's hand.

To the newlyweds,

With so many possible uses, I can think of no better wedding gift than a library table from Chippendale's. I'm quite sure you will find that one perfect way to use it.

Yours in service,
David Fitzwilliam
P.S. Please don't mention this to Mr. and Lady Comber. I shouldn't want there to be any jealousy.

Reading the missive over Dahlia's shoulder, Anthony chuckled. "I cannot decide if he's trying to cause trouble or if he is pretending ignorance," he murmured.

Dahlia gave him a quelling glance. "He knows exactly what he's done, and if I were a betting woman, I would say an exact replica has been delivered to the townhouse in Bruton Street," she claimed, her hand skimming over the surface of the table. She leaned over it to study the inlaid pattern, her body bent nearly at a right angle. "It's even the perfect height," she added, lowering her chest to the tabletop as she bent her elbows and rested her cheek on the back of her hands.

Anthony's chuckle turned into a struggle to breathe. "My sweet, you really shouldn't do that," he warned.

"Do what, Tony?" she replied, angling her head to look back at him.

When he saw the expression on Dahlia's face, he shook his head. "Are you... are you quite sure?"

He blinked when she merely arched a brow and grinned.

AUTHOR NOTES

Where did these characters come from?
    If you are a regular reader of my *Aristocracy* series of books, you probably recognized a few of the characters in this book. For stories about the earlier lives of David, Daniel, Clarinda, Adam, and Diana, you'll want to read *The Dream of a Duchess*, *The Widowed Countess*, and *The Secrets of a Viscount*.

Cambridge University Terms
    The academic year starts on 1 October, and finishes on 30 September. There are three terms per year: Michaelmas (October—December), Lent (January—March) and Easter (April—June). Each teaching term (also known as Full Term) is eight weeks long.

Hyde Park Corner and Stanhope Gate
    Since the year in which this story takes place, the entrances into Hyde Park have changed dramatically. Back then, a renovation designed by Decimus Burton had begun in 1825, its intent to create an urban space

dedicated to "celebrate the House of Hanover, national pride and national heroes." The Cumberland Gate, Stanhope Gate, Grosvenor Gate, the Hyde Park Gate with its screen of columns at Hyde Park Corner, and, later, the Prince of Wales's Gate in Knightsbridge, were all created in the classical style.

Six streets converged at the southeast corner of Hyde Park: Park Lane (from the north), Piccadilly (northeast), Constitution Hill (southeast), Grosvenor Place (south), Grosvenor Crescent (southwest) and Knightsbridge (west). Apsley House, immediately north of the junction, was the home of the first Duke of Wellington.

The Triumphal Arch, which is now known as the Wellington Arch, became the centerpiece of Hyde Park Gate, but due to traffic congestion at Hyde Park Corner, the arch was moved to Constitution Hill in 1883.

Stanhope Gate was located on Park Lane at the junction of South Audley and Curzon Streets. The Dorchester Hotel (which replaced Dorchester House) and Barclays Bank are currently located at that corner, although the buildings that preceded them were not yet in existence at the time of this novel.

Your Invitation!

Do you crave historical romance filled with passion and red hot chemistry?

Come join me and my author friends in the Face-book group, Historical Harlots, for exclusive giveaways, chats with amazing HistRom authors, raunchy shenani-gans, and more! https://www.facebook.com/groups/2102138599813601

ABOUT THE AUTHOR

A self-described nerd and student of history, Linda Rae spent many years as a published technical writer specializing in 3D graphics workstations, software and 3D animation (her movie credits include SHREK and SHREK 2). Getting lost in the rabbit holes of research has resulted in historical romances set in the Regency-era as well as Ancient Greece.

A fan of action-adventure movies, she can frequently be found at the local cinema. Although she no longer has any tropical fish, she follows the San Jose Sharks and makes her home in Cody, Wyoming.

For more information:
www.lindaraesande.com
Sign up for Linda Rae's newsletter:
Regency Romance with a Twist
Follow Linda Rae's blog:
Regency Romance with a Twist